Game
On

Kyra Lennon

Also by Kyra Lennon

The Game On Series

<u>**Game On (Game On Book 1)**</u>
Praise for Game On
"Loved this book! Radleigh might be loathsome, but he's magnetic! Kyra has a witty style and excellent character development." <u>- Elizabeth Seckman</u>, Author of *Past Due*

"Game On is a moving, emotional, very real contemporary romance filled with fun, friendship, laughter, and a look on the human condition" <u>- Clare Dugmore</u>, Writer

<u>**Blindsided (Game On Book 2)**</u>
<u>Praise for Blindsided</u>

"Once again, Kyra Lennon has brought some fantastic characters to life, and as with Taylor in Game On she hasn't shied away from a love-to-hate character Mischa." - Annalisa Crawford, Author of *Cat and The Dreamer* and *That Sadie Thing*

"I absolutely loved this book! It was such an easy read, had it done in two sittings, and the love story was so cute and sweet. I think it was a perfect fit for Jesse, because he deserves this kind of love story." - Becca Ann, Author of *Reasons I Fell For The Funny Fat Friend*

<u>**Sidelined (Game On Book 3)**</u>
Praise for Sidelined

"I've always loved Kyra's no-mess writing style. She lets you into her character's heads that it didn't matter what the clothes they wore looked like, or where they lived, how they sat, and all those details that tend to get overdone at times. I pictured everything because those characters felt so real to me it's like I could call Bree up on the phone and beg her to take me shopping." - <u>Cassie Mae, Author</u> of *How To Date A Nerd* and *Switched*

"It goes without saying Kyra Lennon is a fantastic writer. She manages to keep an intricate plot exciting and fresh." - Confessions of a YA and NA Book Addict

Play On (Game On Book 4)
Praise for Play On

Kyra Lennon's writing makes it so easy to slip back into the world of the Westberg Warriors - it's like meeting up with old friends. This time the focus is Freya, slowly coming to terms - or not - with the death of her boyfriend. The characters are so well drawn, with flaws and redeeming features - and Lennon gets right to the heart of their emotions. Once again, I'm looking forward to the next book in the series, because I need to know what happens next! - Annalisa Crawford

Nobody Knows (Razes Hell Book 1)
Praise for Nobody Knows

"This was a fabulous read. Touching and full of insecurities and trauma. And feelings. Lots of feelings. Seriously, I defy you not to be moved by this beautiful story, especially the ending. Bring on #2." - Jo Evans, A British Bookworm's Blog

Acknowledgements

I have a seriously large amount of people to thank for helping me to get this book out into the world, but I'm going to try to keep it short! To Angela Cothran, Morgan Shamy, Leigh Covington, Elizabeth Seckman and Rachel Jackson, I'd like to say a gigantic thanks for your advice and hard work in helping me whip Game On into shape. It was a long road, and I appreciate every word of encouragement you gave me to guide me to this point.

Clare Dugmore – what can I say? Without you, this story may never have reached completion. I literally could not have done it without your encouragement. You have been my number one cheerleader since I met you, and that is why I'm sitting here writing my acknowledgements, and not cowering in the corner, afraid to let anyone see my work! For your friendship, wise words, unwavering belief in me and many, many hours of laughter – I thank you.

Chapter 1
Rebel By Name

I stormed out of the locker room, letting out a growl of annoyance. My heavy footsteps bounced off the stone walls, echoing around me, but not loud enough to drown out the sound of his voice in my mind. The clicking of my heels aggravated my throbbing temples until I thought my head would explode.

'Come on, Leah. Admit it. You want another chance.'

As if.

I walked up the stairs to the training ground's lavish restaurant where the wait staff greeted me with a smile I was too angry to return. I craved vodka but alcohol wasn't permitted, not even after hours. I ordered an orange juice and promised myself a proper drink later. Dealing with such a sleaze every day I was astounded I didn't have a fully-fledged drinking problem.

Radleigh 'Rebel' McCoy thought being the star of the Westberg Warriors made him a Big Deal. Maybe to the fans, but to me, he was a royal pain in the arse. If I'd known signing a contract with the Warriors would lead to such a high level of stress I would definitely have had second thoughts about scrawling my name on the dotted line.

The restaurant was always full at the end of the day, and the noise of chattering men did nothing to ease my aching head. Instead of going home after five hours of intense soccer training, the players preferred to eat on site. I could only assume the harder they trained, the more energy they needed before getting into their fancy sports cars and driving back to their mansions where their supermodel wives and girlfriends waited to boink their aches away.

Easy on the snark, lady. Your small town mentality is starting to show.

Chuckling in spite of my rage, I propped myself against the sleek black bar. If the room hadn't been so full I would have rested my flaming cheeks against the cool marble to extinguish my fury.

"Miss Walker."

Oh boy.

I closed my eyes for a second, hoping I'd imagined the sound of his deep, over-confident voice but I could sense him behind me. *Eau de Self-Importance* swirled in the air around me.

"Mr McCoy."

"Can I buy you a drink?"

There are only two types of people who would offer to buy a drink for a woman they'd only just finished arguing with. Idiots and egomaniacs.

Radleigh McCoy was no idiot.

"No. Thank you."

A shiver rippled across my skin. Instead of being repelled by the brush-off, he moved closer, his breath tickling my perfectly straightened hair. My impulse was to drive my elbow into his ribs but I thought better of it. Too many witnesses.

Once the bartender handed me my drink, I turned to face McCoy. I use the term loosely, though. At six feet four he towered way above my mere five feet two inches.

"Are you still here?" I asked, as if I couldn't feel the imprint of his rock hard abs on my back.

"I was hoping you'd keep me company." His ice blue eyes danced with amusement.

"Radleigh, I only put up with you because I have to. Am I not making myself clear?"

His lips curved into a grin. "I love how you say my name with that cute British accent."

Since I moved to America over a year ago, I'd heard that line a lot. It didn't irk me nearly as much coming from other men, though. I stepped around him, making a mental note never to use his first name again.

"Excuse me."

I breezed across the restaurant as coolly as possible with anger surging through me. To him, it was all a bit of a laugh. Witty banter to unsettle the new girl. For me, it was a challenge to get through the day without knocking his head off his shoulders.

"Easy tiger," Will Carter obviously spotted the murderous look in my eye as I threw myself down into the chair beside him.

"Why? Of all the soccer stars in the world, why did I get stuck with Radleigh McCoy?"

Freya Phillips gave me a knowing smile. "There's a reason your job was always available, Leah."

Freya sat opposite Will at the table. They were both soccer coaches, and the first people I'd met on the team aside from the manager, Richard Bailey. Freya was pretty much the only reason I'd been able to accept my job. The Warriors had needed me to start immediately but when I applied for the position in Los Angeles, I lived in Boston. Sleeping on sofas until I found my own place didn't appeal at all, so Richard introduced me to Freya. She needed someone to share the rent on her apartment, and I needed somewhere to live. We connected instantly, chatting like old friends, and we hadn't stopped talking since.

"What did he do?" Will asked.

"Today, or since I started working here?"

Will shrugged. "Let's say since you started working here."

"Okay, on my first night, he tried to chat me up. You know how the story goes. *'You have the most beautiful eyes, I'm very rich, want to see my bedroom?'* Blah, blah, blah."

"And because you turned him down, he's more determined than ever," Will guessed, with amazing accuracy. "You did turn him down, right?"

"Of course," I told him, insulted by the insinuation I would drop my knickers for a glass of wine. "Do you think I'd risk my job for a quick tumble in the sheets with him?"

"Okay, okay. I'm sorry."

Another groan escaped my lips. "I don't understand. Thousands of women would kill to sleep with him, I've seen them screaming at him like he's a rock star. Why bother with me when I'm obviously not interested?"

"He likes a challenge," Freya answered. "It's a game to him."

"Well, I don't want to play."

My eyes flicked towards the bar where McCoy chatted to some of his teammates. Like me, he'd changed out of his training gear already. Even if he hadn't, he would still have stood out among the sea of royal blue and black in the room. He had an elusive presence many men thought they had, but few truly possessed. The biggest problem was, he knew it.

"You need to be careful. Many women have quit their jobs here because of the way he treated them."

"Please! I may be struggling at the moment, but I won't be forced out of a job by an over-sexed, over-confident-"

"I'm serious." Will halted me before I started swearing in an unladylike manner. "Richard didn't want a woman taking the physiotherapist job because of how McCoy is but you impressed him so much, he couldn't pass you up."

"He called you 'feisty,' which you are." Freya grinned.

5

"What I'm saying is," Will went on, "you're tough, but so is he. Nobody has ever fought against McCoy and won. The best thing you can do is keep your head down and wait for him to get bored."

Saturdays without a match were my favourite days. Training didn't start until ten, but as early as nine-thirty, a few staff members milled around the training ground, grabbing a quick bite to eat or getting bottles of water to take onto the field.

The sun streamed in through the glass wall of the restaurant, and rays of light bounced off the sparkling cutlery laid out in preparation for lunch. The Warriors' restaurant could easily have been mistaken for a hotel dining room if it weren't for the unmissable view of the pitch. The decor reminded me of a beach hut with its soft sand coloured walls and laminate wood floor. Huge potted plants surrounded large pillars, and artsy photos of Los Angeles hung behind the bar. The tracksuited team members looked out of place amongst such delicate furnishings, but there was no denying it was a great spot for relaxation.

Freya and I headed into the restaurant after helping ourselves to some coffee from the machine as McCoy and teammate Bryce Warren were leaving.

Thank you, God. Thanks for ruining my day before it's even begun.

Will's words about lying low around McCoy weighed heavily on my mind. He was right, of course, but holding my tongue while being irritated was not a skill I possessed.

"Morning," Bryce greeted us, and we smiled in response.

Bryce Warren was beefy with a capital B. Okay, so it's not entirely professional to get a kick out of rubbing a player's muscles, but every job has to have some perks. Bryce's biceps were mine.

"So, anyway," McCoy said, "you should've seen her, man. She was stacked!"

Clearly we'd inadvertently interrupted a conversation that would have been more at home in the locker room. The stench of testosterone filled my nostrils and Freya and I walked on, not wanting to be subjected to any more of McCoy's bragging. Unfortunately for my bullshit sensitive ears, they stopped by the coffee machine.

As McCoy poured himself a drink, Bryce said, "So, what happened?"

"What do you think?" McCoy laughed. "I left her in bed this morning. She was pretty tired."

"I'm surprised you had the energy after that woman on Wednesday night!"

The mind boggled.

The guys strolled back into the restaurant, still laughing, but halted when they reached our table.

"Did you have a good evening, ladies?" McCoy asked.

"Yes, thanks," I answered, reminding myself to stay calm.

"Another night at home alone?"

"Well, we don't all have an endless parade of desperate groupies following us around so we can engage in meaningless sex."

Dammit.

"You don't know what you're missing."

"Oh, but I do. In the morning, the world will be treated to another detailed news story about some bimbo's night of passionate love making with the great Radleigh McCoy, complete with photos of said bimbo exposing too much of her cleavage and complaining about how you never called her, but hopes you'll be in touch soon to rock her world again. Sounds divine."

McCoy's grin faded, his blue eyes turning cold. I'd only ever seen him use that look out on the field when someone crossed him, and it was usually followed by a spectacular foul. The chances of him tackling me in the middle of the restaurant were pretty slim so I gave him my most charming fake smile until he took the hint and walked away.

"Well, that put him in his place." Freya giggled. "Urgh, I can think of nothing worse than spending a night with him. He's so self-involved, I bet he shouts out his own name when he reaches orgasm."

My mouthful of coffee burned the back of my throat as I choked out a laugh.

I didn't *want* to pick a fight with him, but if he thought I was going to let him walk all over me, he had another think coming. I'd clashed with men's egos over and over in my line of work, but I hadn't been broken yet. I'd be damned if I'd let Radleigh McCoy be the one to grind me down.

****

The morning passed without any major problems. As soon as the clock struck twelve, Freya, Will and I got changed and headed out of the training ground for some retail therapy.

Rodeo Drive thrilled me more than any place I'd ever been. It was a work of art for people who love to shop, with its pristine stores and palm tree lined pavements. I wouldn't be able to afford anything for a while, but just walking along the immaculate paths and breathing in the air of wealth was a dream. Freya and I dragged Will in and out of designer clothing stores, browsing the rails for things I could buy when my first pay check came in.

After three hours, I'd purchased an $800 dress.

Call me weak, but I hadn't splurged on anything so frivolous since I lived in London and discovered Manolo Blahniks. Before I could spend any more of my savings, I pleaded exhaustion and we went home.

I still struggled to think of Freya's apartment as mine. She insisted I spread my personal belongings around so I'd feel more comfortable and it helped, but I was very aware almost everything had lived there long before me. It was a gorgeous place to live, though. The building contained six flats on three floors, all overlooking the ocean. The view seemed to stretch for miles. For a beach lover like me, there was nothing better than looking out at the endless blue, listening to the calming sound of the waves.

Any thoughts of relaxing flew right out the window when we saw Radleigh McCoy waiting by the entrance to the apartments. He casually leaned against the wall like it was the most normal thing in the world for a famous soccer player to hang out outside the home of two women who couldn't bear the sight of him. The moment he spotted me, he straightened and squared his shoulders as if preparing for battle.

My stomach lurched.

"Freya, does he usually lurk outside your apartment?"

She shook her head, her blonde ponytail swinging wildly. "He's never been here before."

"Oh joy. This should be fun."

As we approached, McCoy smiled and eyed our insane amount of bags. "Looks like you've been busy."

"What do you want?"

Unfazed by the bluntness in Freya's tone, he said, "I wanted to talk to Leah."

"Can't it wait until work?"

He shrugged. "I guess, but I'm here now."

Freya silently asked if I needed her to stay and I shook my head. How much trouble could he cause in broad daylight? She took my bag from me and headed inside, glancing back before she ducked into the lift.

The second she disappeared out of sight, McCoy stepped towards me, pressing me against the door. He placed his hands either side of me, trapping me in place. My breath caught in my throat at the suddenness with which he'd advanced. He leaned in closer, not with any force, just so our bodies lightly touched.

Oh, he smells good.

He usually smelled like the other players, a weird mixture of grass and sweat. I'd never been close to him when he was freshly showered. The scent and his unexpected nearness made my head spin a little, momentarily throwing me off balance.

"We need to talk."

Focus.

With a shake of my head, I cleared the fog clouding my brain. "So talk. But get the hell off me unless you want to hear me scream."

With a hint of a smile, he dropped his hands to his sides but didn't step back and I had to tilt my head up to look at him.

"I think we should make a deal," he said.

"Oh, really? What could you possibly offer me that I would want?"

Apart from you not to smell so good.

"I'd like to call a truce. I'll leave you alone and be a good little boy, and in return, you start being nicer to me in front of my friends."

"You're kidding?" I narrowed my eyes. "You came all the way over here because I made a tiny dig at you in front of Bryce? He should be aware of what you're like without me having to enlighten him."

"Well, he's known me long enough to accept all my faults, not that I have many, but that's not the point. Some people don't know me so well. You included."

"I know enough."

"Maybe you're wrong."

"Sure. You shoved me up against the door because you're a kind, sensitive guy, not because you get horny every time a woman so much as looks at you."

"Not *all* women."

His eyes locked onto mine and it became glaringly obvious how he charmed so many into bed. With well-timed words and a face that would have made Greek gods envious, Radleigh McCoy possessed all the skills to charm a girl's pants off.

I put my hands against his chest and pushed him away. I didn't trust him for a second, but I was willing to play along, for the time being at least. *If* it worked, and I got a break from his constant come-ons, it would be worth it.

"You've got yourself a deal. But if you make even one more inappropriate suggestion towards me I will not be responsible for my actions."

A filthy grin spread across his face. "Is that a promise?"

"Jesus, you can't stop for a second!"

"Sorry." He held his hands up. "I'm sorry. Starting now, I'll be the perfect gentleman."

Without another word I turned away, tapped in the security code and leapt through the doors into the building, my heart pounding unnaturally fast. The moment I stepped into the lift, I sagged back against the mirrored wall.

It wasn't fair. It wasn't fair that I'd stumbled across the kind of man I used to find irresistible, or that he'd managed to stare right inside my head to locate my weaknesses. The thrill of being wanted while pretending not to be interested was a game I'd played over and over during my youth. I'd *thrived* on it. I'd done more than my share of getting mixed up with men who were all ego and muscles, and Radleigh McCoy reminded me exactly why I'd given them up. Danger, the chase. It was never worth the pain in the end.

Unfortunately, my body hadn't got the memo yet.

Chapter 2
Mini Clones Of Bree

"Ahh, that's freaking cold!"

"Sorry, Jesse. This will feel better soon, I promise."

"I've never had an ice massage before. Now I know why!"

The blond soccer player writhing with discomfort on my table had suffered a Grade 2 ankle sprain during the last Warriors match after an aggressive tackle. He'd taken a nasty fall, and with the weight of his opponent's boot stomping down on it, he was lucky his ankle hadn't broken.

"It's not so different to applying an ice pack," I told him, circling the ice cup over his injury. "If this doesn't help, I swear I'll never do it again."

Jesse laughed in spite of his soreness. "I'll hold you to that."

"Has there been any improvement since Sunday?"

"Not much. Painkillers help but once they wear off I'm back where I started."

The frustration was clear on his face. I'd seen the same expression many times over the years. Working with sports injuries was mostly rewarding, but I'd watched grown men crumble because their careers had been ruined by something which, for others, would merely be an inconvenience. Jesse's case wasn't career-threatening by any means but his sprain would put him out of action for at least two weeks, maybe longer.

"These things take time," I said. "I'll do my best to get you back on the field as soon as I can."

"Hmm, I'm not sure if I trust you and your voodoo techniques!"

"Hey." I laughed. "This is legitimate. I can't believe you've never had an ice massage before."

13

"I'm new, like you. I was scouted in high school. I've been playing soccer since I was a kid but I've never had this level of care before."

His words triggered something in my head. When I first joined the Warriors, I did some research about the players so people wouldn't think I was a complete noob. Not only was Jesse Shaw scouted in high school, he was the youngest player the Warriors had ever signed. Originally from Phoenix, Jesse's parents moved to Westberg so he could work with the team he'd supported his whole life. The fact he didn't mention what a big deal he was only multiplied my respect for him. If he could keep his feet on the ground while working alongside some of the biggest egos in the sporting world, he'd go far.

"I'm sorry," I said again, choosing to pretend I didn't know the truth. "My ignorance about the team is becoming all too clear right now. I can tell you a few things about English teams. Over here, I'm lost."

"In England you call it football."

"It *is* football. It physically hurts me to say soccer."

A knock on the door interrupted our laughter. I glanced up to find Will standing in the doorway.

"Leah, Richard's looking for you. Are you nearly done here?"

Concern was etched on Will's face. The only other times I'd seen him look that way were the rare occasions he found a crease in his shirt.

"Kind of. I need to finish this massage and strap Jesse up then I'm free."

"Okay. Richard said to tell you to go to his office as soon as you can."

He attempted to duck out into the corridor but I called him back. "What's going on?"

"Not sure. He sounded pretty serious."

14

Memories of my last few days flicked through my head like the highlight reel of a silent movie as I searched for an event worthy of getting me into trouble. Nothing sprang to mind.

"Thanks, Will. I'll go and see him when I finish up here."

Will gave me a reassuring smile before getting back to his duties, and I continued working on Jesse's ankle.

By the time I was done, my panic levels had reached epic proportions. My palms were sweaty as I walked towards my boss' office; something which never happened. Talking to Richard had only ever been pleasant and I wasn't crazy about the idea of that changing.

Richard Bailey was a legend, highly regarded as one of the top U.S soccer players of all time. In his youth, he played for the Westberg Warriors and as well as being a skilled goal scorer, he was once the hottie of the soccer world. Twenty-five years on his looks had faded a little. The stress of managing such a high profile team had aged him but he was still as fit, if not fitter than most of the guys he trained.

"Hi," I said, peering into his office. "You wanted to see me?"

His head snapped up. "Leah, yes. Come in. Sorry to pull you away from work but I need to clear something up."

I stepped inside, closing the door behind me. "What's the problem?"

"Radleigh McCoy has made a complaint about you."

It took a moment for the words to sink in. *He* made a complaint about *me?*

"Don't worry," Richard said. "I had to follow this up but I know how McCoy is. If people don't bow down to him he thinks they're disrespecting him. I just want to hear your side. He says you're treating him differently than the other players and you've been bad-mouthing him."

Oh, in his filthy-minded dreams!

15

"Bad-mouthing him? Richard, with an ego that size, do you think he'd even notice an insult?"

I hadn't intended to blurt out exactly what was on my mind, but Richard gave an almost undetectable smile. "Good to see you've got the measure of him."

"Damn right I have. He's got a bee in his bonnet because I… well, I *did* answer him back in front of Bryce Warren on Saturday. Otherwise, I've been nothing but professional with him. Geez, if anyone should be complaining, it's me!"

"You have a complaint to make about McCoy?" Richard asked, halting my verbal diarrhoea.

The last thing I wanted was for Richard to think I couldn't deal with him. After all, part of the reason he hired me was because I was 'feisty.' He had unknowingly given me the perfect opportunity to report McCoy for his behaviour towards me but I had no intention of letting either of them think I couldn't cope.

I shook my head. "It's nothing I can't handle. He's just been a bit … suggestive."

Richard's eyes darkened. "Leah, if he's hassling you, you need to tell me because I take this kind of thing very seriously."

"It's nothing," I insisted. "But if things change you'll be the first to know."

Especially since he's been so petty.

"So what happens now? Do I get an official warning or something?"

Richard shook his head. "Nothing official. You don't even deserve to be here now. However, if you can be extra nice to him for a few days you'll be doing me a huge favour. I can tell him I've had a word with you, and everyone's happy."

He was playing it fast and loose with his definition of happy. Being 'extra nice' to McCoy sounded more like a punishment than a prize but when the alternative was a black mark against my name, I had no choice but to take it.

I excused myself, taking a few deep breaths before heading out to the pitch. Freya's comment about McCoy playing games echoed in the depths of my mind. Less than forty-eight hours ago, he'd attempted to call a truce, yet I'd had my arse hauled into Richard's office over something I hadn't even done.

Game on, McCoy. Game. On.

Most of the team were running laps with the coaches keeping a close eye on them. I spotted McCoy almost immediately among the throng of players, and willed him to fall on his bum so I had a legitimate excuse to "accidentally" inflict some pain on him using the handy disguise of treatment. My wish was denied. He sped the length of the field without a stumble and his teammates met him with much praise at the end.

Git.

I lurked on the sidelines until I caught Will's eye. He whispered something to Freya before jogging over.

"What did Richard say?" he asked, wiping beads of sweat from his forehead. The sun was so scorching, even the short distance he ran made him melt from the heat.

"McCoy made a complaint about me. He told Richard I've been bitching about him."

Will let out a laugh of disbelief. "That was a fast move, even for McCoy. Richard didn't believe him, did he?"

"I don't think so, but he couldn't be seen to be ignoring a complaint."

"I don't think you need to worry about this, Leah. Richard doesn't like McCoy any more than the rest of us but he thinks the world of you."

Richard had taken me under his wing from the beginning, perhaps because I was so far away from home. He seemed quite protective of me. However, having the boss on my side wouldn't last long if I couldn't find a way to work in blissful harmony with the team hero.

"I'm not worried as much as annoyed. Being friendly to McCoy might kill me."

"It's a sacrifice we all make," Will said dramatically, making me laugh. "You wanna hang out after work?"

"Depends. Freya, Bree and I plan to abuse the facilities this afternoon. We're swimming and hot-tubbing but you're welcome to join us."

Bree was the bubbly, ditzy wife of Jude Collinson, the team's goalkeeper. She often travelled to away matches with us, mainly because at twenty years old, she didn't like being left at home alone. I couldn't blame her. Rattling around in their enormous house even with security at the touch of a button was enough to make anyone uneasy. We formed a friendship during my first week when she came to me for help after she broke a nail. I couldn't help her, obviously, but she thought my accent was "like, totally awesome," so she stayed around to chat.

Bree *really* likes to chat.

"Hmm, and interrupt girl talk?" Will asked. "I think I'll pass."

****

I sank into the warm water, letting out a small sigh of relief as a stream of bubbles massaged my back. The day's tension began to slip away, replaced by calm.

The silence was perfection. Instead of shouts and whistles, the only sounds were the hot tub's low hums and the small ripples created by the jets caressing my tense muscles.

I didn't care that Freya and Bree were late, or that I'd had another crappy day. All that mattered was closing my eyes and letting the waves wash my worries away.

Think happy thoughts. Family, friends, cupcakes, designer handbags. The sound of my niece and nephew laughing, the smell of clean laundry.

The scent of a freshly showered Radleigh McCoy?

Startled, I opened my eyes

It was bad enough I had to share a city with him, I didn't want him invading my head space too. I closed my eyes again and tried to shove him out by picturing my home in England. Whenever my new life got a little crazy, I let my mind take a trip to familiar shores. There was a distinct irony to the habit because the idea of living in the Cornish countryside again made me shudder. The images of Cornwall's lush fields and stunning sea views however, always put me at ease. Visions of McCoy faded, and I transported myself to the glorious beaches of Newquay, where I'd spent many hours sitting on the soft sand, listening to the gentle sounds of the ocean.

"Hey, Sleeping Beauty. Wake up!"

The sound of Freya's voice made me smile and without opening my eyes, I said, "I'm not sleeping, I'm exorcising a demon."

I heard Freya and Bree climbing into the hot tub, and Freya laughed. "McCoy?"

"Yup."

"What did that meathead do now?" Bree asked, forcing me to lift my eyelids.

Her green orbs widened with interest and she was literally bouncing at the idea of hearing some gossip. Her red curls swung around her shoulders, the ends dipping into the water. "Ooh, is he still hitting on you?"

"You don't have to sound so happy about it."

19

"Leah, it's flattering! He thinks you're cute, which you totally are."

"Are you forgetting who we're talking about? This is Radleigh McCoy, womaniser extraordinaire, and you just called him a meathead!"

"He *is* a meathead. A super handsome meathead."

Bree was a breath of fresh air among the soccer wives and girlfriends. She didn't have a single bone of snobbery in her body, and she took no pleasure in the bitching and backstabbing that often went on. If scientists could make mini clones of Bree to hand out to everyone, the worldwide reduction in depression would be enormous.

"His looks don't make up for the fact that he's disgusting. Or for him reporting me for things I didn't do."

Her smile slipped into a frown. "I'm sorry, I didn't know."

I shrugged. "It's not your fault he doesn't like me."

"It's not about liking," Freya said. "McCoy is all ego and he's used to getting his way. He doesn't like being told he can't have what he wants."

"He doesn't want *me*." I rolled my eyes. "He wants the woman who turned him down."

"Yes. But that's you."

"I can't be the first woman who ever said no to him."

"I don't know," Bree mused. "Women can't get enough of him and he can't resist a pretty face."

"But Leah isn't just a pretty face," Freya pointed out. "She's a pretty face with a kick-ass attitude."

"Well, so are you," I said. "Has he ever hit on you?"

"No. Maybe I should be offended because he'll usually mount any woman with a pulse, but actually, I'm relieved."

"How about you, Bree?"

She shook her head. "I've seen him looking at me but he's never tried anything. He wouldn't dare go near a teammate's wife."

Bree clearly had more confidence in McCoy's restraint than I did. If he could show up at my flat and lie about his intentions, he'd have no problem betraying a colleague if he thought he would get away with it.

I had no idea what made me so interesting to him. Perhaps he assumed me being new meant I'd be an easy target. Too bad for him, being a pushover is not in my nature.

Chapter 3
I'll Never Be That Drunk

Travelling around America for away matches never got old. It fascinated me to visit different states and although we rarely got a chance to thoroughly explore, I always found time to indulge in one of my favourite hobbies. Collecting tacky souvenirs. It was a hobby I'd picked up as a teenager when I worked in a gift shop. We sold all kinds of bizarre crap tourists wouldn't have touched on home turf, but with their brains in holiday mode, they purchased it in bundles. My bedroom was full of random junk I'd bought from different cities, though I never really viewed it as junk. One day, I could look back on all my mementos and remind myself of the fun I'd had, and the places I'd been.

The week of my - let's call it "surprise" - meeting with Richard, we travelled to Arizona on Friday in preparation for a match on Saturday evening. The last few days of dodging McCoy had been trying, and I was more than ready to blow off some steam. Freya, Will and I made plans to find the best club in Phoenix and let our hair down for a few hours to relieve some of the stress.

After training, I took a nap so I'd be refreshed for our evening out, but a call from Bree woke me mid-afternoon. She begged me to go to her room to see the piles of new clothes she'd bought and I knew if I didn't go I'd never hear the end of it.

For an hour and a half, we rummaged through her insane amount of purchases like we were at the world's most upmarket jumble sale. She insisted on modelling almost every item – including the newest additions to her sexy lingerie collection. Good thing I was confident about my body or I'd have felt extremely depressed standing so close to a girl whose figure would have made Barbie weep with envy.

Bree's one-woman fashion show exhausted me, but she eventually released me and I joined Freya and Will for dinner in the hotel restaurant to fuel up for the night ahead.

"Hey," Freya said. "We thought you'd got lost!"

"I almost did." I took the seat opposite her and perused the menu. My stomach growled. "Bree wanted me to check out the newest additions to her wardrobe, and treated me to full demonstrations of how she plans to seduce Jude in her new underwear. I didn't think I'd get out alive."

"Death by designer labels. Not a bad way to go."

I smiled in agreement. "I invited her to the club with us later, I hope you don't mind."

"Of course not. The more the merrier."

"Excuse me," a deep voice said from behind me. "Did you guys mention something about a club?"

I turned my head to see an unfamiliar man tilting his chair backwards on two legs. His huge afro tickled my cheek and I shuffled sideways to escape his mop of hair. His skin was dark and smooth, and his chocolate brown eyes were the kind you could get lost in.

Sure Leah, because with all the drama with McCoy, what you need is another man on your mind.

"We sure did, buddy," Will answered. "You wanna come?"

"That okay?" he asked looking at Freya and me in turn.

"Fine by me," Freya said. "Leah?"

"Yeah, no problem," I replied, trying hard not to trip over my own tongue.

"We're meeting in the lobby at nine-thirty."

"Cool. I'll see you then."

Before he returned the front two legs of his chair to the floor, he gave me a smile I had trouble returning. The corners of my mouth twitched as if I had some kind of

23

unattractive tic, and heat rose in my cheeks.

Smooth.

Nobody said another word until we finished dinner, by which time, my face had - thankfully - returned to its normal colour.

"Okay, spill," Will said as we stepped out of the elevator and into the corridor. "What was with the blushing? Do you like Miguel?"

I gave a casual shrug, betraying my interest. "He's cute. Who is he?"

"Miguel Vega. He's our goalkeeper coach. This is his first day back in two weeks. Not sure how you missed him when you first started though."

My first week had been a blur of nerves, fake confidence and trying to memorise the names of the players. I ended every day so frazzled I barely remembered my own name, so it wasn't a big surprise Miguel had passed me by.

"You could do a lot worse than Miguel," Freya mused. "He's a nice guy."

"Plus, I think he was checking you out," Will added.

"Okay, slow down." I held up my hands in an attempt to stop them before they began planning the wedding. "I said he's cute, I didn't say I want to have his children."

"Do you blush over every man you think is cute?" Freya asked with a grin.

"Well no, but that doesn't mean I need to be forced on him."

"I'll introduce you later," Will said, ignoring my comment.

I nodded, resigned to the fact Will and Freya wouldn't let it drop. In spite of my fake coolness, a little buzz of excitement zapped at my insides.

****

"Oh dear God."

I spun around in circles, surveying myself in the bathroom mirror. I hadn't tried on my ridiculously expensive dress since the day I dented my bank balance to make it mine.

Has it always been this short?

It couldn't have been. I'd never have paid insane amounts of cash for something so tiny, not even on a shopping high. Can dresses shrink from being squashed in a suitcase among other clothes? Or maybe I'd grown an inch or two.

Ha. Not possible. I hadn't grown so much as a millimetre since I was thirteen.

"Leah, have you finished? I need to shower!"

I unlocked the door and went back into the bedroom where Freya hovered, waiting to get ready.

"Hey there, sexy lady!"

I stared at her to check if she was joking. She wasn't.

In the full length mirror in the corner of the room, I eyed myself critically again. I couldn't deny I looked good in red, and the spaghetti straps helped to show off my tan.

But it was so short.

"I think I look a bit… slutty."

"You do not!" Freya placed her hands on my waist. "What's the point of being cute and petite if you're not gonna flaunt it?"

"Don't you think Will might assume I'm trying too hard to impress a certain crazy haired coach if I wear this? I think I'll get changed."

I started towards the bathroom again, but Freya stopped me.

"Leah, we're going clubbing! All the girls will be wearing short dresses, and you don't have to worry about what anyone thinks. You're so British."

Freya often mocked me for *occasionally* being a stereotypical reserved Brit but I grew up in the countryside, in a place where you couldn't so much as sneeze without people knowing and having something to say about it.

You're not there anymore. You're free to do, and wear, what you want. Stop being so sensible!

"And you're sure I don't look like a five dollar hooker?"

"I'm sure."

Checking myself out in the mirror a third time, I sighed. "Okay, I'll be brave."

At nine-thirty we headed down to the lobby to meet Will, Bree and Miguel. The sight that greeted us made my mouth drop open. In addition to the people we were supposed to be meeting, were Jude Collinson, Jesse Shaw, Jesse's girlfriend Taylor, Bryce Warren, and Radleigh McCoy.

"Well you did say the more the merrier," I murmured, giving a small laugh.

"Don't worry. They'll all go off and do their own thing when we get to the club."

I figured Freya was right and as we approached them, Will popped out from the crowd, halting as he took in our appearance.

"Whoa."

"Put your tongue away," I said with a smile.

Will grinned. "You two look … wow."

His eyes lingered on Freya's simple black dress, then down her long legs as if she were the most beautiful woman in the world. Actually, there was a strong possibility Freya really *was* the most beautiful woman in the world. Her high cheek bones were striking and her smile could power the bright lights of Vegas for a week.

If she weren't my best friend, I would have hated her.

"Where did all these people come from?" Freya asked, peering over Will's shoulder.

"Word spread and this is what happened."

"But how? We only invited Miguel and..."

Bree. A vision of her bouncing down the hotel corridor, knocking on everyone's doors and telling them about the night out hurtled into my mind. I opened my mouth to share my theory when an unexpected shiver rippled across my skin. The kind you feel when you know someone's watching you. As I turned, a smile spread across McCoy's face. His eyes flashed hungrily, like a hunter seeking out its prey.

I tried to focus on how insulting that was, not how good he looked in his black trousers and white shirt. The top two buttons were open, allowing a glimpse of his well-toned, not to mention completely hair free chest. His smooth torso amused me the first time I'd seen him whip off his shirt. Soccer players were meant to be oozing masculinity, not baby oil.

We hadn't spoken a word to each other since he reported me to Richard. He shot me occasional smug glances, but my decision not to take the bait and scream at him for going back on his deal had kept him away.

"Okay," Will said, "we'll need a couple of cabs to get us all to the nightclub, so we'll split up and meet there."

Murmurs of agreement rippled through the crowd and I turned to locate Bree. She and Taylor were complimenting each other's outfits, not that there was much of Taylor's outfit to admire. A piece of pink floaty material masquerading as a dress hugged her trim figure. With her skinny legs, she slightly resembled a stick of candyfloss.

"Damn, that dress looks good on you," a far too familiar voice said from behind me. "It'll look even better on my bedroom floor later."

Urgh.

"Get lost McCoy." I didn't bother turning around.

"Can't I even compliment you?"

"The only thing I want from you is space, so back off."

"Okay, but if you change your mind -"

"I'll never be that drunk. And stop staring at my cleavage."

McCoy laughed. "You're good."

"And you're predictable. Have a nice evening."

The Blue Tattoo nightclub obviously had an excellent reputation. Hundreds of people moved to the loud, energetic music, their bodies illuminated by the coloured lights. With the beat of the music pumping through us, Freya, Bree and I boogied our way to the crowded bar, Will and Jude close behind. The others hadn't arrived yet which was fine with me. I wanted to have at least half a glass of something alcoholic inside me before Will introduced me to Miguel.

"I can't wait to get down there." Freya looked over the wooden railing to the enthusiastic clubbers below. "I need to dance!"

"All those sweaty teenagers waiting to grope you," Will teased. "Charming."

I laughed. "Hey, I haven't been groped in years. This might be my lucky night."

"Leah!" Bree shrieked. "I thought you were a good girl!"

"I have my moments," I told her, winking.

The atmosphere of the club had me feeling a bit wild and I knew once I started dancing, I may not stop. This was *my* night. I intended to make sure I enjoyed every second.

The rest of the Westberg posse arrived shortly after but only Miguel joined us. Will introduced us, then dragged Freya, Bree and Jude away so we could get to know each other.

Not only was Miguel laid back and easy to talk to, he had the cutest dimples in his cheeks when he smiled. By the time our drinks were ready, those first feelings of attraction had grown into the early stages of '*I want to make him mine,*' moving rapidly towards, '*If he doesn't kiss me tonight I may as well swap my suspenders for slippers.'*

"So how are you settling in over here?" Miguel asked, once we'd found a small vacant table to sit at. "Los Angeles is a lot different than England."

"Actually, I've been in the U.S for a while. I just moved from Boston, but it's still a big change. I love it, though. Everyone's been really welcoming."

Well. Almost everyone. Some people have been a pain in the arse. My eyes darted across the room, to where McCoy sat with Bryce Warren, both of them surrounded by women. At least if he was occupied with them, I wouldn't have to worry about him ruining my night by bothering me.

Miguel smiled knowingly. "Is McCoy giving you trouble?"

My shoulders sagged. Stupid of me to kill a perfectly pleasant conversation by letting McCoy enter my head. "Urgh, yes but I don't want to talk about him. I don't even like being in the same room with him."

"Don't let him bug you. He's basically harmless, and if he gets too much, Richard's pretty good at keeping him in line."

Harmless? Not what I'd heard. I didn't want to waste time debating it, though. Miguel's dark brown eyes were distracting and gorgeous. They sparkled when they met mine.

"Tell me more about you," he said. "What do you do when you're not working?"

Grateful for the subject change, I smiled. "Well, not too much yet. I'm still finding my way around. I love the beach, though. I like to sit out there after work sometimes and watch everyone surfing and stuff."

"Do you surf?"

"Never tried. I'd like to, though."

"I'd be happy to teach you sometime. I mean, if you want me to."

His dark skin reddened a little when he made the offer, and my stomach fluttered. I definitely wanted him to.

As much as I enjoyed Miguel's company, my feet were starting to tap in anticipation. I was gagging to party with my girls so when he went to buy another drink, he told me he'd meet me on the dance floor. I weaved through the crowds to find Freya and Bree surrounded by men with hungry eyes. They seemed oblivious to the attention, absorbed in the pounding beats. It didn't take long for me to get caught up in the rhythm too. I didn't even notice McCoy behind me until my killer heels crunched down on his foot. I whirled round to apologise but when I saw him, I swiftly changed my mind.

"Ow!"

Even with the volume of the music, I heard his yelp loud and clear.

"You shouldn't have been so close," I said, raising my voice over the noise. "Go away. I'm trying to enjoy myself. Although, stomping on your foot has helped improve my evening."

"I never knew you were a sadist." McCoy grinned. I didn't even want to imagine what sick perversions swirled around his brain.

"Did you want something?"

"Yes." McCoy placed his hands on my waist and pulled me close. "I want to dance with you."

This was the second time I'd been pressed against him, and the second time his closeness made my breath catch. The heat of his body ripped through me like fire and I gripped his wrists, pushing his hands away. "This is *not* the kind of music for dancing like that and even if it was, I wouldn't be dancing with you."

"Why not? What did I do to you?" His eyes challenged me to mention the complaint he made but when I held firm, he said, "What's with you and Miguel?"

"Are you spying on me now?"

"And you accuse *me* of being arrogant. No Leah, I don't need to spy on you. With you in that dress and the height of Vega's afro, it's pretty hard not to see you. So, you like him?"

"None of your damn business."

He shrugged. "A one night stand's probably what you need. Maybe then you won't be so uptight all the time."

I hated it. Hated how he made me so angry, and how I always reacted. Even though my head screamed for me to walk away, my mouth refused to let me.

"A quickie in some groupie's hotel room might satisfy you," I snapped, "but that's not my thing."

"How do you know if you've never tried it?"

"I have! It made me feel cheap and dirty, and that's why I don't do it anymore!"

He stared at me in surprise. He'd been trying to get under my skin, he hadn't expected me to confess the sins of my past.

Nice work. Now he thinks you're a harlot, he'll never leave you alone. His eyes continued to bore into me, still with the expression of surprise, as if he'd thought he had me all figured out until the moment I opened my mouth.

Yeah. People aren't always the way they seem.

A warm hand tugged at my arm. "Leah, come dance!"

Bree bounced on the balls of her feet like a toddler waiting for her mum to quit talking and start playing. Her enthusiasm waned when she noticed McCoy staring intently at me, his eyes heavy with questions. I could almost see her brain trying to figure out a way to save me from dealing with him.

"Mr McCoy." She flashed her most charming smile. "May I have this dance?"

Bree subtly winked at me, and gratitude flooded through me that she was so well versed in the girl code. She stepped forward and McCoy's gaze travelled up and down her curvy frame. It took all of my strength not to throw myself in front of her to protect her from his leering, but she took it in her stride.

"I would love to dance with you, Mrs Collinson," he answered, taking her hand.

I mouthed the words, 'thank you,' as he whisked her away. With a slight twinge of guilt, I moved back towards Freya and Miguel.

Miguel's dance moves were as wild as his hair. His craziness allowed me to let loose and I immersed myself in his zany dancing spirit, shoving my revelation to McCoy to the back of my mind. He probably wouldn't even remember in the morning anyway. Miguel kept me far too entertained to worry. He made me laugh until my ribs hurt, and it was in the middle of one of those fits of laughter that Bree caught our attention by squealing, "Yes! They're free at last!"

She grabbed my hand and dragged me along behind her to the middle of the dance floor where four raised, well-spaced poles stood. Judging by the people who'd been using them earlier, I thought they were for staff only, but I spotted several other clubbers racing towards them too. Bree had obviously been keeping a close eye on them and we just managed to beat out a group of young girls dressed as nuns.

"Sorry," Freya called. "No sinning for you!"

Bree pulled herself up on to the platform.

"You're kidding?" I asked, already knowing full well she had her heart set on shaking her booty in front of the masses of strangers.

Bree shook her head. "Come on!"

Freya had already started dancing and as she swung round the pole towards me, she laughed and gestured for me to join her. The alcohol I'd consumed had lowered my inhibitions so I smiled back at her before stepping up to one of the available poles.

"Imagine it's a man," Bree said with a cheeky smile on her face.

Laughing, I placed my hands on the cool metal pole and wiggled towards it. I spun around, swaying my hips from side to side and sliding up and down. Bree abandoned her pole to join mine, mirroring my moves perfectly. I looked round at her and grinned.

"Go Leah," she giggled before returning to her own pole.

I started to get a feel for it so I hoisted myself up into the air and swung round, bottom leg straight, top leg slightly bent.

As I whizzed round the pole, I let out a shriek. One of my expensive black heels flew off my foot into the crowd.

Fuck!

I landed - lopsidedly - glancing around like Cinderella for my missing shoe, praying it hadn't injured anyone. I was lucky not to have broken McCoy's toes earlier, but a flying six-inch heel could take someone's eye out.

I scanned the people nearby, searching for someone who looked angry but my eyes rested on a smiling Miguel.

He held my shoe up.

What are the chances …?

Shaking my head in amusement, I took off my other shoe then stepped back up to the pole to continue my dance. I felt less self-conscious this time, fired up knowing Miguel was watching me. Pulling out every sexy move I had, I didn't care if I looked ridiculous because there was one man who seemed to be enjoying every second.

When the song ended, I stepped down from the platform, hot, sticky and exhilarated.

If things don't work out at Westberg, there may be a career in pole dancing for me.

Miguel greeted me with a grin and handed me my disobedient heel.

"Sorry," I said, slipping my shoe on. "I didn't hurt you, did I?"

"No." He laughed. "And even if you had, the dance more than made up for it!"

High from the buzz, I slid my arms around him, touching him for the first time. His body was toned but much softer than I'd expected. It was comforting, like having my own life-sized teddy bear.

"Did I just make a complete fool of myself?"

"Not at all. In fact, from the way the guys in here are staring at you I'd say they would kill to be in my position right now."

I began to respond but a disturbing sight caught my eye over Miguel's shoulder, halting me before I spoke. Amongst the throng of happy clubbers, I noticed McCoy entwined with Taylor. His hands firmly held the exposed skin at her waist and she was grinding her hips against his.

"Oh hell."

Miguel turned to follow my gaze. "That's not good."

My eyes darted around, seeking out Jesse and hoping he hadn't seen them. I spotted him by the bar, staring in their direction, and my heart instantly went out to him.

"I should go and talk to him. He looks like he needs a distraction."

"Okay, I'll wait for you down here."

I gave him a quick hug, before making my way off the dance floor towards Jesse.

"Hey." I placed a gentle hand on his shoulder.

With a half-hearted smile, he said, "So you saw them too."

"I did. I don't think you should read too much into it, though."

"Leah, that's practically foreplay!"

It was hard to disagree. Taylor whispered something in McCoy's ear and he smiled like a man who was about to get lucky.

First me, then Bree, now Taylor? Not to mention all those other girls who'd thrust out their chests in front of him earlier. The man had no shame.

"Taylor's yours. You know that."

"I thought so too but now I'm not so sure. Of all the people in here, why did she choose McCoy? Why the man who made me want to be a soccer player?" He let out a deep sigh. "When I got selected to play for Westberg, I couldn't believe I was going to meet McCoy and play on the same team as him. I guess he is as much of a dick as the papers say."

The pain on Jesse's face made my heart break a little. Eighteen years old, starting out in his career and his life, only to think it was all over because the girl he loved was rubbing herself up against the man he idolised.

"Jesse, listen." I turned him to face me. "I'm no fan of McCoy but the only thing he cares for, besides himself, is the Warriors. He would never screw you over by taking your girlfriend."

I desperately hoped Bree was right in assuming McCoy wouldn't touch his teammates' women because I couldn't think of any other way to wipe away Jesse's sadness.

"What about Taylor?" he asked. "Can I trust her?"

"I don't know. But she's young, and being here with all these super famous people is probably really exciting for her."

"Did you behave that way when you first got here?"

"No," I said with a laugh, "but I'm eight years older than her. I don't look that good half naked. If I did, Bryce Warren would almost certainly have got a lap dance."

Jesse's face finally broke into a smile. "Hey, for an older woman, you've got it goin' on."

I playfully bumped my hip against his. "Come on, kiddo, let's get out there and show them you're not worried."

"I can't. Sprained ankle, remember?"

"Not a problem." I took his hand. "You stand still and I'll dance around you. That'll make her come running back!"

My prediction was correct. While we were laughing and dancing foolishly together, Taylor unwrapped herself from McCoy and joined us. Thankfully, she didn't seem upset by my dancing with her boyfriend. I didn't want to heal one rift, then immediately start another. I left them alone, satisfied I'd done my good deed for the day.

We arrived back at the hotel at three in the morning, and almost everyone was completely hammered. Miguel and I shared a taxi with Freya and Will, both of whom were staggering around, giggling. Freya had removed her shoes and she still couldn't walk straight. She and Will fell against each other as they tried to stumble through the revolving doors, then promptly collapsed on the floor, laughing hysterically.

"Do you think we should help them up?" I asked, unable to suppress a chuckle at how ridiculous they looked.

"In a minute." Miguel took my hand, and laced his fingers through mine. "Tonight's been cool. Maybe we can go out again sometime?"

I nodded. "I'd love to."

"I'll give you a call later, after we've had some sleep. We can grab a drink or something."

"Sounds good."

Miguel gave me a shy grin. "I'd really like to kiss you goodnight."

Funny how he'd gone from a confident party animal to an unassuming gentleman once we were alone. In the club, surrounded by people there hadn't been a hint of nervousness. Just the two of us in the cool night air, it was different.

Taking a small step closer to him, I said, "Well, it's only fair. You did find my glass slipper, after all."

His smile widened and he leaned in towards me. Just as his lips were about to touch mine, I pulled away slightly, resting my forehead against his.

"Wait. Please tell me there isn't a rule in our contracts that says we can't date?"

Miguel placed his finger under my chin and gently raised my head so he could look into my eyes. "There's no rule. Staff and players can't date, but there's nothing to say staff can't date each other."

A sigh of relief left my body. "Okay, good. I'd hate it if we couldn't do this."

I brushed my lips against his. They were so soft, so welcoming. His arms circled around my waist, gathering me into him to block out the late night chill. Heart pounding, I snuggled into his warmth.

It had definitely been a night to remember.

Chapter 4
Jude Collinson Is a Very Good Looking Man

I woke up at nine o' clock on Saturday morning to the sound of Freya retching in the bathroom. My stomach churned but I forced my tired body out of bed and tapped on the door.

"You okay?" I called.

"Yeah," Freya replied in a voice that said she was anything but.

My legs gave way due to the speed at which I'd got up, and I sat back down on my bed, massaging my aching temples.

The toilet flushed and Freya came out of the bathroom. Her long, blonde hair was unusually messy and tangled, and her skin as pale as a vampire before its next feed. She staggered over to her bed, moaning, "Never let me drink again. I had a great time, but -" she paused, "- we had a great time, right?"

"We did."

"Good. I don't remember much." She let out a pathetic laugh as she lay back on the bed. "I can't believe I got into this state."

"It doesn't hurt to go wild now and again."

"Says Little Miss *I'm not going out dressed like that*," Freya teased, her voice coming out as a mumble because she'd covered her face with her hands.

As my mind unfogged, a soppy grin crept across my face.

At least half an hour had passed before Miguel and I had gone to our rooms after stumbling out of the cab. After agreeing to arrange a date, we stood outside the hotel, kissing like a pair of hormonal teenagers until we got so cold we had no choice but to go inside. I couldn't wait to be with him again but my gut growled with hunger, and what I wanted more than anything was to indulge in a traditional English fry-up.

"I'm going to order something to eat," I said, reaching for the phone. "I'd ask if you want something but I'm guessing not."

Freya shook her head, her face whitening further at the idea of food, so I called room service and ordered breakfast for one. I'd just closed my eyes against my pounding headache, when my mobile rang. I answered quickly so as not to disturb Freya's hangover. "Hello?"

"Good morning, Leah."

The sound of Miguel's voice made me smile, not least because it proved the night before hadn't been a figment of my imagination. I'd been single for so long, I wouldn't have been surprised if the whole thing had been a fantasy created by my male deprived mind.

"Hi," I said. "How are you?"

"I'm good, thanks. Did you sleep well?"

"I did, but my head is thumping and I'm starving."

Miguel chuckled. "I didn't want to call too early to be sure I didn't wake you."

"Don't worry, you didn't. Freya puking woke me up." I yelped as her pillow hit me with more force than she should have been capable of mustering. "And now she's bullying me!"

"*You're* bullying *me*," she mumbled. "I'm dying here!"

"So, do you want to meet up before training?" Miguel asked while I giggled at Freya's response. "Nothing heavy after last night. Maybe we could watch TV in my room or something?"

For the average woman, his offer would definitely have fallen on the lame side. To me, a morning of television sounded like bliss. It would be much easier to talk in his room than in the hotel bar and more importantly, there wouldn't be anyone staring, trying to decide if anything was happening between us. The gossip circuit worked non-stop at Westberg, and I was in no rush to be at the centre of everyone's speculations, especially since I didn't know how things with Miguel would be away from the adrenaline of the club.

"Good plan," I told him. "Give me an hour or so to get ready, though."

"Okay. I'll see you soon."

Putting the phone down, I smiled to myself.

"Got a date?" Freya croaked.

"Not a date as such. But I'm going to see Miguel once I've eaten and fixed myself up a bit. I don't look too rough, do I?"

Freya heaved herself onto her side to face me. "Not at all. You're a little pale, but once you've eaten you'll be fine. I'm going to look like this forever!"

"No you won't. You need some more sleep. And you really should drink some water."

"I did. It made me sick."

"What a state to get into," I said, suppressing a laugh at how pitiful she looked. "Will you be okay if I leave you here on your own?"

She nodded. "Yeah, don't worry. If I need anything, I'll call Will. I should call him anyway to find out if he's as hungover as I am."

"I think it's a safe bet he's got his head down the loo."

After munching through my breakfast, I took a shower then changed into my work clothes. The black and royal blue Westberg Warriors tracksuit wasn't the most flattering outfit in the world, but there wasn't much point dressing in my every day clothes, only to change again in a couple of hours. I pulled my hair back into a ponytail, checked on Freya once more, then made my way to Miguel's room with nerves bubbling inside me.

Tommy Salinger opened the door. It hadn't occurred to me how inconvenient sharing a room could be until I saw the amused grin on his face.

Fabulous. The news I'm spending the morning in Miguel's room will be spread through the team in no time.

Tommy let me inside, where Miguel was lounging on his bed flicking through the television channels.

"Hey," he said. "How's the headache?"

"Better. I just needed something to eat and a cup of coffee. Actually, I could use several more cups before work."

"I think I can arrange that. Come sit down."

My British upbringing told me I should perch daintily on the edge of the bed instead of launching myself at him for a kiss, which was what I wanted to do. It didn't help that Tommy was still watching us, smirking.

"Okay," he said. "I'm gonna head out."

"See you later." Miguel gave him a wave.

"Have fun, and don't do anything I wouldn't do," he added, winking before he stepped outside.

"He's clearly from the Radleigh McCoy school of subtlety," I said, dryly.

McCoy hadn't crossed my mind since I saw him dancing with Taylor at the club. In fact, I couldn't recall seeing him again afterwards. He'd most likely hooked up with one of the other scantily clad youngsters who were drooling over him, and disappeared back to her place for another night of debauchery.

Miguel laughed and patted the space on the bed beside him. "I don't bite."

"Glad to hear it." I kicked off my trainers and slid across the bed towards him. I nestled under his arm as his lips sought out mine in a kiss that already seemed so familiar.

41

"Now I know I didn't imagine last night," Miguel said, stroking my cheek.

"I know what you mean. I felt sure I'd wake up at home in L.A and find none of this really happened. Which would have been disappointing."

"It sure would."

The two of us stayed curled up together until we absolutely had to get up for work. It didn't matter that we didn't speak much. Being wrapped in his arms, doing something as simple as watching television was heaven. I felt safe with him, and I hadn't experienced that with a man in a long while.

****

Training only lasted for two hours on match days. Just as well, because after our night out, nobody was functioning properly. We weren't supposed to drink the night before a match but over half the team had spectacularly broken that rule. Freya and Will did a stellar job of hiding their hangovers, but the moment we were free to leave, we all went straight back to the hotel to nap for a few hours before we had to be at the stadium again.

The afternoon's rest made all the difference to the Warriors, and when they showed up for work again, they were refreshed and raring to go. Half an hour after they arrived, the players were out on the pitch doing some gentle exercises and I was in my designated treatment room, waiting for Jude so I could strap up his knee before the game. He'd been complaining about pain earlier, possibly caused by him busting moves after several beers at the club, and worsened during training. Keeping the joint well protected for the match was critical but I intended to send him to the hospital for a check-up when we got home.

I filled the waiting time by thinking about Miguel. God, I'd turned into a complete sap, and I hadn't even known him for a full twenty-four hours. We intended to meet Freya and Will in the hotel bar for a quiet, alcohol-free drink after the match. We hadn't spoken much that morning; we were too tired, but I couldn't wait to spend more time with him and get to know him better.

A sharp rap on the door startled me, but it wasn't Collinson who appeared. Instead, Richard stepped into the room.

"Leah, have you seen Radleigh?"

Oh sure, he's always with me because, you know, we get on like a house on fire.

"No," I answered. "Why?"

"He hasn't shown up yet.

There was no mistaking the stress on Richard's face, and this wasn't the first occasion I'd seen him in a McCoy-induced tizzy.

"Well, if I see him I'll tell him to hurry up," I said.

"I need you to do more than that. I gotta get back on the field with the guys, so can you call him and tell him to get his ass in gear?"

"Me? But… why? Why not Will or Freya, or… anyone?"

"Everyone's busy."

"I'm busy too," I told him, jumping up from my seat and opening up my medical bag to rummage for bandages. "I have to deal with Jude's knee and if I don't-"

"Leah," Richard interrupted, smiling at my sudden eagerness to work on anything but talking to the man I loathed. "Please. I need McCoy here. Think of this as a way to practice being nice to him."

My boss was no fool. He knew I'd been keeping away from McCoy in order to avoid ripping his head off. Unfortunately, no matter how much I wished I didn't have to talk to him, it would happen eventually. Richard was just forcing my hand.

"Okay," I said, trying not to sigh out loud like a teenager who'd been asked to tidy her room. "You'd better give me his number, then."

I pulled out my mobile and typed in the digits Richard gave me. I didn't bother saving them to my phone. I had no intention of using the number again.

"Thanks, Leah."

"Sure," I answered as he sped out of the room.

I took a long, slow breath as I stared at McCoy's phone number, reminding myself to remain even-tempered no matter what he said.

I pressed the call button before I could change my mind. He answered after the sixth ring.

"Leah. What can I do for you?"

With those words, he shattered the air of calm confidence I'd built up.

"How did you know it was me?"

"You're part of the team. I have all the team phone numbers, in case of emergency."

I felt certain that was some kind of privacy violation but I didn't want to waste time debating it. *Give him the message, get back to work.*

"Richard asked me to call you because you're supposed to be here by now."

"I'm running late."

"Are you on your way?"

"Not yet. I've just taken a shower."

"You're still at the hotel?" I asked, battling to keep an incredulous squeal out of my voice. There was running late, and there was taking the piss. He was most definitely taking the piss.

"Yes I'm still at the hotel."

"Are you even ready for this evening?"

"Why? What did you have in mind? My room, room service, wine?"

"I meant are you ready for the game?" I corrected, with fake politeness of an Oscar winning standard.

"I'm always ready for a game," he said, his voice taking on a much huskier tone. "I just need someone to play with."

The desire in his voice robbed me of the last of my already fragile composure which, in turn, made me furious with myself, and then with him as he laughed.

"I have to go," I said. "But … be here as soon as you can. Bye!"

I hung up, my face flushed and hot with rage. *Damn you, McCoy.* He always found the right way to unsettle me in any situation. In spite of my determination to show him I wouldn't be pushed around, he always seemed to have the upper hand.

And his voice, thick with innuendo. Ten years ago, hell, even five years ago, I wouldn't have thought twice about taking him up on his offer. Things had changed since then. *I'd c*hanged.

McCoy eventually showed up at the stadium having missed an hour and fifteen minutes of training, and was promptly ripped into by Richard. I ducked out of the office to the pleasant sound of my boss telling him if he was ever late again without a good excuse, he would be issued an official warning.

It was music to my ears.

When the match began, I took my seat with the coaches. Miguel sat behind me, and although we couldn't engage in any public displays of affection, he occasionally leaned forward to whisper something in my ear on the pretence of talking about the game.

"Hey." Freya nudged me in the ribs. "Can you two knock it off? You're making the rest of us feel sick."

I craned my neck to look round at Miguel and in perfect unison we said, "I don't know what you're talking about."

"Oh come on now!" Freya laughed. "Speaking the same words so soon?"

"We were discussing how well Collinson is doing in spite of his knee injury."

"Ohh. So Miguel wants to take *Jude* out to dinner next week to, what, celebrate his goal saving achievements?"

"Jude Collinson is a very good-looking man," Miguel said with mock seriousness. "He'd be lucky to have me."

"That's true. Perhaps Leah and Bree could hook up, too?"

Freya wasn't speaking loudly, but something about the suggestion of two women getting together alerted the senses of every man within a five foot radius. It was like they all had some kind of built-in lesbian radar. Heads turned in our direction and Jesse said, "On behalf of the team, I want to say we totally support this idea."

"Keep dreaming lads, I haven't kissed a girl since Uni."

Jesse let out a small groan. "Do you have photos?"

"Kidding!" I laughed. "I'm strictly men only!"

Our sordid conversation came to an abrupt halt as the crowd got louder, and chants for the Warriors filled the stadium. We all turned our attention to the pitch where Cody Rivera sped towards the opponent's goal, expertly weaving his way through Phoenix's poor defence. He paused for a moment, weighing up his options and as he was about to be tackled, he hammered the ball the width of the pitch where

McCoy waited. As the ball came to him, he leapt in the air to head it into the goal. It was as if he had springs on his feet as he soared. Instead of making contact with the ball, he was blocked by another player and their heads cracked together in mid-air. The ball was kicked away, but while Phoenix's number twelve landed with barely a stumble, McCoy crashed to the ground.

Everyone on the Warriors bench jumped to their feet, shouting, and the referee blew the whistle and ran to McCoy. Time seemed to stand still as we waited for him to get up but he didn't move. Richard and Will walked briskly on to the field to assess the damage to their star player, the medics quickly following.

I'd never seen anything like that before. Sure, I'd seen sportspeople with bones sticking out of their bodies at weird angles, but I'd never witnessed such a violent bashing of heads. I truly thought I was going to vomit right there in front of everyone.

"Is he going to be okay?" I asked, watching McCoy's lifeless form being carefully manoeuvred on to a stretcher.

"I think so," Freya said. "It's probably just a concussion."

My eyes widened in surprise at the casual way she'd said *concussion*. People die from head traumas, and he'd been hit incredibly hard.

The more time that ticked away without him moving, the more nauseous I became. It was probably only minutes before he was carried off the pitch but it seemed like hours.

Shake it off! You've witnessed things far more horrific than this.

Miguel wrapped a supportive arm around my waist. "Come on, Leah."

I let him usher me off the field into the tunnel, my legs shaking the whole way.

"You must think I'm a complete wimp." I leaned against him a little. "I'm not usually this pathetic, it's just… head injuries freak me out, and McCoy's always so… I don't know. It was weird seeing him like that."

Miguel tightened his arm around me. "I don't think you're a wimp. I think you're sweet to be so concerned."

There was no sign of McCoy in the tunnel, but Richard was pacing the floor, speaking into his mobile.

"The match will go ahead," he said. "Call me as soon as you know anything."

Richard snapped his phone shut and wearily rubbed his eyes. A long-term injury to McCoy could throw Westberg's chances of winning any trophies way off course, and even though Richard usually stayed calm under pressure, he was clearly concerned about Radleigh, not to mention the club's standings if he didn't make a quick recovery.

"Leah," he said, his voice strained, "is everything okay?"

I nodded. "I think so. I … is McCoy-" I trailed off as a fresh wave of nausea washed over me, my mind replaying the moment his head smacked into Phoenix's defender's.

"We were wondering if he's okay," Miguel finished, tightening his arm around me.

"Not sure yet," Richard answered. "He came round in the ambulance which is a good sign. Will's with him, he'll keep me updated."

The only person who disliked McCoy more than me was Will. Even in my stunned state, I couldn't help but see the humour of Will being the person with him.

"I need to get back to the match," Richard said. "I'll let you know if I hear anything more."

Chapter 5
How Evil Do You Think I Am?

Even without McCoy we won the match 3-0, but the team celebrations were a little subdued. Away wins usually ended with bucket loads of drinks, however, everyone was still tired from clubbing the night before and too worried about McCoy to fully enjoy another drinking binge. I waited up with Miguel and Freya for news but after trying to call Will several times and not getting through, we gave up and went to bed.

It had taken me hours to fall asleep. Many times I'd imagined knocking McCoy out cold myself, but seeing him unconscious for real was a whole different matter. I still hadn't shrugged off the unease I'd felt when it happened, and it was as annoying as it was uncomfortable. It had become the norm to push any thoughts of McCoy right out of my head, so having him nestled inside my brain for the night made sleep even more difficult.

A call from Richard woke me early the next morning. Freya must have already gone to breakfast. She'd left her bed sheets in a tangle and half on the floor. I'd barely seen or heard her move all night, yet she'd still managed to make a mess.

Maybe this *is why she and Will aren't dating. The untidiness would give him the shakes.*

I pressed the answer button on my phone and listened as my boss informed me McCoy had suffered a concussion, and was brought back to the hotel after he'd been seen by a doctor. Hearing he wouldn't suffer any long term damage was a relief, but the relief soon diminished when Richard asked me to check on him. Apparently my concern qualified me to play nurse while Richard and Will put together a plan in case he wasn't fit to fly home.

I was never filled with enthusiasm about talking to McCoy, but visiting him meant I could legitimately satisfy my curiosity without feeling weak for wanting to find out how he was.

At room 316, I knocked on the door and was greeted by Bryce.

Damn, I love my job.

There were a million women who would have loved to make an early morning call to McCoy and Warren, and I got paid for it.

"Hi," I said, "I've come to visit the patient."

Bryce glanced over his shoulder at McCoy, before turning back to me. "Good timing. I've got to go. Take it easy on him, he's a little sensitive."

"How evil do you think I am?"

"I don't think you're evil," Bryce said, with a smile. "I think he's extra touchy today."

"Don't worry, I'll play nice."

Bryce winked as he slid past me, leaving me to enter McCoy's room.

Wow, this place needs a clean. I didn't envy the hotel staff who'd have to throw out all the crap they'd managed to accumulate over the last two days. The bin was overflowing with God knows what, and Bryce's clothes were strewn all over. The air smelled a little musty, probably due in part to the mess and the closed window. I'm no neat freak, but my fingers twitched to at least pick the shirts up from the floor.

McCoy was lying on his bed wearing boxer shorts and a scruffy grey t-shirt. He'd never looked so rough, and yet the glimpse of the tribal tattoos on his biceps still made my pulse quicken, and shifted my attention from the grossness of the room.

Such a shame his muscles were his only redeeming quality.

"Morning," I said, closing the door behind me. "I'm here to mop your brow."

McCoy glared at me, his blue eyes lacking their usual sparkle. "No thank you."

"What's up? You think I'd come in here while you've got concussion to taunt you?"

"Why else would you be here?"

"Richard wanted me to check on you. He's coming by later but he got caught up so you're stuck with me."

"Next time tell him to send someone different. Hannibal Lecter has a better bedside manner than you."

He looked murderous as I sat down on the edge of his bed. Something deep within me wanted to torment him a little bit, but no matter how much of an arse he was, I couldn't be too cruel when I knew he was suffering.

"Come on, McCoy. I'm here now, so you may as well talk to me. How are you feeling?"

"Like I got knocked out and wasn't allowed to rest because Bryce woke me every three hours to make sure I was still alive. How do I look?"

Surprisingly good. Even with dark circles under his eyes and stubble on his normally clean shaven face.

"You look like hell," I told him.

His eyes narrowed. "You love seeing me like this, don't you?"

"Like what? You're concussed, not dying."

"To your great disappointment."

Any hopes a bang on the head would result in him not being such an argumentative prick quickly slipped away. I got that his ego was bruised since he'd been knocked out in front of thousands of people but, regrettably, it wasn't *my* fault. Taking it out on me when I was doing Richard a favour wasn't fair.

"Believe it or not," I said, "I'm glad you're okay."

"You know what? I don't believe it. Now you've done your good deed for the day, you can go."

"Oh for Christ's sake." I stood up. "I'll tell Richard you're fine, and next time he can come and check on you himself!"

I began to walk away but as I reached the door, I turned back. I don't know what made me do it, but I was just in time to see McCoy's hand fly up to his head and he squeezed his eyes closed.

The change happened in an instant. He'd been his usual, annoying self, then in the split second I'd turned away, something had happened. I ran back over to the bed and sat down, placing my hand on his arm.

"Are you okay?" I asked, unable to disguise my panic. I couldn't have him dying on my watch. Nobody would ever believe it was an accident.

"Yeah." His voice was strained as if concentrating hard to block out the pain. After a moment or two he relaxed. Me? My heart was still thundering. "I'm okay," he said. "I slept badly and sometimes my head gets real painful."

"Is that supposed to happen?"

He shrugged. "I'm seeing the doctor again later, I'll find out then."

"Maybe you should get some sleep. Get into bed."

"Careful, Leah. People will start to think you care."

The grogginess in his voice made me a little more compassionate than I would usually have been and I laughed at the truth of his words. "Shut up and do as you're told."

With great effort he got to his feet, and I pulled back the covers for him.

"Are you always this bossy?" he asked.

"I'm not bossy. Now stop bloody questioning me and get in."

With a dramatic sigh he got into bed and I put the covers over him, like a potty-mouthed Florence Nightingale.

"Try to rest, okay?"

He nodded and closed his eyes again.

"Thank you," he mumbled, and I laughed again.

"God, you *must* be ill."

A ghost of a smile flickered across his lips, but he stayed quiet. When I was satisfied he wasn't in any more pain, I stepped out into the corridor to call Richard.

"Hey, Leah. How's he doing?"

"Not so good. He's tired and his head was hurting a lot a second ago. Is the doctor coming soon?"

"Yeah, he just called. He should be here within the next thirty minutes. From what I can tell though, McCoy won't be fit to fly home today. We'll have to wait and see what the doc says, but it might be a couple of days before he can go anywhere and because it's a concussion, I don't want him left alone."

The next match wasn't until Wednesday which meant whoever stayed behind had a little over two days to get back to L.A. Bryce was the ideal person to stay with him, but Richard would never risk having two top players out of the upcoming game.

"So what's the plan?"

"I'm still trying to figure it out with Will. Unless-?"

I laughed out loud at his unspoken question. "Yeah, sure. Two minutes alone with Radleigh and I'd probably finish him off!"

Did I just say Radleigh? I must be getting soft.

Richard chuckled. "Worth a shot."

In a moment of mischievousness, I pictured the irritation on his face when I'd told him Richard had asked me to check up on him. I didn't want him to suffer any serious discomfort, but the opportunity to watch him squirm for a couple of days was too good to pass up.

Evil, Leah. Evil.

"You're really considering this aren't you?" Richard laughed.

"Maybe. It seems like a bad idea but, what do you think?"

"I think it would be a good chance for you to work on building some kind of amicable relationship with him. We can cover you if you're sure. I know he's sick, but I don't want to leave you here if you're not completely comfortable."

His tone shifted and I hated that I'd let slip about McCoy's flirting. I didn't want to be viewed as weak. I was perfectly capable of handling him.

Sort of.

"I'll be fine," I assured him.

Arrangements for me to stay in Phoenix until Tuesday were made. I didn't even have to switch rooms, which meant I could continue to enjoy the view over the hotel gardens for a bit longer. No doubt they'd look even better after I'd poured the contents of the mini bar down my throat.

When I broke the news I was staying to Freya, she looked at me as if I'd volunteered to streak during the national anthem. She wasn't the one I was worried about, though. I had to tell Miguel, and I had no clue how he'd take the news I'd need to postpone our first date to stay with McCoy.

"You're an angel," he said when I eventually caught up with him. "Not many people would volunteer to stay behind with him."

"How do you know I'm not just a slacker?" I teased. "This is like a mini holiday for me."

"A holiday spent nursing an injured soccer player?"

"I don't plan to spend a second longer with that berk than necessary."

My words felt a little harsh in light of the fact McCoy was actually nicer when he was ill than when he was well. However, once he got better, I was convinced he'd go back to his usual self.

"Berk?" Miguel laughed. "Is a berk the same as a jerk?"

While I was used to using American dialect a lot of the time, it went right out the window any time I got annoyed, angry or upset. Thankfully, I'd had little need for the words "berk," "knob," or "tosser" since I'd been in Westberg.

"Pretty much," I said. "I like my Britishisms."

"I like them too. Maybe you can teach me some more on our date."

"Oh, you're quite the romantic, aren't you?" I slid my arms around his waist. "Nothing says first date like learning to insult people using British slang."

"How about if you teach me while we're having a moonlight picnic on the beach?"

He couldn't have known, minus the insults, he'd described my ideal date. Walking along the sand in the cool evening air was one of my favourite things to do. The idea of sharing it with Miguel was perfection.

"I'd love that."

Miguel sighed. "Is it okay that I'm going to miss you? I know we only met two days ago, but-" he trailed off, smiling sheepishly.

I didn't think it was possible to like someone so much so soon but when he leaned down to kiss me, he proved me wrong.

See what you missed out on while you were running around with bad boys?

Miguel was everything I'd never had.

"I'll miss you too," I told him. "As soon as McCoy has the all clear, I'll be on the next flight home."

He kissed me once more before heading into his room to get his things. With a sickeningly happy spring in my step, I wandered back to my own room to pick up my laptop. I'd decided, as there was nothing else for me to do, I'd sit in the bar and take advantage of the free wi-fi.

Oh, and enjoy a glass of wine or two.

Before I allowed myself to enjoy my afternoon of freedom, I had to stop by and check on Radleigh, just to be sure he was still in the land of the living. That way, I'd be satisfied I'd done my bit for the day before taking a well-earned break.

When I reached his room, I knocked gently and waited while he came to the door.

He still looked awful, the worst I'd ever seen him. He'd thrown some jeans on, but his hair was a mess and his shirt crumpled. The blackness under his eyes was highlighted by his ashen face.

"I didn't wake you, did I?" I asked.

"No. Couldn't sleep. I tried though."

"Well that's something, I guess. I just wanted to check how you are before I go and chill out in the bar."

"I'm bored, tired and my head still hurts, but I'm okay."

"Can I get you anything?"

"I could use some company."

He rubbed his eyes, then opened the door wider and shuffled back to bed.

Not exactly what I'd had in mind. In fact, it was the last thing I'd expected him to say, especially after the way he'd greeted me earlier. Perhaps my concern had eased his irritation a little.

"I don't know," I said. "You're supposed to be resting."

"I can still rest if you're here. Please, Leah?"

Idly wondering if that was the first time he'd ever said please in his life, I stepped into his room and closed the door.

"Just for a while," I told him. "I have plans to laze around."

"There's a spare bed and a television in here. Make yourself at home."

Excellent, just point me towards the mini bar.

After six games of - sober - Minesweeper, Radleigh hadn't said another word.

"Do you want me to go?" I asked. "You're very quiet."

"I'm supposed to be resting," he quoted, turning his head towards me.

"I know. But you said you wanted company."

"I do."

Narrowing my eyes at his deliberate attempts to be awkward, I turned my attention back to my laptop to sort through my emails. Amongst the usual bunch of spam, my spirits lifted when I noticed an email from my brother drop into my inbox. I hadn't heard from him in a few weeks because he and his family had recently moved. I couldn't wait to hear all the news from home.

Hi Leah, I promise to send you a more detailed email soon but things have been manic. For now, I want to send you some pictures of the kids because Mum said you were desperate to see them. We miss you so much and Jamie has sent something special for you!

Love Josh, Christina, Jamie and Grace xx

P.S. Since you've been working with "soccer" players, Jamie has developed a new hobby.

I scrolled down and let out a squeal. The first photo showed Jamie playing on his swing in the garden of their new house, wearing a t-shirt with a picture of Cody Rivera on the front.

I chuckled to myself at Jamie's attire. *A new hobby indeed!*

The next photo showed Grace pushing a tiny, brightly coloured pram. She was so beautiful with her dark curly hair and cheeky smile. The final picture was of Jamie, with Grace sitting on his lap on the grass.

I spotted a link to a webpage underneath the photos which took me to a video clip. When I pressed play, my hand shot up to my mouth as Jamie's face filled my computer screen.

"Hi Auntie Leah," he said, bouncing up and down on his chair. "I miss you very much and I wish you could come to our new house soon. My new bedroom has pictures of your football team in it! Mummy says you live too far away though, and you won't be able to come to my birthday party in two weeks but that's okay because I'm going to ask her if she can send you a piece of birthday cake. I have to go now, Mummy told me not to talk too long! I love you!"

There was a brief pause as he turned the webcam off, then the screen went blank.

Although the message from my nephew made me smile, a lump rose in my throat. Seeing how much the kids had grown made me ache. We hadn't taken full advantage of video calls and I promised myself we'd change that as soon as they were settled in the new house.

"What was that?" Radleigh asked, and I quickly wiped my eyes.

"It… it was a message from my nephew, and some photos."

"You okay?"

"Yeah." I took a ragged breath. "I'm just being pathetic."

"Can I have a look?"

I nodded and carried my laptop over to his bed, placing it in front of him before sitting down beside him.

"That's Jamie." My finger lightly brushed my nephew's photographed cheek. "He'll be eight in two weeks, and this is Grace, she's only sixteen months. They're my brother's children."

"Cute kids."

"Yeah, I really miss them."

I stared at the photo, wishing more than anything that I could scoop them out of my screen and hold them close to me.

"She looks like you." Radleigh pointed to Grace.

"Everyone says that. Whenever I took her out, people thought she was mine."

Radleigh smiled. "I bet you loved it."

"I think I'm a bit old for playing Mummies and Daddies now."

I closed my laptop again so I wouldn't spend too long brooding, and wiped away the last of my tears. Radleigh rested his hand over mine, startling me. I pulled away as if his touch scalded me.

"Sorry," I said. "I'm sorry."

"I wasn't hitting on you. I was-"

"I know."

I couldn't bring myself to look at him. I went back to the other bed, feeling like a complete idiot. Really, it was no surprise I was defensive after all the times he'd tried to touch me, or drag me into an embrace.

"You're not gonna leave now, are you?" McCoy asked.

"You want me to stay?"

"Yeah, I do. I feel like crap and I don't want to be on my own. From what I can tell, you don't either."

He had a point. Spending the evening alone would mean suffering from homesickness. At least if I stayed with Radleigh, I'd have someone to talk to.

Once I'd relaxed again, I took my shoes off and curled up on the bed. As Radleigh was bed-ridden, we ordered food then watched part of a comedy movie, which we had to turn off half way through because the laughter made his head hurt.

"I was enjoying that." I switched the television off and went to sit beside him on his bed, where he was covering his eyes with his arm.

"You're a bitch," he moaned. "I'm in pain. This is your fault for making me watch that movie."

"You're such a drama queen. Besides, you were enjoying it, too."

"Until it gave me a headache."

"Because you were laughing, because you were enjoying it," I finished, with a smugness that rivalled his.

He peered up at me from behind his arm. "You're not half bad to be around when you're not being uptight."

"Well, you're not half bad to be around when you're not being a sleaze. If you can keep this up when we're back at work, I might be able to get through the day without wanting to strangle you."

He smiled, a smile that lit up his eyes for the first time all day. "I'll do my best."

Before I had a chance to respond, my mobile bleeped, alerting me to a text.

I grabbed my phone and clicked to read.

I think you are well fit. Did I get that right? :D

I threw my head back, dissolving into giggles. Clearly Miguel was taking his British slang lessons seriously.

Very good! You're a top bloke. Xx

A few seconds passed before his reply. ***Oh come on, you're really testing me now! Xx***

Keep practicing! Xx

I put my phone down on the bed, amused and warmed by Miguel's messages. After reading them, all I wanted to do was curl up in my own room and talk to him, so I stood up. "I think it's time for bed."

"Why? You need to go talk dirty with your boyfriend?"

So much for him not being a sleaze.

Choosing to ignore his comment, I slid my phone into my pocket and picked up my laptop. "Is there anything you need before I go?"

He finally put his arm down by his side, allowing me to see exactly how tired he looked. "You could stay here."

"I don't think so," I told him. "That would be unprofessional."

"I've built a career out of being unprofessional."

I almost smiled. He certainly didn't gain his nickname for playing fair.

"I built mine by working hard and gaining a good reputation."

He shrugged, and I took that as my cue to leave. After a relatively drama free day, I didn't want it to end in an argument neither of us had the energy for. We were both still alive after eight hours together. I figured I could chalk that up as a win.

Chapter 6
There's a Teenager Inside Every Man

I woke up the next day more rested than I'd felt in ages. Perhaps it was because I'd fallen asleep knowing I wouldn't have to fight with my alarm clock in the morning.

Or perhaps it was because I'd spent two hours on the phone to Miguel, making plans for our date. He asked me a million questions about food to make sure he didn't poison me with the picnic he'd planned, all while trying not to give anything away, and we spent the rest of the time continuing to get to know each other. It made me want to see him even more. We'd hardly had any time together yet, but every time we spoke, I realised how many things we had in common, and he was so easy to talk to. There were never any awkward silences, or moments when I worried I might have said something stupid. I'd never had anyone like that in my life before. Most of my relationships in the past had been built on two things. Games and tension. Neither of those things are conducive to a healthy relationship, which was why I chose to stay single for so long. Moving out of the UK was admittedly a dramatic way of re-starting my life, but it worked. I'd always been independent, and I'd often lived away from my parents, but in America, everything was a true fresh start. Excitement with men was less important because there was always something new and exciting to discover about my new surroundings. Sure, I'd been on a few dates, but not with anyone I was desperate to see again. Not until Miguel.

Time couldn't move fast enough for me, but going home heavily depended on how quickly Radleigh recovered from his head injury.

He had a visit from the doctor in the morning and I sat with him, every muscle in my body tense throughout the examination. Thankfully, the doctor gave him the all clear to fly home the next day, as long as he promised to take things easy.

Radleigh pretended to be cool but he was obviously relieved to be on the mend. He called Richard to tell him the news, while I called the airline and booked us seats on the following afternoon's flight to Los Angeles.

Even though the doctor gave good news, Radleigh was still under strict orders to keep resting, which limited our activities. After lunch, he asked me to accompany him for a walk around the hotel grounds and I wasn't cruel enough to make him go alone, especially when he was still so unsteady on his feet.

We wandered leisurely along the pathway through the beautifully mowed lawn towards the river that flowed at the bottom of the gardens, the sunshine on my back warming me through the thin material of my khaki shirt. We sat down on a bench overlooking the stream where ducks were swimming, and dipping their heads under the water in play. Radleigh leaned back rubbing his neck, completely oblivious to the beauty around him.

"You okay?"

"My neck's a bit stiff from being in bed for so long. I'll be fine when I can move around again."

"You can't rush it. You've still got to take it slow for a while."

He nodded, obviously humouring me. The man thought he was a superhero.

"Your dad was a soccer player too, right?" I asked, remembering a profile I'd read on him. I had no idea I'd retained any of the information until the question slipped out of my mouth.

"Yeah, and my grandfather too. One day I'd like to have a son following in my footsteps."

"After all the women you've slept with, you might already have a whole soccer team you don't even know about."

A jolt of guilt hit me hard, unexpectedly. *Nope, still not okay to joke about that.*

"Ha ha," Radleigh said, blind to my discomfort. "My dad played with Richard in Missouri for a while, until Richard transferred to Westberg."

"Wow, so Richard's known you your whole life?"

He nodded. "Pretty much."

Richard had never given any indication he knew McCoy before he played for Westberg. In fact, my boss showed mostly disdain for him in matters that weren't directly related to his talent on the field. I suspected McCoy's complete lack of respect was the biggest problem.

"I screwed his daughter," Radleigh said, in response to my unspoken question.

I rolled my eyes. "Of course you did."

As he attempted to explain his behaviour, I walked around the bench to stand behind him and batted his hand away from his neck so I could massage his shoulders. I wasn't quite sure what possessed me to do it. I guess healing pain was instinctive.

"Oh God," he moaned, halting his piss poor excuses for defiling the boss' daughter.

I ran my thumb slowly but firmly up and down the back of his neck, trying hard not to enjoy the feeling of his muscles beneath my fingers. "Control yourself."

"If you knew how good this felt, you'd understand."

"It's supposed to feel good, it's not supposed to be a turn-on."

"Okay, let's swap places and we'll see if you can still make the same statement."

64

"Shut up or I'll stop."

"Don't even think about it."

Knowing my touch had such an effect on him made me feel … powerful, like it was finally me who was in control. Dominance wasn't usually my thing, but when it came to McCoy, I really got a kick out of it. I hoped he'd keep quiet because I wanted to continue torturing him for a bit longer.

"What would Miguel say if he knew you were giving me a massage?" he asked. "If I found out my girlfriend had been rubbing some other guy's shoulders, I'd be pretty pissed."

With two short sentences, he took the power back again. Just like always.

"First of all," I said, increasing my force, "until you stop screwing around, that's something you don't need to worry about. And second of all, I'm fairly sure Miguel would understand this is a professional massage, nothing more."

"Hey, take it easy!" Radleigh hunched up at my vice-like grip. "I get the message. I shouldn't have said anything, and I can't take an argument right now, so please can you forgive me and maybe ease the pressure?"

I dropped my hands down to my sides and sighed. "Why do you always annoy me when we're actually managing to have a normal conversation?"

He turned around, fixing me with a grin. "I enjoy flirting with you. I went too far."

"You always go too far."

"Well if you weren't so damn hot, I'd be able to control myself."

"You're not a horny teenager, you're a grown man!" I tried to ignore the stirring sensation inside me at his words. Not even a hint of hesitation about saying what he thought. What he wanted.

"There is a teenager inside every man," Radleigh stated. "Even Miguel."

"Miguel is nothing like you."

"And *you* are nothing like him."

"You don't know anything about me."

An internal battle was happening inside him, I could see it in his eyes. To his credit, he kept his thoughts to himself but it didn't mean I couldn't hear and feel every one of them.

The same way he seemed to hear and feel every one of mine.

****

On Tuesday morning, I did something a little crazy. To prove I didn't buy into Radleigh's unspoken theory I had more in common with him than Miguel, I agreed to spend the morning exploring Phoenix with him. I needed to pick up a tacky souvenir from Arizona for my collection anyway. Perhaps if he got to see me at my dorkiest, he'd realise we were worlds apart in terms of, well, everything.

Radleigh came to my room a little after nine, while I was trying to straighten my hair. I let him in and told him to make himself comfortable while I finished off.

My hair was being particularly stubborn, and looking at the frizzy mess in the bathroom mirror, I sighed. Some days it was easier to avoid the hassle and scrape it back out of the way. It wasn't like I had anyone I needed to look good for.

When I stepped out of the bathroom, Radleigh was sitting on the edge of my bed, talking on his mobile phone. I put my straighteners into my suitcase then hunted round the room for my key card.

"No, she's out of the bathroom now," I heard him say, and the words halted my search. *Why is he talking about me?* A jolt of realisation made me spring into action and I snatched my phone from his hand, shooting him a poisonous glare. If I hadn't been so considerate and stopped myself listening in, I might have realised sooner that he'd answered *my* mobile.

"Hello," I said, annoyance prominent in my tone.

"Leah?"

"Bree, sorry about that."

"Um, why is Radleigh McCoy in your room so early?"

"We're going to look around Phoenix. Why?"

"Are you dressed?"

"What?" I laughed. "Of course I am!"

"He said you were in the shower."

Suddenly, everything slid into place. Radleigh leaned back on my bed, smirking. I picked up the nearest thing to hand, which happened to be my hairbrush, and threw it at him, enjoying the satisfying smack as the wooden handle hit his arm.

"Bree, I was not in the shower! McCoy is just being a pillock. You don't think I would have let him in here while I was…" I trailed off, reluctant to use the word 'naked' in front of him, "… showering."

"Well, I… no. But I panicked when he answered the phone because it's early and-"

"You thought I'd gone over to the dark side? Bree, I am immune to sexual predators like McCoy."

He grinned at me as if he was proud of the title. I had to turn away because his smug smile made me want to throw something else at him.

The next nearest thing was a heavy lamp.

"So, everything's okay?" Bree asked.

"Everything's fine."

"Oh good. It would be *so* icky if you did anything with him!"

"The only thing I plan to do with him involves a shovel and a big hole in the ground. Can I call you back later?"

"Sure." She giggled. "Bye Leah."

Taking a long breath, I turned back to Radleigh. "Why the hell did you answer my phone?"

"I thought I was doing you a favour." He smiled.

"No you didn't, you smug piece of crap. You were trying to cause trouble."

"Relax. Bree wouldn't have told anyone."

"That's not the point! I don't want her or anyone else getting the wrong idea about us!"

"Maybe she got the right idea." He tilted his head back slightly the way he always did when he was challenging me. "Maybe the reason she believed what I said is because she knows you're into me."

"Or maybe you have way too high an opinion of yourself."

I tried not to think about the unavoidable fact he had every right to. For the first time since he'd arrived in my room, I looked at him properly. The dark circles under his eyes had gone, and the colour had returned to his cheeks. The tattoos on his upper arms were just visible, peering out from underneath the short sleeves of his black t-shirt, and my eyes kept drifting back to them as he spoke.

"That doesn't stop what I said being true." He stood up. "You could have gone home with Miguel but you chose to stay here with me. And I saw the look on your face when you came to visit me. You were worried."

"You were in pain. I'd have been worried about anyone in that condition."

"It was more than that."

"You're delusional."

68

"Cut the crap, Leah. You didn't stay here because you had to. You stayed because you wanted to."

"I stayed because nobody else wanted to be stuck here with you!"

I turned away, ready to open the door for him to leave but he grabbed my wrist and pulled me to him. As I stumbled against him, my fingers twitched with longing as they gripped the taut muscles beneath them. Without giving me a second to think, his hands grasped my hips and his mouth crushed against mine.

His lips were infuriating. Soft, full, and unquestionably hungry. Every time they brushed against mine, my anger was replaced by excitement, and something resembling relief. His tongue found mine, dancing in rhythm as his hands dug into my sides, keeping me close.

'No, no, this can't happen!' a voice said from the depths of my mind. *'This is all wrong.'*

I moved away from him slightly, my heart racing. I couldn't speak. I could barely breathe.

"Don't even try telling me you want me to stop," Radleigh said.

Desperation tinged his voice and while I hesitated, he lowered his face towards mine and kissed me again.

Oh God!

My head spun, my legs weakened and when his hand snaked underneath my shirt and touched my bare skin, for a second I was more than willing to let him keep going. *This* was what I was used to. Heat, fire, *need.*

Are you insane? He tried to have you fired for Christ's sake, and now you're letting him grope you? Make. It. Stop.

It was like being doused with a bucket of cold water and I pushed him away.

"Leah-"

"Don't," I snapped, holding my hands up. "Don't ever do that again."

Radleigh stared at me for a moment with an expression I couldn't read. I hated how he read my thoughts so well yet I didn't have a clue what went on inside his head. After letting his eyes burn through me for a moment, he turned and walked out.

I threw myself down on my bed, trying to slow my racing heartbeat. Trying to shift the feeling of his hands on my hips, and the taste of his kiss out of my mind.

Too late.

Letting out a groan of frustration, I rolled over onto my back, wishing I could rewind the morning and start again. With one kiss, he'd forced me to face up to what I'd been denying since the moment we met. I wanted him. Purely physical, but I wanted him all the same.

There weren't many guys like McCoy. Sure, there were thousands with misplaced cockiness, but not so many who had a reason for it.

Growing up in England was dull. All through my schooldays I kept the same bunch of friends, and every weekend we struggled to find ways to entertain ourselves.

When I turned sixteen, we started hanging out in one of the two local pubs in Zellor, Cornwall on Friday nights. We were allowed in, provided we kept out of trouble and stuck to non-alcoholic drinks. That was okay with me. I got drunk on the atmosphere. For me, the best part of our nights out was the men. The variety. It was like being in a sweet shop with permission to take whatever you wanted.

So I did.

I lost my virginity a week before my seventeenth birthday in the alleyway alongside the pub. Not my finest moment, I admit. In one year I bedded guys my age, older men, married men. I didn't care about seeing them again, I just wanted the buzz from being with someone new.

In short, I was exactly like McCoy.

I let out a deep sigh, moving my focus back to the present. To Radleigh. I wasn't a teenager anymore and my decisions needed to be made on more than a passing physical attraction, however strong. I had so much more to lose. My job which I loved more than any I'd had before, and Miguel.

I hugged my pillow close to me as I thought of him. I'd been so looking forward to seeing him again. Now it would be tainted by the guilt of what I'd done. I couldn't even justify it by saying, *"It was only a kiss"* or *"Miguel and I haven't even been on an official date yet"*. Nothing excused my actions. I was no longer a clueless teen, and I should have stopped the kiss sooner than I did.

Perhaps I hadn't changed nearly as much as I thought. Deep down, I was still a small town girl who wanted a bit of fun.

Chapter 7
Dream On, Muscle Man

The second the plane touched down at LAX, I finally relaxed.

I was home.

After throwing Radleigh out of my hotel room, we barely spoke another word to each other. There weren't many words left to say. Whenever he looked at me, I expected him to resume his usual spiel about how it would only be a matter of time before I gave into him again but he never did. Maybe the kiss was enough for him to have satisfactorily proved his point.

Out of politeness, I said a quick goodbye to Radleigh before speeding out of the airport. His father was collecting him, so I escaped in a cab before I was forced to meet any more of the McCoy family.

On the way home, I called Miguel to tell him I'd landed. He sounded so happy to hear my voice. I usually felt the same way, but everything I said was blackened by my stupidity. It would be even harder face to face, but I'd have to wait until the morning before jumping over that hurdle.

Freya wasn't in when I arrived back at the apartment, so after dumping my bags in my room, I kicked off my shoes and threw myself on one of our comfy loungers on the balcony. The weather was glorious. It's difficult to stay unhappy when the ocean is sparkling in the sun, and people are laughing as they soak up the rays. Even with so much on my mind, the beauty of my surroundings made me smile. I'd never been much into religion, but I thanked God every morning for everything I had.

While cursing him for giving me Radleigh McCoy.

I had no idea how much time passed before Freya came home. I'd somehow located the off switch for my brain, and sat virtually comatose until she nudged me from my stupor.

"Hey beautiful, welcome home!"

Her words sounded bright but the sparkle in her tone didn't quite reach her eyes. I sat up. "What's wrong?"

"Wow, you're good," she said, giving into a laugh. "It's usually only my mom who can read me so well. I'm okay, though. How are you? How was Phoenix?"

"Freya, I called you yesterday, don't change the subject."

She paused for a moment. "You wanna order a pizza and drink wine? May as well make this into a girly evening if I'm gonna pour my heart out."

The sadness in her eyes caused a physical pain in my chest and I leapt up to give her a hug. My own inner turmoil seemed insignificant while she clung to me with what felt like deep gratitude.

"We can do whatever you want," I told her.

"Okay. You pour the wine and I'll order the food."

In less than an hour, we'd settled ourselves on the floor in the living room. A bottle of white wine rested on the coffee table next to our piping hot Hawaiian pizza.

"I don't even know where to begin." Freya ignored the pizza and reached for her glass of wine. "Whatever I say is going to sound insane."

"Try me. What happened?"

Freya took a deep breath, letting her blonde hair fall in front of her face a little to hide her. "Will's seeing someone. One of his ex-girlfriends, Heather, tracked him down a few months ago to let him know she was moving back to Westberg. I didn't think anything of it at the time but she's here now and they went out last night."

"And?"

"They had fun. He hasn't stopped talking about her all day, which is fine. I mean, really, it's fine. I'm happy for him, but at the same time I feel so… I don't know."

About bloody time. There seemed to be an unspoken bet between everyone on the team about when Freya and Will would get together.

"Really?" I asked. "You have no idea?"

She sighed. "I have an idea."

"Freya, why didn't you tell him you liked him before?"

She looked up at me, confusion in her eyes. "I didn't know. I didn't realise how much I… I care about him until someone else came along."

How was that possible? Denial I could understand, and even trying to play it down, but she must have had an inkling she felt more for him than friendship. Especially since it was so obvious to the rest of the world.

Sensing my thoughts, Freya said, "You've never misjudged your feelings for someone?"

"No," I told her, honestly. "I've lied to myself but deep down I always knew the truth."

Just like with McCoy. Those weren't real feelings, though. More like… poorly thought-out lust.

"That's not what happened here."

A sombre silence hung between us. "Things with Will and Heather might not be serious," I said, eventually.

"Maybe. But whenever we're on our own together, I'll be forced to hear about her. I can't exactly tell him to stop, can I?"

"You could tell him how you feel."

"Would you do that? Would you put years of friendship at risk for something that may not be reciprocated?"

"I don't know. But I'm not sure I'd want to live with the constant question of what might have happened if I'd been brave enough to admit the truth."

Freya and I stayed up late, talking about what she should do next while drinking more wine than was entirely necessary. Witnessing Will's blossoming relationship was going to be torture for her. She was adamant she couldn't reveal the truth, though. *'If he had any feelings for me, he wouldn't be dating her,'* she'd said. I understood her reasoning, but in reality, I believed Will and Freya had been misreading each other's signals for so long, they couldn't see what was clear to everyone else.

With potential drama brewing between Freya and Will, and having to face Miguel after kissing McCoy, I had no enthusiasm for work on Wednesday morning.

Instead of heading straight to the pitch, I holed myself up in my office for a while. I figured I had ten minutes clear before anyone would look for me. Settling myself in my desk chair, I flicked through a magazine I'd bought but never got round to reading. An article entitled *"Ways To Make Him Ache For You"* caught my attention and I chuckled as I perused some of the suggestions. I always found it odd that people looked to magazines for sexual advice. I couldn't ever imagine an occasion when I'd be in the middle of sex and suddenly think, *'Hang on, now what was that tip I read about in Cosmo…?'*

I hadn't managed to read more than tip four of ten when someone spoke my name, startling me out of my self-help trance.

I hadn't even heard the door open.

"Hello," I said, quickly closing the magazine.

Richard grinned. "I didn't see a thing."

"I was only looking." I sounded like a teenager who'd been caught watching porn, and Richard laughed.

"Your secret's safe. I just wanted to come in and say thanks for staying with McCoy. He didn't give you any trouble, did he?"

"No. In fact, he was actually pleasant for the first day. It was when he started to get better that he went back to his usual smug self."

"A sure indication he's back to normal, then. Even so, I'm taking him out of tonight's match just in case he isn't fully fit. I don't want to risk his health by putting him back into action too soon."

I doubted Radleigh would thank him for the night off, even if it was for his own good. He'd been desperate to get back to work even while he was in pain, so having to sit the game out when he was so much better would piss him right off.

"It's only for tonight though, right? He'll be playing again by the weekend?"

"We'll see. He can do some light training today, and if he's okay, we'll step it up a little more tomorrow."

"Knock knock."

My heart jumped into my throat then descended into the depths of my stomach, where it churned with guilt as I looked into Miguel's beautiful brown eyes.

"Hi," I said, as he stepped into my office.

Richard's eyeballs swivelled back and forth between us, and he smiled. "I'll leave you to it."

"Won't be long, boss," Miguel told him. The second we were alone, he drew me into a hug. "I missed you."

"I missed you too."

The words felt phony as they left my lips but instead of dwelling on my stupidity, I kissed him softly, forcing my... *indiscretion* with McCoy out of my head.

"I know we don't have too long here," Miguel said, "but I wondered if you wanted to go on that first date tomorrow night?"

"I would love to."

"Good. Because I already ordered the picnic food."

I laughed. "Oh, very confident!"

"I wasn't confident." He kissed me again. "I was hopeful."

"Well, I don't plan to disappoint you."

"You could never disappoint me," he said, and my stomach lurched again. He was so trusting, so open. I wasn't sure just how much of his adoration I deserved.

****

I had a packed schedule, but being busy made the hours whizz by. Just when I thought I was going to get through the day without dealing with McCoy, he barged into my office fifteen minutes before the clock signalled leaving time.

"What did you say to Richard?" he demanded, slamming the office door behind him so hard my pinboard fell off the wall and thudded onto my desk. His eyes burned with rage and I stepped back as if his glare had thrown me off balance.

"What do you mean?" I asked. "What about?"

"About me, Leah! He's taken me out of the match!"

Oh, I should have known this would be my fault.

"You were there when the doctor gave me the all clear! Tell Richard and get me back in the game!"

"Take it easy. This decision was not mine, and you've had all day to talk to Richard. Yelling at me won't change anything."

"You could change his mind. You've got him wrapped around your little finger!"

Not true. I got on well with Richard, but business was business and once he made a decision, it couldn't be changed. McCoy knew it too, so throwing a hissy fit at me was a complete waste of breath, not to mention dangerous while he was recovering from a concussion.

"First of all," I said, "if you want me to do something for you, ask nicely. Screaming at me isn't going to make me rush to help you. Secondly, Richard is doing this for you. For your health. So quit acting like a spoilt brat and enjoy the time off."

"What am I supposed to do tonight?"

"Why don't you flip through your little black book and call one of your many, many lady friends?"

"Excuse me," a third, softer voice said from the doorway.

McCoy and I had been so involved in our argument we didn't notice Taylor watching us through wide eyes.

"Hey Taylor," I said. "What are you doing here?"

"I'm looking for Jesse."

"Try the restaurant. I think I saw him heading that way."

She nodded her thanks, but her eyes lingered on Radleigh and she smiled in a way that suggested they had a secret. He smiled back in response, and not-so-subtly leered at her arse as she walked out.

"She's barely past the age of consent," I said. "Back off."

He flicked his head round to look at me. "I can't help it if she's got a great ass."

"Are you sleeping with her?"

His lips curved into a smug grin, his frustration about the match forgotten. "Jealous?"

Was that a yes?

"I'm serious. There are plenty of available women who would happily service your penis, so leave Taylor alone."

"Relax. I'm not sleeping with her. I do have some morals, you know."

There was no reason for me to trust his word, but if I pushed the issue, I would be faced with more of his idiotic theories I asked because *I* wanted to service his penis.

"Are we done here?"

When McCoy's only answer was his famous, irritating smirk, I finished putting my things away, picked up my bag and walked out.

****

Even with the cloud of McCoy hovering above me, I refused to let him ruin my date with Miguel.

He picked me up from my apartment a little before sundown, and hand in hand, we walked the short distance to the beach.

Miguel had gone to a huge amount of effort to make our date perfect. He had a picnic basket made up especially for us after his very careful questioning about my tastes. Lucky for him, I'll eat anything. He chose roasted beef tenderloin in red wine sauce with red peppers and potatoes, Caesar salad, and brownies for dessert. It was a million miles from the ham sandwiches and ice creams I had at picnics when I was a kid.

After we'd eaten, we cleared up, and went for a walk along the sand. Evenings in Los Angeles were always cool, and Miguel wrapped his arm around me as we strolled. Some other couples were enjoying the moonlight, plus a few teenagers chatting, and the occasional person staring out at the waves.

"I wonder what he's thinking about," I said, as we passed a man in his forties, dressed in a business suit, and idly drawing patterns in the sand while he watched the water.

"Maybe he's not thinking anything."

"He's definitely thinking. I used to do the same thing at home in England. When I needed to clear my head after work, I'd drive to the beach and sit for hours looking out at the sea."

"What did you think about?"

"All sorts of things. Mostly how to escape from my little town."

"Why?"

"Bad memories, I guess."

Miguel didn't press me, and I was glad because divulging the details of my past on our first date probably wasn't wise.

"So you don't miss it?" he asked.

"Sometimes, but I couldn't live there again. I miss my family, though. My mum keeps hoping I'll go back, but even if I lived in the U.K, I wouldn't want to live in the town I grew up in. It's too small. Everyone knows each other's business."

"How did you end up in America?"

I smiled. "A twist of fate."

"Tell me more."

"Well," I began, "four years ago, I moved from London back to Zellor to be with my family after a bad break-up. One of my friends, and when I say 'friend,' I mean someone I'd known since birth but was never very close to, invited me on a trip to Boston. She had a friend there. The person she originally planned to go with backed out, so I was her last resort. I thought it might be fun. I'd meet some new people, get away from home and live a different life for a couple of weeks. As it turned out, my friend fell for her mate's brother, which meant I spent most of the time alone."

"So, she invited you because she couldn't think of anyone else then ditched you when you got there? Some friend."

Laughing, I said, "It actually worked out for the best. I enjoyed looking around, making my way on my own. I fell completely in love with Boston, and the moment I got home, I wanted to go back. So, I set about finding out how to move to America and ... here I am."

"I know this is totally selfish, but I'm glad you're not homesick. I would hate it if you went away."

I smiled up at him. "Thanks for tonight. It's been good to be together away from work."

We stopped walking, and Miguel pulled me in to him. "Does this mean we can go out again?"

"Yes. That's exactly what it means."

He lowered his head to kiss me, and I closed my eyes, waiting for his lips to brush against mine. His arms protected me from the sea breeze, wrapping me in warmth. The sound of the waves rang in my ears.

"Miguel, do you have to go home tonight?"

He shook his head. "I don't have to."

"Do you want to stay with me?"

His eyes stared into mine and he placed a hand on my cheek. "I would love to stay, angel. But that's not why I planned this date. I just wanted the evening to be perfect for you."

Angel.

I loved that. Every word he spoke calmed me, made me feel cared for and safe. I wasn't used to it. Didn't want it to stop.

"I know," I told him. "It was so perfect, I don't want you to go."

Smiling, he kissed me again. "Then I'll stay."

****

There's something wonderful about waking up in the arms of a man, and knowing there is nowhere else either of you would rather be. Sex on the first date wasn't something I'd planned, but the evening had been so perfect, so romantic.

Freya barely concealed her amusement when she saw us emerge from my room, but she restrained herself from making a comment. It was only when she got me alone in the kitchen that she quietly squealed her delight, and we jumped up and down, gigantic grins on our faces.

Miguel and I held hands as we entered the training ground. We may as well have held a neon sign saying, '*We had sex,*' because everyone stared at us in a way that told us *they knew*. Nobody said a word, though.

Well, almost nobody.

Radleigh cornered me on my way out of the hydrotherapy pool, of all places. Too bad I'd left my towel in the changing room so I couldn't cover up. He was sweaty and dressed in his training gear, but the sight of him still knocked the breath out of me for a second. His eyes unashamedly travelled the length of my body.

"Will you please stop looking at me like that?" I snapped. The water dripping from my hair was not cold enough to cool my burning cheeks.

"Like what?"

Like you're going to throw me on the floor and ravage me!

"You know what I mean."

There was nothing I could do to stop him, short of running away. That would have been a tempting option if I hadn't been so determined to prove he didn't have an effect on me.

"I saw you with Vega this morning," he said.

"You and everyone else."

"Did he stay with you last night?"

"Why? Are you jealous?"

I shouldn't have gone down that road, but he sounded slightly put-out and I couldn't resist playing on it.

"Yes, I am. A couple more days in Phoenix and it would have been me."

I rolled my eyes. "Dream on, muscle man."

The first hint of a grin played on his lips. "Don't try telling me you didn't feel anything when you kissed me. If we were still at the hotel, you would have spent the night with me, not him."

Every time I thought his arrogance couldn't get any worse, he stepped up to prove me wrong.

"Are you trying to take credit for my night with Miguel?"

"I *am* taking credit for it. You wanted me in Phoenix, but you got scared so you came home and screwed him instead."

There wasn't a grain of truth in his words. Well. I did want him for that brief moment when he sucked my brain out through my lips, but I sure as hell knew better than to give in to it, and it had *nothing* to do with me and Miguel.

"Nothing to say?" he asked, smirking.

"Only that I can't believe your nerve. Stay away from me, McCoy. I mean it."

Chapter 8
Respect Is a Two Way Street

Over the next four weeks, there were many mornings when I woke up snuggled into Miguel. Freya was cool with him staying over, but sometimes I stayed at his apartment to give her a break. It felt wrong to show off my happiness when she was still trying to handle her feelings for Will.

She had chosen to stay quiet and wait to see what happened with Will's new relationship. The unfortunate consequence of her decision was that she had to suffer while he babbled on about Heather. Freya covered her pain well at work, and even put a brave face on at home most of the time. It wasn't half as easy as she pretended, but she was way too tough to let herself fall apart.

One particularly difficult afternoon, Freya left work early, bailing on her plans to meet Will and me for dinner in the Warriors' restaurant. It wasn't the first time we'd been alone since Freya realised how she felt about him, but her storming out of the grounds without speaking to anyone was a first.

Will and I sat in our usual spot in the restaurant, by the window in the far corner, waiting for our meals to arrive. Will twitched in his seat, obviously preparing to ask questions, yet not wanting to put me in an awkward position.

"Okay," I said, eventually, "you need to stop fidgeting. You look like you've got worms."

He stopped moving, but smiled at my bluntness. "You're such a charmer."

"I try."

After another slightly uncomfortable pause, Will said, "Something happened with Freya today. I'm damned if I know what it was though."

"Well, why don't you walk me through it?"

"We were having coffee and she asked me about Heather. I told her we went out to dinner with my parents and she flipped out."

Dinner with the parents. Things were getting serious.

"What did she say?"

"She muttered something about how it was soon for me to introduce Heather to my family. When I pointed out we've been together for over a month, and she met my parents when we dated before, she bit my head off. She said it must be nice to have such a long history with someone then walked out. She didn't even finish her drink. I know we haven't been hanging out as much since I've been with Heather but that's what happens when someone starts dating."

The man was clueless.

"So, things with you and Heather are going well?" I asked, trying to steer the focus away from Freya.

He sighed. "I like her a lot. She's pretty, she's caring, we have a lot in common. But she's recently divorced. Her husband cheated on her and she's real clingy. She calls several times a day, even while I'm at work. I understand why, but she's not giving me any room to breathe."

Interesting you never said that in front of Freya.

"Well," I said, "I suppose it makes sense if her husband screwed around. Even so, dating you when you're on the road a lot isn't the most sensible idea if she's insecure."

I was caught between the proverbial rock and hard place. Freya and Will were the perfect couple who never were, but if I encouraged Will to stick it out with Heather, he would never be with Freya. If I advised him to break up with her, he'd get hurt.

So to sum up, I was better off shutting the hell up.

"You know something." Will's eyes fixed onto mine. "Something about the way Freya's been acting."

Shaking my head, I replied, "Don't involve me in this, Will. Please."

Will stared at me thoughtfully for a moment or two. "I'm sorry. You're right. I should talk to Freya."

Dinner ended up being pretty tense once Will realised I had the answer to Freya's mood, and I couldn't wait to escape.

When I got home, Freya was in our small but trendy kitchen, frying noodles. She only cooked when she needed to distract herself from something, and although the smell was heavenly, I knew most of the food would probably end up in the bin. I filled her in on the things Will said, and she gave me a grateful hug for not revealing the truth. I stayed with her for as long as I could, but I had to shower and change before Miguel came over. I offered to cancel for her, but she refused to let me.

Miguel and I had spent a lot of evenings holed up in my bedroom watching movies, talking, laughing. It wasn't just because I didn't want to flaunt my relationship in front of Freya. We liked the privacy. We didn't always stay in, but after the drama between my two best friends, I couldn't find the energy to do much more than laze around on my bed and make plans with Miguel for our next day off.

In the middle of a debate about whether we should spend the day on the beach or doing something more energetic, Freya knocked on my bedroom door to tell me my brother was on the phone.

My heart jumped into my throat. If he wanted to talk, he usually sent me a text to arrange a time for us to have a proper chat. The fact he'd called the apartment meant whatever he had to tell me couldn't wait.

Untangling myself from Miguel's arms, I took the phone from Freya. "Josh?"

"Hi Leah," he said, the brightness in his voice instantly calming me down. "How are you?"

"You scared me half to death by calling so suddenly!"

"Sorry," he laughed. "I'm not interrupting anything, am I?"

"Well, I was hanging out with my boyfriend, but I think I can spare a few minutes to talk to my big brother."

I hadn't mentioned Miguel to my family yet. I wanted to make sure I had something worth telling them first. My mother already thought I should be married with kids, and I couldn't be bothered to sit through another lecture about my terrible track record with men.

She didn't know the half of it.

"You've got a boyfriend already? You little hussy!"

"I will hang up right now."

"No, don't," Josh said, still chuckling. "I want hear all about him. Is he a footballer?"

"He's a coach. His name's Miguel."

"Aw, Jamie will be so disappointed. You'd score major points with him if you dated Bryce Warren or Radleigh McCoy."

He couldn't have known how much of a nerve he'd hit, but I bristled at the mention of Radleigh's name. Over the last few weeks, he'd backed off a little, but not nearly enough to keep me from wanting to throttle him whenever our paths crossed.

"He likes McCoy?" I asked, unable to keep disgust out of my voice. "Can't you persuade him to pick a better role model?"

"Who could be a better role model than a world class football player?"

"Trust me, there are a million more respectable people he could idolise."

"I'll tell him, but I doubt he'll listen. I'm just the uncool dad, remember?"

Nothing could be further from the truth, but I enjoyed winding him up so I didn't correct him.

"So, should I buy him something soccer related for his birthday?" I asked.

"That's what I wanted to talk to you about. I don't want you to send anything over."

"What? Josh, I -"

"I don't want you to send anything," he interrupted, "because we want to come over and see you."

The squeal I let out made Miguel jump. At the other end of the phone Josh said, "Bloody hell, you nearly deafened me!"

"Sorry." I giggled. "Josh, are you serious?"

"Yep! I'm taking two weeks off and we're coming to America!"

"Really? When?"

"I'm not quite sure yet. Can you send me over your schedule so we can work something out?"

We chatted for a little longer, and I promised to email him with my work schedule as soon as I got off the phone. By the time we hung up, I was bouncing around the room like Bree after a bikini wax.

"So, your brother's coming over?" Miguel asked, laughing at my elation.

I threw myself into my spot on the bed. "Yes! I have to email to let him know where I am and when, and he'll figure out the rest."

I honestly couldn't think of anything better than having them visit me. I'd been sure the next time I saw them would be in England. It didn't occur to me they might come to me.

"Look at you," Miguel laughed, his fingers gently stroking my cheek. "This is the most relaxed I've ever seen you."

"Really? I'm always relaxed with you."

He shook his head. "This is different. You look…"

"What?"

"Even more beautiful than usual."

He made me feel every word he spoke. I loved how everything that came out of his mouth was honest, uncensored. He said whatever he was thinking in the moment, not because he wanted anything from me, but because he meant it.

I wriggled closer to him, kissing his soft lips, and thanking whatever guardian angels were looking over me for making my life so good.

I should have known it wouldn't last.

The high from talking to Josh and being so happy with Miguel carried me through the next day. It's funny how having something to look forward to makes everything seem brighter. Not that life was particularly murky before, but it was good to have an event on the horizon other than work.

At around four-fifteen that afternoon, everything changed.

Technically, I had forty-five minutes left of my working day but somehow I'd managed to get through everything with time to spare. It seemed a shame not to reward myself for being so efficient, so I headed up to the restaurant for a sneaky coffee, and to watch everyone else slaving away.

On my way up the steps, Radleigh passed me, his eyes shooting out vibes of anger. He didn't even stop to make a dig at me. If he hadn't bashed into my arm as he sped by, I'd have thought I'd imagined seeing him.

"No, really, it's fine," I muttered, continuing towards the welcoming aroma of coffee and food.

Right away, something seemed off. There were usually waiters milling around, or at the very least, someone standing behind the bar just in case anyone came in early. It was *not* okay to keep a Westberg Warrior waiting.

I guess I should take the silence as a sign to find something else to do.

But the room wasn't silent. I could hear someone taking deep, shuddering breaths and sniffling.

At the sound of my footsteps, a blonde head snapped upwards, looking in my direction in panic.

"Taylor?"

She wiped her eyes and tried to fake a smile, but it was too late.

So. McCoy thundered past me, and Taylor was curled up on a chair sobbing her heart out. It didn't take a genius to put it together.

"Are you okay?" I asked as I approached, not sure I wanted to know but too far in to creep away.

She shook her head, tears still streaming from her eyes. I'd never seen her face so pale, and her whole body was trembling. I pulled up a chair beside her, my distaste quickly replaced with concern.

"What happened?"`

"I ... I don't ... I can't say. I can't."

"You've been seeing McCoy, haven't you?"

Surprise flashed across her face. "No," she said. "No. I'd never cheat on Jesse. Never."

Well, that was a relief. I couldn't deal with being dragged into the middle of another relationship drama. Freya and Will were bad enough, without stumbling into a Radleigh/Taylor/Jesse love triangle.

"So why are you crying?"

"McCoy... he told me to meet him here. He said he wanted to talk to me."

The Warriors restaurant seemed like a weird place to request a meeting to get into her pants, but he certainly had enough authority to make the wait staff disappear if he needed them to.

Taylor tried to steady her breathing. "He's been bothering me for a while. At first I didn't mind him flirting. It was flattering, you know? He said some stuff about... about wanting to sleep with me." Her cheeks flushed bright red. "I mean, not so blatantly. He dropped hints. I told him to stop and he did for a while, but-"

"But what?"

"I agreed to meet him today to make sure he got the message. I thought I'd be safe here."

She dissolved into sobs again, and I held her close to me, stroking her hair until she was ready to speak again.

"He told me he isn't going to give up," she said. "Then he... he..."

An array of disturbing images hurtled into my mind. How long had they been alone?

"What did he do, Taylor?"

"He put his hands on me... on my shoulders then my waist, and he pushed me against the wall and tried to kiss me. He only let go when I slapped him."

It all sounded familiar, but this wasn't the same as what he did to me. He hadn't scared me. Taylor was terrified. She clung to me, her tears dampening my shoulder, but I didn't let her go. She swanned around in designer clothes, oozing confidence, but seeing her so fragile reminded me she was little more than a child.

The look of fury on McCoy's face as he'd stomped past me embedded itself in my brain. I'd never seen him look that way before, but perhaps I shouldn't have been so surprised. He always went for what he wanted, even if it was off limits.

Especially if it was off limits.

"This is all my fault." Taylor's voice trembled. "I guess I made him think I -"

"Taylor," I interrupted, "even if you'd walked past him naked, it wouldn't have given him the right to touch you. You told him to leave you alone, and he didn't."

"But I-"

"No. This is not your fault, and this needs to be stopped right now."

"How? I don't want to make trouble. I just want him to leave me alone."

"Oh, he'll leave you alone. I'll make sure of it."

"You're not gonna say anything to him, are you?"

In my mind, there were two options. Talk to him, or talk to Richard. After all, McCoy had sexually harassed her at his place of work. If I went to Richard, there was no way it would remain a secret. Not that he deserved to have it kept under wraps. But for Taylor's sake?

"What do you want me to do?" I asked.

"I don't know." She put her head in her hands. "Do you think talking to him will make a difference?"

"Maybe. Maybe if he knows you've told someone he's bothering you, he'll back off."

She took a minute to mull over my offer. "It's worth a shot."

"I'll try," I promised. "But if he does anything like this again, it'll need to be taken to Richard. Perhaps the threat of destroying his career will make him stop."

The way her shoulders slumped forwards told me she was too broken to disagree. I sat with her for the next thirty minutes, until the staff began to filter back into the restaurant. She had to meet Jesse and she was adamant she didn't want him to find out about McCoy, so I went with her to the restroom so she could freshen up and reapply her make-up. Although she'd washed the tear stains from her cheeks, the worry hadn't left her eyes, but she plastered a smile on her face and I gave her a hug before sending her out to Jesse.

It had taken almighty restraint to hold in my anger while I was with Taylor, but by the time I left her, I was ready to unleash.

How could he do that?

Why the hell couldn't he take a hint? It wasn't normal to believe that *'Leave me alone'* translated to, *'I want to shag your brains out.'*

I sent Freya a quick text to tell her I'd be late meeting her then went up to the gym, where I knew McCoy would go as soon as training ended. He always went to the gym after training.

I reminded myself to approach him with some degree of tact and calmness. Thanks to his completely unfounded complaint against me, I was already on dodgy ground. Knowing my explosive temper, particularly where McCoy was concerned, it would be difficult to keep the conversation professional.

'Well that would be because your interest isn't strictly professional,' a rogue voice said from inside my head. It had cropped up so fast, I hadn't had chance to block it out. *'Not true,'* I argued with myself. *'Admitting he's good looking is not the same as being interested in him. This is about Taylor.'*

As I pushed through the doors to the gym, prepared to wait, I found him already there, running on one of the treadmills. One step ahead of me again. I forced my gaze away from his powerful legs, took a deep breath and said, "I need to talk to you."

He hadn't heard me come in, and my entrance almost caused him to slide off the treadmill and smash his face on the floor. He caught himself just in time and deftly jumped off before he was thrown.

"What the hell, Leah?"

"You need to listen to me, and listen carefully because if I have to bring this up again, it'll be in front of Richard."

He picked up his towel from the floor and wiped the sweat from his face. "What's got your panties in a bunch?"

"I'm not playing around, McCoy. I talked to Taylor."

I watched as his face clouded over. There was something very satisfying about seeing his confidence turn to uncertainty. "What's she been saying?"

"Guilty conscience?"

"What's she been saying?" he repeated, a little more forcefully.

"She says you've been hassling her."

He rolled his eyes, making me want to jam my fingers into his ice blue orbs and scratch them right out of his head.

"That's crap."

"Is that it? That's your whole defence?"

"What do you want me to say? I don't have time to defend myself against little girls who make up stories about me. And I'd expect after being warned about treating me unfairly, you would do your job properly for once and treat me with a little respect."

His words stung. I'd done nothing but work damn hard since I'd taken the job, in spite of him belittling me at every turn. Somehow he always succeeded in turning every conversation into a threat or a come-on, and it was getting old.

"Respect is a two way street, and you've shown me none. Now, I'm asking you *nicely* to leave Taylor alone. She's thinking of going to Richard."

I meant to make a sweeping exit after I'd delivered that information, but I couldn't resist waiting to witness his reaction. It was worth sticking around to watch the colour slowly draining from his cheeks.

"What exactly am I being accused of?"

"Wow. Do you force yourself on so many women that you can't keep track?"

Confusion, then clarity crossed his face. "Force myself on…? Leah, she's only saying this because I turned her down."

"Oh please, when have you ever turned a woman down? I've seen the way you look at her."

"I'm serious. She threw herself at me, I told her it was never gonna happen, and now I guess she's out for revenge. I'm telling you, I've done nothing wrong here."

"I don't believe you." I watched him closely. "I saw the state she was in. You don't think kissing someone after they've told you they're not interested is wrong?"

"I've never kissed anyone who wasn't into me."

I shivered involuntarily under his gaze. "Don't even start. Whatever happened between us has nothing to do with this."

"Sure it does." The smirk returned to his face. "The idea I would hit on somebody else has made you crazy with jealousy. Admit it."

The fact that thought had already crossed my mind made me more uncomfortable than the way he was staring at me. I refused to turn away, even though his grin was tormenting me.

"You need to take this seriously," I said. "If she makes this official, you could be fired."

He shook his head. "She has no case against me. She has no proof, no witnesses, nothing that says I've been near her."

Only because you made sure of it.

"Well you'd better hope she doesn't find any because if she does, you can say goodbye to your career."

"What would it take to get you on my side?" Radleigh asked, stepping towards me. "Maybe the possibility of Miguel finding out you kissed me?"

I should have seen that coming.

"You're doing nothing to convince me of your innocence."

"Leah, come on, this is bullshit! It's all in her head!"

The level of agitation in his voice stopped me in my tracks.

Is he telling the truth?

No, of course not. Taylor was a mess. But if I kept looking into Radleigh's eyes, I felt sure he'd somehow hypnotise me into believing his version of events.

"For someone who didn't do anything wrong, you look extremely guilty."

"Screw you!" he snapped, throwing his towel on the floor. After shooting a final glare in my direction, he stormed out of the gym, the door slamming hard behind him.

For the rest of the day, I couldn't force him out of my mind. The things he'd said, and the things Taylor told me played in a continuous loop until I thought my brain might melt from working overtime. The worst part about the whole situation was that I wanted to believe him. I'd found McCoy to be pushy, persistent and infuriating, but not once did it cross my mind that he'd force himself on someone. Why would he need to? For every woman who turned him down, there were probably ten more who were willing to get on their backs – or whatever the preferred position was – for him.

Taylor's distress made it real though. If she had thrown herself at him, he wouldn't have hesitated for a second. I'd seen the '*I wanna get in your pants*' glint in his eyes on more than one occasion.

He did it.

And I was the idiot who *let* him kiss me.

Chapter 9
We'll Be Announcing Our Engagement Any Day Now

It wasn't a huge surprise when I received a phone call from Richard, summoning me to work early the next morning. I'd expected Radleigh would instantly figure out some kind of counter-attack to help him wriggle out of Taylor's accusations. Throwing something at me to deflect from what he did was definitely his style.

To say I was nervous was an understatement. Freya drove me to meet my fate, sacrificing an extra hour in bed to ensure I arrived on time. I gave her the key to my office so she could nap on my couch if she wanted, then went to find Richard.

"Don't look so worried," he said, with an amused grin. "It's nothing you've done wrong."

"Oh, good. The last time you called me here it was because of McCoy."

He tapped his pen against the edge of his desk. "Well…"

"Really? What now?"

Richard put his pen down and looked at me closely. "When McCoy made the complaint about you, you said he'd been suggestive towards you. I wondered if you wanted to elaborate on that."

My stomach dropped. This had to be about Taylor. It was too much of a coincidence to be anything else. I'd barely slept the night before because every time I'd drifted off, my dreams flashed with images of McCoy and Taylor. Of him touching her, and her fighting to get away.

"Does this have anything to do with a certain young blonde who happens to be dating Jesse Shaw?"

Richard's brow furrowed. "You know?

"Yes. I know."

Cheers, Taylor. I risked my already unstable work relationship with McCoy to confront him and you reported him anyway! Oh well. At least she'd done the right thing eventually. Richard was far better equipped to handle this kind of thing than me.

"Why didn't you tell me?" Richard asked.

"Because Taylor didn't want me to."

"Well, she changed her mind. She was in a really bad way, Leah. You should have come straight to me."

I hated that I'd disappointed him, but when Taylor made me swear I would do as she asked, I couldn't betray her trust. She needed someone on her side, not stabbing her in the back.

"I'm sorry," I said. "I wasn't prepared to go against what she wanted. What would have been the point in telling you if she wasn't planning to follow through with the complaint?"

"I thought you of all people would know why. I thought you had the measure of McCoy."

"Oh, I do. But I couldn't drag an eighteen-year-old girl through the drama of a sexual harassment case when she wasn't sure about making a complaint in the first place."

Plus, what if he really didn't do it?

Richard waved a dismissive hand in the air to let me know we'd have to agree to disagree. "The reason I wanted to talk to you was to ask if he ever did anything like this to you. Has he ever tried to touch you in an inappropriate way, or made you afraid to come to work?"

The question made me feel sick. Yes, he'd tried to kiss me but I'd let him, and he'd tried to make me dance with him at the club, and pushed me up against the doors at my apartment. I never felt fear, though.

You are sick.

I shook my head. "I've never been scared around him, but I'm not a teenager who doesn't know how to handle idiots. I can see how he might seem intimidating to her. It doesn't matter about me, though, does it? It's what he did to her that's important."

"Yes. But if there was someone else, someone who could give a bit more weight to the allegation, it would make my job easier."

"What's the procedure in situations like this? For one thing, he totally denies it. It won't be easy to prove."

"Not unless a witness appears," Richard agreed. "First I need to talk to him."

"And if he continues to say he didn't do anything?"

"It's all in Taylor's hands to decide what to do next."

"You believe her, don't you?"

"What I believe isn't important. Until I have proof one way or the other, my main concern is keeping this quiet. If it gets out, it'll ruin McCoy. If he did it, that's what he deserves. If he didn't... I'm not risking my best player's reputation. Taylor was very upset, and I doubt anyone would fake that level of fear, but these things happen. I need to be sure before I do anything else."

"Is there anything I can do to help?"

"Can you send McCoy here to see me? I've got some work to do before training starts, and I don't want to draw attention by hauling him in here in front of everyone. I've already tried calling him but I can't get through."

"I can do that," I said, even though I'd hoped I wouldn't have to talk to him.

"Thanks," Richard answered, with a smile. "I appreciate your help with this."

I gave him a half-hearted salute, then left his office and went back to my own.

Freya was sitting in my desk chair, holding a cup of coffee. There was another steaming mug beside her which she handed to me.

"I thought you might need this."

"I need a double vodka, but coffee will do for now."

I smiled gratefully as I took it from her, and she said, "What happened?"

"What always happens when Richard calls me to his office? McCoy."

Her eyebrows nearly disappeared off the top of her head. "He hasn't-"

"Not another complaint against me. A complaint against him."

"What did he do?"

I knew Richard wanted to keep the whole thing a secret, but Freya was the most trustworthy person I knew, and if I didn't talk to someone I was in serious danger of going round the bend.

"Wow," she said, after I'd given her a brief rundown of the situation. "He really can't take no for an answer, huh?"

"Apparently not. Freya, I'm so sick of him."

Sick and tired. And frustrated with myself.

"Hey." Freya stood up and rested her hands on my shoulders. "Don't let him get to you. This is not your problem."

I wanted tell her the real reason I was so freaked out. That my relationship with Miguel was potentially in jeopardy because of one stupid kiss with Radleigh. But how could I possibly admit to anyone that I'd fallen into the trap so many other women had slipped into?

It was one moment. One badly judged moment. Nothing more.

"You're right," I said, more calmly. "This is his fault. I need to chill out. Now I'd best go and find him. Maybe it won't be as bad as I think."

Freya gave me an encouraging smile and I stepped out of the office and made my way towards the locker room.

I wasn't sure if Radleigh had even arrived yet, but if he had, that's where he'd be. As I approached, I spotted Bryce walking down the stairs from the restaurant, coffee in hand, heading in the same direction as me. He hadn't changed into his training clothes yet, and his close fitting blue t-shirt hugged his muscles.

Lucky t-shirt.

"Hey, Leah. What's up?"

"I'm looking for Radleigh. Is he here yet?"

Bryce nodded. "Yeah, he's in there." He jerked his head towards the locker room. "Want me to get him for you?"

"Yeah, I guess so."

He chuckled. "I see you two are still getting on well."

"Fabulously. We'll be announcing our engagement any day now."

Bryce gave in to a fit of laughter and I smiled. "I'm sorry, I'm a little stressed today and it's way too early to deal with McCoy."

As if the mention of his name had summoned him, Radleigh walked out of the door. His eyes narrowed when he saw me and Bryce laughing, but he didn't say anything. The tension was palpable as Bryce winked at me before leaving me alone with McCoy.

Alone with McCoy was the last place I wanted to be.

"Richard wants to see you in his office," I told him. "Now."

"You told him about Taylor, didn't you?"

"No. Taylor told him. I only found out a little while ago."

Everything about him, from the way he'd squared his shoulders to the look in his eye told me he didn't believe me.

"I have nothing to say. I'm not going."

"Fine. If you want to make this worse for yourself, that's up to you. I'll tell Richard you can't be bothered to give your side of things."

I began to walk away from him, wishing with every fibre of my being that he'd be fired over this incident so I wouldn't have to spend every hour of my working day being so completely pissed off.

His footsteps followed mine and I walked faster, hoping to dive into my office before he could say anything else.

"Why did you trust what she told you?" he asked, catching me up before I escaped.

The stupidity of the question nearly floored me.

"Why? Because you left her in a quivering mess! It's about time you understood when a woman says no, she's not playing hard to get, she just doesn't want anything to do with you!"

"Oh, like you didn't want anything to do with me?"

I looked around, hoping to hell nobody was nearby to hear what he'd said. The words echoed around us.

"Get over yourself," I hissed. "I didn't ask for that kiss, you-"

"You responded! So before you start pretending you're innocent-"

"I'm not pretending to be innocent, I'm saying that forcing yourself on women might not be something you'd be above doing!"

"Oh, I see." His eyes glimmered with malice. "Are you gonna tell Richard I 'forced myself' on you? I'm sure he'd be interested to hear how you handled it!"

My insides burned with anger at the way he kept bringing the kiss up every time I challenged him. Was this how my life was going to be now? Forced to remember my mistake, waiting for McCoy to spill it to Miguel if I pushed him far enough?

"If you weren't guilty of throwing yourself at Taylor, you wouldn't be going to so much trouble to unsettle me. If you want to tell Richard what happened between you and I, go right ahead. Even if I lose my job, I'll be happy if it means you get what you deserve!"

Instead of waiting for him to respond, I slipped back into my office, slamming the door behind me, and almost jumped out of my skin when I saw Freya was gone and Miguel was sitting on my desk.

He smiled, so he couldn't have heard the argument I'd had with McCoy. When he took in the expression on my face he said, "It's too early in the morning for you to be this mad."

I slunk towards Miguel and let him wrap me in his arms.

"What's wrong, angel?"

"Bad day," I mumbled into his shoulder.

"What happened?"

I took a deep breath and informed him of the situation with McCoy. Again, even though I wasn't supposed to divulge any of the information, I *needed* to tell him. Since we'd been dating, I'd softened. Whenever things started to fall apart, I wanted to cuddle up to him and talk instead of pretending everything was fine. It was something I always had in me, I'd just never been with anyone who allowed me to be so openly honest and soppy. I wasn't afraid to be honest with Miguel.

"What a way to start the morning," he said.

"Yep." I sighed. "I could do without any more run-ins with McCoy, but now this has come up …"

"You don't *have* to fight with him," Miguel pointed out. "Why don't you try walking away?"

I raised an eyebrow. "Don't you know me at all?"

Miguel began to laugh. "Leah, you're not an argumentative person. You could do it if you tried."

I shook my head. "McCoy is different. He's so smug and so arrogant, and so-"

"Okay," Miguel interrupted, sensing the rant threatening to explode from me. "I know. But you'll have to find some way to control it. Think of something calming. What relaxes you?"

"You."

"So think about me," he replied, leaning in to kiss me.

'I always think about you when I fight with him,' I thought, guiltily, but shrugged it off as I returned Miguel's kiss.

"I hate to leave you so soon," he said, "but work is calling me."

"I know, for me too."

"Cheer up! Isn't it next weekend you're going back to Boston?"

My mood instantly lifted at the thought. Before I'd accepted my job in L.A, I'd accepted an invitation to my friend's wedding reception. Alison was one of the first people I met when I moved to Boston. She was a physiotherapist at the hospital I worked at and she introduced me to Stacey, who wound up being my roommate. Alison's wedding to her long-term boyfriend Michael was an event I'd been looking forward to, and even though the wedding ceremony was family only, I didn't want to miss the evening celebrations. Richard approved my days off because it was planned before I moved to Westberg, so I had three full days away from work, most of which would be spent with my Boston buddies.

"Yes. I can't wait. I wish you could come with me."

"Me too. I'm already jealous of the guys who'll have the chance to dance with you."

"There'll be no dancing. Not slow dancing anyway. I save that for you."

Miguel's eyes softened like he wanted to say something more but instead, he kissed me again.

"We still on for dinner tonight?" he asked.

"Absolutely."

A couple of hours later, after tending to Bryce's groin strain, another sprained ankle, and sending Jude to hospital after he re-injured his knee during training, I had to meet Cody Rivera on the pitch to go through some simple exercises with him. I'd recently started treating Cody for spondylosis - a disorder which affects spinal function - after he complained of back pain and stiffness. He was officially out of any matches for the next few weeks but he came to training every day to watch. Such was his dedication, he didn't mind doing his exercises out on the pitch so he still felt like a part of the team.

Rivera already knew the exercises. My job was to stop him overexerting himself. He was desperate to get back to work, but his enthusiasm caused him to push too hard, risking making his condition worse.

I loved working out on the field. First of all, it meant I wasn't stuck in my stuffy office in the blazing heat. It had air conditioning, but it didn't compare to being out in the open. Secondly, I got to see Richard, Will, Freya and Miguel put the Warriors through their paces. It fascinated me to watch them working together, all so focused and strict.

Cody was doing knee lifts when some shouting caught my attention. A certain amount of noise was normal, but someone had yelled out for Richard and I whipped my head around to see what was happening.

I'm certain my heart stopped beating for a second.

Miguel was on the ground between the goalposts, tightly holding the ball he'd saved. Radleigh towered above him and drove his foot into Miguel's stomach, a dangerous look on his face. The shock forced Miguel to lose his grip on the ball but McCoy kicked him again, harder than before. Everyone on the pitch ran over to stop him, but he managed to get one last blow in before he was dragged away, leaving Miguel curled up in pain.

I sped across the grass even though my legs were shaking from the brutal beating I'd just witnessed. Richard called for the medics, and I knelt down beside Miguel.

"Leah," he mumbled. "I'm okay."

Gently stroking his cheek, I said, "Really?"

He gave a weak laugh. "No, but I will be."

The medics were quick to reach us and I stepped aside so they could help him to his feet. He was shaking, and clutching his stomach.

"We're gonna take him to the E.R," one of the medics said. "He'll need to be checked for broken ribs and any other internal damage."

Internal damage? If McCoy had seriously injured Miguel I'd kill him with my bare hands.

"Can I come with you?" I asked.

Miguel shook his head. "If you come it'll be a lot of waiting around. You should stay here and keep working."

"Are you sure? Because I don't mind waiting around."

"I'm sure," he told me. "I'll call you as soon as I've been checked over, okay?"

"Okay," I agreed. "I'll see you later."

As the medics took Miguel away, Freya put her arm around me. "Are you okay?"

No words came at first. The past few minutes had rushed by in a blur. One minute I'd been supervising Rivera's exercises, the next I'd seen Radleigh kicking the crap out of my boyfriend.

"I don't understand," I said. "What happened?"

"McCoy flipped out when Miguel saved his goal. I've never seen him do anything like that before."

I knew he was angry about Taylor telling Richard what he'd done, but it never occurred to me he would be irate enough to lash out that way. The image of his foot thudding into Miguel's stomach kept playing over and over in my head.

My eyes flicked around the field but Radleigh was nowhere in sight. Without thinking, I ran off the pitch and straight to the locker room, barging in without knocking. McCoy was rifling through his sports bag, but glanced up as I entered. His blue eyes had never looked icier. Did he even care that he'd put Miguel in hospital? I wanted to scream at him, but the fury burning through me made it impossible to speak. After glaring at each other for what seemed like an eternity, Radleigh said, "Get out of here, Leah. I have nothing to say to you."

And release.

"How about an apology?" I snapped. "You took out your aggression on an innocent person and that is not on!"

"You're right. It's not right to take out your aggression on an innocent person but that's what Taylor's doing to me!"

"So you thought beating the crap out of Miguel would make you feel better?"

"Yes. And it did."

I shook my head in disgust. "You weren't beating up Miguel, you were using him to attack me. What you did was personal. You may as well have kicked me because I felt every single bit of pain you inflicted on him! What kind of person would take pleasure in hurting someone else?"

"Maybe someone who was falsely accused of harassment! Someone who couldn't make anyone hear what they're trying to say! Someone who is so damn angry that they had to get rid of the frustration somewhere!"

"You can protest your innocence all you want, but you're not fooling me. And if you wanted to get rid of your anger, you could have gone to the gym and beaten the hell out of a punch bag, but instead you used Miguel because you knew it would hurt me!"

"And you say I'm arrogant," he muttered sarcastically.

"So tell me," I challenged. "Tell me what you did to Miguel had nothing to do with me?"

"It had everything to do with you! You -"

"Stop right there!" Richard bellowed.

McCoy was standing over me, yelling, and while I hadn't been in the least bit afraid, I understood why Richard would think I might be. McCoy took a step away from me as Richard advanced on him.

"What the hell are you doing?" he demanded. "First you're accused of harassment, which I would have thought would be enough to make you lay low for a while, but instead you took your anger out on Vega! Now you're yelling at Leah as if it's her fault you're in this mess! With the accusation Taylor made against you and what you just did, you're being issued with a four week suspension, effective immediately."

I had never seen Richard so wound up. His entire body was tense, his face red with rage.

Radleigh stared first at Richard then at me before growling, "That's not fair."

"Well get used to it," Richard told him. "Because it's happening."

Miguel came out of the hospital a few hours later, and thankfully, the only damage McCoy had done to him was severe bruising. Just because his ribs weren't broken, it didn't make me any less angry. After my confrontation with Radleigh, it had taken me hours to calm down. I'd stopped vibrating with rage but a steady stream of fury still flowed through me. I wasn't just angry, though. Every clash I'd ever had with Radleigh had prompted his attack.

I felt guilty.

Freya drove me to Miguel's apartment after work, and as I climbed the steps to his Spanish style home, I stopped to glance around at the neighbourhood. The beauty of it always knocked me out. The terracotta roofs and the perfectly manicured lawns were so different to my beachfront flat. It was peaceful and private, and although curtains probably twitched when someone unknown walked by, it felt like the neighbours were more likely to fling open their doors and say hello instead of calling the people next door to ask why there was a stranger in their midst.

Opening the door to Miguel's apartment, I called out to him. His answer came from the living room where he was sitting in his gigantic leather chair with an ice pack over his ribs.

"Hey," I said softly. "How are you feeling?"

"Like I've been kicked in the stomach by a big-footed soccer player," he replied with a smile.

I dropped my bag down in the hallway and walked over to where he sat.

"Let me see."

Miguel lifted the ice pack, then carefully shifted his t-shirt to reveal an array of purple and black bruises across his stomach.

"It looks worse than it is."

"Liar."

He grimaced. "I'm lying a bit, but the painkillers help. I've got the next few days off, but after that I'm still going into work to help where I can. Richard said I can go in and out when I want."

"Did he tell you he suspended McCoy?"

"Yeah. I'm not sure that was a smart move, though."

"What?" I screeched. "After what he did to you, he's lucky he wasn't fired!"

He smiled at my concern. "Four weeks without him on the team is a long time. And if Jude has to take leave for his knee-"

"Minimum of six weeks," I interrupted. "We got the call before I left."

"Crap."

It surprised me that I'd started to care about the team. Obviously I cared about the players, they were my workmates, but I didn't realise I was interested in how they would fare in the soccer league. To have McCoy and Collinson out would be a huge blow, and talented as the others were, it would be a struggle without them.

My eyes rested on his bruises again and I felt another stab of guilt.

"I think this was my fault."

"Your fault? No, Leah-"

"It *was* my fault. He did this to you because he and I argued earlier. I'm so sorry."

Miguel reached out and took my hand. "Don't blame yourself, angel."

"How can I not? If I hadn't-"

"McCoy's got a temper, and whether you'd argued with him or not, he would still have been angry about being accused of harassment. You didn't cause what happened."

He was wrong, but I didn't have the heart to carry on trying to convince him. The damage was already done.

111

"Look on the bright side," Miguel said. "He's been suspended. Now you won't have to deal with him for a while."

I didn't deserve him.

He'd been viciously assaulted, and all he was thinking about was the fact my life would be easier without McCoy around.

I leaned over to kiss him on the cheek, but he turned his head so our lips met. He put his hand up to my cheek.

"I love you, Leah."

Warmth began to spread through me as I took in his words. There was never a time when I believed a person more than at that moment. He wasn't saying it because he wanted something from me, or because he thought I wanted to hear it. He *meant* it. I had no idea if four weeks was too soon – there were no mind games involved, this was brand new territory. What I *did* know was that I felt differently for Miguel than any other man I'd dated in the past. Safe. *Happy*.

I smiled, kissing him again. "I love you too."

Chapter 10
Oh God, Let Me Be Hallucinating

I'd gotten quite used to my life being an odd mix of spectacular and awkward, and the next week pushed me to my limits. After Miguel told me he loved me, everything in my life felt brighter. I spent as much time as I could with him, nursing him back to health with my own special method of ice packs and riding him like a – slightly injured – pony.

Another thing making me happy was seeing Jesse being selected in the starting line-ups, instead of being brought on in the final minutes of a game. With McCoy out, Jesse was given the chance to prove why Westberg made him their youngest signing and his reputation grew with every match.

The downside was that Taylor still hadn't told him about Radleigh. His suspension for attacking Miguel made a great cover story to hide the harassment claims, so Jesse was still completely in the dark. No matter how much I tried to encourage Taylor to tell him, she refused, saying she didn't want to cause any more trouble. It was a tough situation to be in. The media interest in McCoy made it difficult for her to figure out what to do next. If the story got out, it wouldn't only mean bad news for him, it would mean Taylor would have to deal with the paparazzi demanding all the details. Nobody needed to be under that kind of scrutiny, especially not an eighteen-year-old girl who'd done nothing wrong.

Leaving L.A for Boston was a welcome relief. After all the stresses of the past few days, and the long flight, I was eager to go to bed but when I arrived at my old flat a little before midnight, Stacey presented me with a glass of wine. It would have been rude not to drink it.

Plus three more.

The next morning I had a long lie-in followed by a lazy breakfast with Stacey before heading to the mall in search of a new outfit to wear to the party. I'd considered wearing my super expensive red dress, but a wedding called for something a little more classy. There's nothing worse than upstaging the bride by accidentally flashing a bum cheek.

After walking around for a few hours, I eventually settled on the simple royal blue one shoulder dress I'd spotted in the first shop I went into, plus a few pairs of jeans and some strappy sandals.

"Stace!" I called, as I struggled through the front door with my bags. "I think I got carried away!"

Stacey came into the hallway looking nervous. She didn't even give into a smile when she saw all of my shopping.

"No kidding," she said, helping me regain the use of my hands, and we piled the bags down on the floor. "Leah-"

She didn't get chance to finish her sentence but she didn't need to. As I entered the lounge, I stopped dead and did a double take.

Sitting on the sofa in his usual, rather smug manner, was Radleigh McCoy.

Oh God, please let me be hallucinating.

"Hello Leah."

About a million thoughts flooded into my head at once and I looked from McCoy to Stacey in utter shock. The first words to tumble out of my mouth were, "How the hell did you find out where I am?"

Radleigh raised an eyebrow. "I know people."

"Well you should tell them if I ever find out who they are, their lives will be at serious risk. How long have you been here?"

"About a half hour."

"I tried to call you," Stacey jumped in, "but I was redirected to your voicemail."

"Why did you let him in?" I asked, turning to her. "You should have told him to leave."

Stacey was an attractive woman, with her blonde hair cut in a sleek bob, and her slight figure. I wouldn't have put it past him to make a move on her. Even more worrying was his very presence in Boston. After his suspension we'd parted on bad terms, yet he sat on Stacey's sofa as though he didn't have a care in the world.

"I'm sorry. He said he was a friend of yours and, well-" she trailed off, and I could almost hear her thinking, *It's Radleigh McCoy!*

"It's okay, Stace. It's not your fault." Turning back to Radleigh, I said, "Get out."

"I want to talk to you."

"So go home and call me. I don't want you here. For one thing, it is completely inappropriate, and for another, I have nothing to say to you."

"Leah, I came all the way from L.A. to see you."

He looked so sure of himself, my heart began to pound.

"Well," Stacey said, "I need to take a shower, so I'll leave you guys to talk."

Radleigh openly leered at her. "Need me to scrub your back?"

Stacey wasn't sure whether to smile or not, but one glance at the incredulity on my face gave her all the answer she needed and she headed for the bathroom.

Radleigh leaned back, tucking his hands behind his head as if he were a regular visitor. "Stacey's real nice. She made me coffee."

"Well, I'm not nice. You have thirty seconds to tell me why you're here."

He let out a deep sigh. "I need you to help me."

"Oh, don't even start," I told him, shaking my head. "Any chance you ever had of me helping you was blown right out of the window when you put Miguel in hospital."

And the chances were slim before. God, just looking at McCoy caused bubbles of anger to rise within me. I couldn't stop seeing his foot driving into Miguel's stomach, or the way we'd argued in the locker room. Being near him made my blood pressure spike.

Radleigh's next retort was lost as there was a knock at the door. It was just after four-thirty, and I was pretty sure Stacey wasn't expecting anyone. I turned my back on McCoy to answer it, and was immediately bundled into a hug by Billy, Stacey's boyfriend. I loved Billy. He had all the looks of a rugged bad boy but really, he was a big softy.

"Leah!" he said. "It's been too long. How are you?"

"I'm fine," I answered, returning his hug. "How are you? And why are you here already? You're not supposed to be picking us up until later."

"Yeah I know," he said, glancing briefly at my shopping bags which were still all over the floor. "But I realised on my way home that the shirt I want to wear tonight is here."

"Help yourself. You know where it is better than I do."

"Thanks Leah." He opened the door to Stacey's room. "Where is Stace anyway?"

"She's in the shower. You know what girls are like. It takes us forever to tart ourselves up."

"You're not wrong." Billy laughed, his voice muffled as he rummaged around in the wardrobe. "Though it's always worth the effort!"

I chuckled. "You're still a charmer, aren't you?"

"That I am." Billy finally reappeared from Stacey's room, green shirt in his hands. "Thanks, Leah."

"No problem."

Billy's gaze shifted over my shoulder, and his jaw dropped. I tried hard not to let out a groan.

"Aren't you going to introduce me?" McCoy asked as I turned to him.

I wouldn't have to if you'd kept out of the way.

"Radleigh," I said, as politely as I could manage. "This is Stacey's boyfriend, Billy. Billy, Radleigh McCoy."

McCoy held out his hand and Billy shook it in complete awe.

"Wow, Leah. You didn't tell me you're bringing Radleigh McCoy to the party."

"I'm not. He's just passing through. He'll be gone before the party starts."

"Actually, I'm staying in a hotel for the night," Radleigh interrupted and I fixed him with a death stare. "I only just got here."

"If you hadn't turned up unannounced, I could have saved you the price of a plane fare."

"See what I have to put up with?" McCoy asked Billy, putting his hand on my shoulder with more familiarity than I liked. It made me think of Taylor, and I shrugged him off, keeping a smile on my face so Billy wouldn't think I was being rude.

Bloody stupid British manners!

"I'm sure Alison and Michael won't mind if you come along. Having a celebrity at his wedding will make Michael's day!"

"Oh, I'm not sure." Radleigh's words oozed fake modesty. "It wouldn't be right to intrude."

How I refrained from rolling my eyes at his little act, I'll never know.

"Besides," I added, "he probably doesn't have anything suitable to wear."

"As it happens, I do. I brought a few extra things along with me."

"Well, that's settled then." Billy smiled. "I have to run but I'll catch you guys later!"

The moment Billy left, I spun round to face McCoy. His eyes glimmered with barely suppressed pride at his bullshitting skills.

"I could kill you. Who the hell do you think you are? You are *not* coming to this party, no way. Make up an excuse, anything. You're not coming."

"Why not? It might be fun."

My hatred for him had never been stronger. Not content with groping Taylor and kicking the snot out of Miguel, he had to seek me out in Boston to make my life even more uncomfortable.

"I'm not about to ruin my friends' wedding by bringing you along."

"But Billy's expecting me. You wouldn't want to let him down, would you?"

I had two choices. I could scream at him and increase his amusement, or take a deep breath and accept that there was no way I was going to get rid of him easily. For the sake of my sanity, and to stop him looking any smugger, I had to calm down.

Gently massaging my forehead to ease the headache that was rapidly coming on, I sighed. "Whatever."

He grinned triumphantly. "What time do you want me?"

"Seven thirty," I answered, unenthusiastically. "If you must come, don't be late. I won't wait for you."

"Lighten up, Leah. We might even have a good time."

"Screw you."

With one last look of superiority, Radleigh headed out the door and I let out a loud growl of frustration.

Stacey poked her head out from around the bathroom door. "What's up?"

"McCoy. I want to throttle him!"

"Easy, Leah. I assume he's gone now?"

"Oh sure, he's gone. But while you were showering, Billy stopped by and invited McCoy along to the party."

She may not have known the situation, but Stacey clearly saw it wasn't a smart move on Billy's part.

"Want my advice?" Stacey asked. "Start drinking. You won't find him nearly as annoying when you're drunk. And if you end up punching him, you can blame the alcohol."

"Sounds good to me."

When Stacey vacated the bathroom, I jumped into the shower to begin my usual pre-party routine. After showering and washing my hair, I slipped into my bathrobe and began sorting out the disaster that was my hair. As I was straightening it, Stacey popped into my room with a glass of vodka and Coke.

"Here." She set the glass down on the dressing table. "I thought this might help calm you down."

"Thanks," I replied, then knocked the drink back in one mouthful.

She sat on the bed chatting to me and pouring us both more drinks as I continued to get ready. It was like I'd never been away.

Just as I was finishing off my subtle make-up with some clear lip gloss, the doorbell rang.

"I'll go, you finish off here." Stacey leapt off the bed.

"I hope it's Billy, and McCoy has decided not to come at all!"

No such luck. The familiar scent of Radleigh's aftershave wafted through the hallway into the bedroom. I went out to save Stacey from the lecherous stare he was probably giving her. When I stepped out of my room he started to laugh.

"Great minds."

Closing my eyes for a moment, I sighed. He was wearing black trousers and an open collared blue shirt in exactly the same shade as my dress. We couldn't have been any more co-ordinated if we tried.

"I need to change." Maybe Stacey had something I'd fit into. Anything so McCoy and I didn't look like twins.

"No," he said. "Don't change. You look gorgeous."

So do you.

Wait ... what?

"Do you two want a drink?" Stacey called, as we walked through into the living room.

I nodded and downed another vodka and coke. Actually, I blamed the four vodkas for making me think that way. Time to start pacing myself. The problem was, without a drink in my hand, I wasn't sure what to do with myself.

I should call Miguel and let him know what's happening.

I didn't know why the thought hadn't occurred to me earlier. Probably because I was too busy chugging vodka straight out of the bottle. I needed to move around in the hope of using up some of the buzz taking over me. I hopped up from the sofa and went into the hallway to get my phone from my bag, but just as I got my hands on it, the doorbell rang.

I swung the door open, and Billy smiled. "All ready to go?"

"Yeah," I replied, as Stacey and Radleigh made their way to the door.

Calling Miguel would have to wait. The cab had arrived, and my hellish evening was about to begin. I wasn't quite sure how I was going to make it through, but I had no choice but to give it my best shot.

Chapter 11
A Man Of Many Talents

Alison and Michael's wedding was held in a lavish hotel in the centre of the city, much to my amusement.

As if I didn't spend enough time in hotels.

An elegant function room had been set up especially for the reception and when we arrived, the DJ played popular music as the guests filtered in.

I was already a little woozy and although I wasn't usually such a lightweight, I didn't normally drink so much in the space of an hour. If I carried on, I knew it wouldn't be long before I started dancing on tables, singing *It's Raining Men*.

Before we went to the bar, Stacey, Billy, Radleigh and I went to say hello to Alison and Michael who were slowly greeting everyone by the entrance.

"Leah!" Alison squealed, hugging me tightly. "I've missed you!"

"I've missed you too," I told her. "Congratulations! You look beautiful."

Alison's wedding dress was a simple straight gown with lace detail across the bodice. Classy and understated, just like Alison.

"Thank you," she beamed, looking up at Michael with the kind of adoration that had made me nauseous before I met Miguel.

"It's good to see you." Michael kissed me on the cheek. He opened his mouth to say more when he caught sight of Radleigh. "Holy crap." His eyes widened. "It's Rebel!"

I was used to seeing this reaction from women, not men. I introduced them and Michael said, "Leah, I thought you were dating one of the team coaches."

"I am but he's not fit to travel at the moment." I threw a pointed glare at Radleigh.

"So Radleigh McCoy was your last minute substitution?" Michael joked, and an alcohol induced hysterical giggle slipped out of my mouth.

"Actually, I had no idea he was coming."

"But… you're wearing matching outfits."

"Purely coincidental."

"We're showing our unity by wearing the team colours." Radleigh laughed, putting his arm around me.

His fingers on my waist filled me with unexpected heat.

Wow, you really are pissed.

"Let's get a drink, shall we?" I suggested, though I knew I couldn't let another drop of alcohol pass my lips.

"Sure," Radleigh said. "What's everyone having?"

Billy and Stacey told us what they wanted and we made our way to the busy bar.

"You're going to do everything you can to embarrass me, aren't you?" I hissed.

"Of course not," Radleigh replied, but I caught a devilish flash in his eyes. "By the way, you really do look all kinds of hot tonight."

"Shut it, McCoy."

He laughed, and we waited to get close enough to help ourselves to drinks. An open bar was a novelty for me. In the UK, open bars at weddings were highly unusual. I always thought that was a good thing. Free alcohol plus over-emotional family members equalled drunken fights and tears. Nobody wants their big day ruined that way.

I glanced around the room while we waited at all the people who had arrived for the party. Everyone chatted animatedly, hugging, catching up, and there were the obligatory children skidding up and down the dance floor, as seemed to be tradition at most parties.

"Leah, what do you want to drink?" Radleigh asked.

Engrossed in people watching, I hadn't noticed we'd reached the bar.

"A Coke, thanks."

"A Coke? With...?"

"Nothing. Just a plain Coke."

"I thought you planned on having fun?"

"Well that plan was ruined when you showed up. Besides, I've already had way too much to drink. I need to slow down."

I actually hoped the caffeine would help sober me up.

"Okay." McCoy shrugged.

We joined Stacey and Billy at a four-seated candle-lit table, and McCoy and I sat down and handed out the drinks.

"So, what's it like being a soccer player?" Billy asked. "I play a little, but nothing close to your level."

"It's unbelievable," Radleigh replied with a grin. "I get to travel all around the country doing what I love, and I meet loads of hot women."

He added the last comment with a sideways glance at me, and I scowled at him.

"What do you do for a living, man?" McCoy asked Billy.

"I'm an accountant. Nothing nearly as interesting as you."

"At least you get to stay at home and be with your woman."

After fifteen minutes of Billy hanging on McCoy's every word, Stacey grabbed my hand and dragged me on to the dance floor.

"I can't stand any more of Billy's hero worship." She chuckled.

"I know, like McCoy's ego isn't big enough already."

We danced to a few cheesy pop songs before heading to the bar where Stacey insisted I at least have a glass of wine. I took it but only drank a sip before setting it down and getting myself another Coke.

A few minutes later Alison approached us, glowing with pride and looking every inch the perfect blissfully happy bride.

"My goodness it's hot in here," she said, fanning herself with her hand as she reached for a glass of vodka and lemonade. I agreed, but Stacey looked a little distracted.

"I'm sorry," she said. "I think I better go rescue McCoy from the Billy fan club. I might try to put Billy in the mood for later with a little dirty dancing!"

Alison and I shook our heads in amusement as Stacey left to re-join her boyfriend.

"So." Alison steered me away to a far corner of the room where it was a bit darker and a lot quieter. "Now we're away from the guys we can catch up properly. How are things with you? Are you still enjoying the job?"

"Hey, come on, this is *your* night! We're supposed to talk about you and the wedding."

Alison grinned. "What's to know? It's a wedding, it was expensive and I will never be able to afford anything again for the rest of my life."

"You can't fool me, Ali. I can see how excited you are."

"Okay, of course I'm excited, I just got married! But I've been gushing about how happy I am for hours. I want to hear about what you've been up to."

"Me? It's all been about work. Apart from meeting Miguel."

The thought of him made me smile, and Alison said, "Wow, that's the happiest you've looked all evening."

"Oh," I moaned, briefly hiding my face behind my hands. "Do I really look that pissed off?"

"No." Alison laughed. "Actually, you look incredible tonight. I just meant your eyes kind of lit up at the mention of his name. Are things getting serious between you two?"

"Well, we've not been together long but... he told me he loves me."

"Ooh, that's a big step forward!"

"Ali, he's such a great guy. He's so caring and honest. I wish he was here."

"Why isn't he?"

"He's... injured." I didn't want to go into the ins and outs of what happened.

"So, how come Radleigh McCoy's here?"

"That is a *long* story so I will spare you the full details. McCoy's been suspended, and he decided to show up at Stacey's to try and persuade me to help him, I think. We haven't had much chance to talk yet. Billy came over to the flat earlier and invited McCoy along tonight, so..."

"I sense animosity." Alison watched me closely. "You don't like him much, huh?"

"I don't like him at all," I told her with a laugh. "But he's here, there's nothing I can do about it now."

"That's not a satisfactory explanation, Leah. You can't leave me dangling!"

I looked distastefully at my glass of coke, put it down on the table and took Alison's glass of vodka and lemonade from her hand, swallowing a huge swig and causing her to burst out laughing.

"Is he *that* bad?"

"Oh yes."

Alison glanced across the room to where Radleigh sat surrounded by children and a few of their parents. He was laughing, and one of the kids challenged him to an arm wrestle. I watched as he pretended to struggle with the determined boy then finally concede making the young teenager beam with pride.

"He looks harmless enough."

I tore my eyes away from him. "He has his moments."

"He's damn good-looking, too. The women in here can't keep their eyes off him."

"I'm used to that. It wouldn't be so bad if he weren't so up himself."

"Are you saying you don't see the attraction?"

"I'm saying there are more important qualities in a man than an incredible body. He's a great looking guy. But that's where his good points end."

"I bet he's an amazing kisser. His lips are incredible."

I tried not to splutter into my drink. After what I'd said, confirming her theory probably wasn't the best idea.

"Alison! You're a married woman!"

"Exactly. I'm married, not blind." She winked. She finished the last of her drink and stood up. "Well, I better be getting back out there."

"Have fun. I'll catch you later."

I rose from my seat and made my way over to where McCoy was sitting alone since his admirers had left him.

"Well, well, well," I said with an amused grin. "I never would have thought you'd have a way with children."

He looked up at me. "I'm a man of many talents."

"You may be able to fool a bunch of kids into thinking you're a superhero, but I am not so easily misled."

"Actually, I was charming them into not using their smartphones to tell the world where I am."

I don't know why it didn't occur to me to think about that before. He wasn't quite famous enough to be stalked whenever he stepped out of his front door, but if he was seen partying while suspended, it would make an interesting story. And if I was seen in any of those photos, it would be a disaster. I could imagine the horror on Richard's face if he found out Radleigh was with me, and what about Miguel?

"Don't look so worried," he said. "Everyone's having too much fun to take any notice of me."

I had no choice but to hope he was right. "Why don't you tell me why you came here?"

"You want to talk about this now?"

"I don't want to talk about it at all, but you came here to talk so you may as well get it out of your system."

Radleigh fixed his eyes on me. "I owe you an apology, Leah. I shouldn't have taken my anger out on Miguel. You were right, it wasn't fair."

I'm not buying this. He appeared sincere, but I highly doubted he'd flown across America just to say sorry. It could never be that simple.

"You should apologise to Miguel, not me. He's the one who got hurt."

"I already did, this morning. He was more understanding than he should have been after what I did to him."

"Well, he's pretty amazing that way. I'm not as forgiving."

"I didn't expect you to be. But I'd appreciate it if you'd put that aside because I want to tell you the truth about what happened with Taylor."

I raised my eyebrows. "A confession?"

"There's nothing to confess. The day she says I kissed her, I did see her. I wanted to talk to her with nobody else around. The truth is, she's been following me for weeks. Every time I looked over my shoulder, she was there. I wanted to tell her once and for all that it had to stop."

That was pretty much the opposite of what Taylor had told me. Same story, different perspective.

"I'm having trouble imagining you wanting to avoid a woman who is desperate to sleep with you."

"Leah, she is nuts. Even *I* have limits."

"So why didn't you tell anyone?"

"Because she's a kid." Radleigh blew out a frustrated breath. "I thought she'd get bored of throwing herself at me. Instead, she kept showing up wherever I was like a creepy stalker."

"And she was so distraught that day in the restaurant because...?"

"I told her there's no chance of anything ever happening between us. I know what you think of me, but even I have rules about not screwing around with my friends' women."

He sounded convincing enough, but I couldn't shrug off everything Taylor had told me, and how upset she'd been. Whatever happened had only just unfolded when I found her in a quivering wreck. There wasn't enough time for her to make up a lie that big and do it so convincingly.

But what if she did?

This was the wrong time and place to think about it. I'd had too much to drink to think it through rationally. Instead of stressing over what Radleigh may or may not have done, I wanted to enjoy my time with my Boston friends and forget about work and McCoy and Taylor.

"Leah, do you want to dance?"

I took in the romantic ballad that was playing and smiled sweetly. "Yes. But not with you."

"I'm the only one who's asking."

"Well, what guy would be brave enough to ask me with you sitting beside me? I'm going to mingle."

Even though I'd told Miguel I'd save slow dances for him, he'd insisted I have at least one. '*It's a wedding,*' he said. '*If someone asks you, accept. There will be plenty of other chances for us to slow dance.*'

I started to stand up but McCoy caught my hand. "Please?"

His pale blue eyes softened in a way I was sure would floor most women. Even slightly drunk, I found the strength to remind myself I couldn't trust him. His eyes were weapons to entice and engage. Not genuine in any way.

"No."

"Leah, come on. One dance. It won't kill you." He raised an eyebrow. "Please."

Ah, what the hell. What I said is true. No other man is going to come near me with him around.

"One dance."

Grinning, Radleigh stood up. I followed him to the dance floor where he gently but confidently snaked his arms around my waist.

"You really do look gorgeous tonight," he said, breaking into my thoughts and bringing me to my senses in one breath.

"Okay, let's cut to the chase." I looked him in the eye. "This is the part where you tell me I've got you all wrong, and you're just a poor misunderstood boy, right?"

Radleigh smiled roguishly. "You're good."

"I've had plenty of experience with men like you. I know all the tricks. I've even fallen for them."

"The tricks or the men?"

"Both."

"I'm sorry. Must have been rough for you."

"Cut it out," I told him, unable to stop myself laughing at the fact he was still trying. "Your corny lines are wasted on me."

His arms tightened around me, almost like a challenge, but I didn't back away. For the first time ever he'd sought permission before putting his hands on me. I wasn't even close to trusting him, but it was easier to be around him when he was merely flirty, rather than a complete asshole.

Radleigh felt so different to Miguel. McCoy was taller, his body firmer. Miguel was fit but not nearly as toned. Hugging him was like hugging a cushion.

I looked up at Radleigh again. "Have you ever been in a relationship?"

I don't know what made me ask but it was worth it to see the surprise on his face.

"Sure I have."

"Any that lasted longer than twenty-four hours?"

"My last relationship lasted for two years. But I haven't been serious with anyone for a long time."

Two years? Wow. I found myself wanting to ask what happened, and how any woman managed to get him to settle down for so long. It was hard to imagine him in a long-term relationship based on what I'd seen of him so far.

He once said you were wrong about him. Perhaps it's true.

The constant back and forth over who McCoy really was gave me a headache at the best of times, but with several drinks inside me, the questions tangled up in my mind. *Just for now, accept him as he is in this moment. No questions. Tomorrow you can go back to second guessing his every word.*

"How come you haven't been serious with anyone for a while?" I asked, taking my own advice.

Radleigh's fingers twitched against my waist as if uncomfortable with my line of questioning. "Haven't found the right woman."

"How could you possibly know that when you don't spend more than one night with anyone?" I teased, and he grinned.

"I haven't found a woman who is good enough in bed that makes me want to call them again."

I rolled my eyes. "You're disgusting. Has it ever occurred to you that life isn't entirely about sex?"

"No," he answered, with mock thoughtfulness. "Actually that hasn't occurred to me."

I stomped hard on his foot to express my indignation, and he winced in pain. "What was that for?"

"For being such a pig."

"Well I'd hate to disappoint you, Leah. I mean, what would happen if you started to like me?"

"The universe would implode."

The smile he gave me reminded me of the way he'd been in Phoenix. Even with concussion, he'd been fun and easy to get along with. That was a very dangerous comparison though, so I shook it off.

Radleigh was about to respond when someone tapped me on the shoulder.

"Sorry to interrupt," Stacey said, "but our cab will be here soon."

"It's okay, Stace. I didn't realise it was so late."

It was nearing eleven thirty, which wasn't late by some people's standards but after the day I'd had, I was pretty tired.

"Time flies when you're having fun," Radleigh said, smirking.

Shaking my head, I turned back to Stacey. "We'd better go and say goodbye to everyone."

She nodded, and it was only then I realised McCoy and I hadn't let go of each other yet.

I dropped my hands from around his waist and a coolness hit me as his warm body moved away from mine.

I linked arms with Stacey and we headed off to say goodbye to Alison and Michael. I hated that I had to leave everyone again, though I promised I would visit again as soon as I could.

Once we had said our goodbyes, Stacey, Billy, Radleigh and I headed outside to wait for our cab. It had gotten surprisingly cold outside and I shivered with the chill of the wind against my exposed arms and legs.

Stacey snuggled against Billy to keep warm and a brief pang of jealousy washed over me, wishing Miguel was with me to block out the cold.

"You okay?" Radleigh asked.

"I'm fine," I answered with a nod.

Talking to him suddenly felt weird. Taking McCoy for who he was "in the moment" wasn't easy. I'd gotten used to searching for the subtext behind everything he said, and while he'd spent the majority of the evening winding me up, seeing the slightly more open side of him showed me he wasn't completely soulless. It didn't come close to making up for all the crappy things he'd done, but maybe…

No. A couple of normal conversations with him doesn't change who he is. He didn't come all this way for you, or to make up for what he did to Miguel. He came for your help to get out of a sexual harassment charge.

With that thought solidified in my mind, I remained silent until we got back to Stacey's apartment.

Stacey and Billy said a hasty goodnight as soon as we got through the door, before stumbling into Stacey's room, leaving me alone with Radleigh.

"Can we meet in the morning for breakfast?" he asked, breaking the awkward silence that hung between us. "So we can talk about the Taylor thing."

I nodded. "I suppose so. My flight home isn't until tomorrow evening. I'll call you when I wake up."

"Thanks."

McCoy slipped his hands into his pockets, then cursed out loud.

"What's wrong?"

"I think I've left my wallet at the hotel. Can I use the phone to call and check if it's there?"

I nodded. I had a horrible feeling I knew where this was heading, but I rummaged under the coffee table for the phone book, then waited while he called. The receptionist told him nobody had handed anything in, and after having a look around, they said it was nowhere to be found.

"Leah -" he began, but I cut him off.

"Yes, you can stay here tonight. But understand it means nothing, and I'm only agreeing because you have no money and nowhere else to go."

"I was just going to ask if you could lend me the cash to get back to the hotel."

"Oh." I felt my cheeks reddening. I should probably have let him finish. "I don't think I have enough. But maybe Stacey -"

"You can't go in there now," he laughed as a shrill squeal and giggle came from Stacey's room.

He was right. He'd have to stay.

"I'll get you some pillows and a blanket." I sighed, heading to the cupboard in the hallway.

I returned a few minutes later with a spare duvet and a couple of pillows, as McCoy piled up his clothes on the armchair. He'd already stripped off his shoes, coat and shirt. I didn't want to hang around to see him take off his trousers.

"Goodnight." I set the bedding down on the sofa.

I found it hard to meet his eye as he stood, shirtless. I'd seen him with his top off a million times when the players swapped shirts at the end of a match, but this wasn't the same. We weren't on the pitch. We were alone in Stacey's apartment, and he looked... different.

"Goodnight, Leah."

Blocking thoughts of Radleigh from my mind, I went to my room, changed my clothes and climbed into bed, hoping my tiredness would send me to sleep within minutes.

At two a.m, I was still staring at the ceiling.

My throat had dried up and I knew I wouldn't sleep at all if I didn't get something to drink, so I dragged myself from the warmth of my bed and crept towards the kitchen.

I needn't have bothered trying to be silent. As I approached the lounge, I heard the sound of the television and when I entered the room McCoy was sitting on the floor, leaning back against the sofa, wrapped in his duvet. Wide awake.

If I'd known he'd be up, I'd have put my bathrobe on. As it was, I had on an old grey t-shirt that only just covered my arse, but there was no point in worrying about it. I wasn't planning on being near him any longer than I had to.

"Leah. Sorry, did the TV wake you?"

I shook my head. "I came to get a drink. Carry on."

In the kitchen, I opened the fridge and pulled out a bottle of cold water, thankful Stacey still kept a good supply. I downed most of it in one go. Once I'd re-hydrated myself, I peered out from around the fridge door. "Radleigh, do you want anything?"

"I'm actually kinda hungry," he answered, looking up at me. "Do you cook?"

"Not at two in the morning."

"Worth a try."

"I have ingredients for making a sandwich though. Or there are some cookies."

"I'll take the cookies."

Closing the fridge door, I reached up to the cupboard and rummaged around for the biscuits I knew would be buried at the back. Stacey always hid them there so Billy wouldn't find them and eat them all. I figured I would replace them in the morning.

"Here you go." I tossed him the packet which he caught expertly.

"Thank you." He ripped into the packaging.

"You could have helped yourself," I told him, stepping into the living room. "I'm not cruel enough to let you starve."

"I'll remember that next time."

"Next time Stacey will know not to let you in."

"Oh don't try and tell me you didn't have fun tonight."

I opened my mouth to retaliate, but changed my mind. We were both barely dressed, tired, and my guard was nowhere near high enough to deal with him. Not when the only things separating us were two feet of floor space, a flimsy t-shirt and a duvet. I picked up my bottle of water and started to head towards the door.

"Leah?"

"Yeah?"

"Cookie?" He held the packet out towards me.

After a moment's hesitation, I smiled. "Yeah, okay."

I stepped towards him and took a biscuit from the packet. As I bit into it I remembered why Stacey always hid them. The chocolate chip goodness melted in my mouth. "Oh wow, I forgot how good these are."

"Well you're not having them back." McCoy smirked, moving the packet out of my reach. I was half-tempted to fight him for them, but decided against it.

"I'll be getting back to bed then."

"Okay, but before you go-" he paused.

"Yes?"

"Thanks. For letting me come out with you, and for letting me stay."

"Technically, you should be thanking Billy and Stacey. Everything that happened tonight was because of them."

"Maybe. But you wanted me there tonight."

With a low growl of frustration I said, "Give it a rest, McCoy."

He picked up the remote and turned off the television. I watched his eyes roam the length of my body, lingering for a moment on my legs before returning to my face. I should have been annoyed with him for so blatantly checking me out, but instead, heat spread through me.

"Goodnight," I said, with a calmness I didn't feel.

"Leah, don't." He threw the duvet aside and stood up. "Don't go back to bed."

Bloody hell, Radleigh McCoy is half naked in front of me. Black boxers. That was all he was wearing.

"I'm tired," I told him, forcing my eyes away from him. "I'll talk to you tomorrow. I want to go to sleep now."

"Sure you do. But you can't, and that's why you got up."

"What are you suggesting? That the thought of you in here kept me awake?"

"It did, didn't it?"

Yes. Just not for the reasons he was thinking.

Well ... not *entirely* for the reasons he was thinking.

"Leah, come on. Why don't you try being honest for once?"

"You don't deserve honesty," I snapped. "I don't even know who you are! One minute you're some sleazy guy, hitting on any girl who walks by, the next you're the perfect date for the evening! Who the hell are you?"

So much for not being honest.

I watched as his brain ticked over for a moment or two. While I waited for a response, my eyes began to travel over his body the same way he'd done to me just minutes before. I gazed at his tattooed arms and his firm stomach, then snapped back to his face as he began to speak.

"I'm Radleigh McCoy, third generation soccer star."

"There's more to you than that. It's just lost under several layers of arrogance."

"And maybe tonight I want to be with someone who knows that, instead of someone who wants to sell their story to the highest bidder. I'm not so complicated. And I don't change. It's you who changes. You think you know me, but whenever you see a different side to me, your opinion shifts."

I was tired. Too tired for the conversation but too curious to stop.

"Exactly how many sides do you have?"

He took a step closer to me and my heart rate quickened as he did so. In a soft voice he said, "I'm just me, Leah.

As I stood rooted to the spot, he slowly leaned in towards me.

"What would happen if I kissed you?" he asked, his mouth so close to my skin that his warm breath tickled my neck.

I couldn't speak. He hadn't even touched me, but I could *feel* him. I closed my eyes against the sensations spreading through me just from his nearness but it was too strong to fight off this time. As I opened my eyes again, I tilted my head upwards, but an image of Taylor's sobbing face flashed into my mind, making me take a step back.

"What would happen if I said no?"

I willed my body to stop wanting him. It wasn't fair. It wasn't fair that he looked so good, or that he was making it so easy for me to give in.

"If you say no we'll both go to bed disappointed. We'll fight, we'll talk, and then we'll end up here again."

"What if I don't want to keep ending up here?"

"If you didn't want to," he said, taking another small step closer to me, "you wouldn't still be here talking about it."

I could see the fire in his eyes, but he didn't make another move. He was giving me the choice. To do something, or to walk away. I reached out and slowly ran a finger down his chest to his abs. My eyes didn't leave his for a second.

I wanted to touch him, I wanted to run away, I wanted to kiss him, I wanted to hit him.

My choice.

My finger gently traced the contours of his stomach, dancing across every muscle, tingling at the softness of his skin.

Decision made.

My lips followed, leaving a trail of soft kisses up to his chest.

Just when I thought I might die from the anticipation of him touching me, McCoy rested his hands on my hips and drew me into him. With one brief look of understanding between us, his lips pressed down against mine, and I wrapped my arms around his back, a small sigh of relief escaping me as his tongue slid into my mouth.

Everything I'd been fighting against for the past few weeks fell away. There wasn't a thought in my head except for the realisation that the feelings I'd tried to push away were impossible to ignore.

His hands slid underneath my t-shirt and I shivered as he touched my bare skin. His touch was firm but gentle and he slowly lifted me off the ground, his lips not leaving mine for a second. As I wrapped my legs around his waist, he carried me out of the living room, and towards my bedroom.

Radleigh sat on the edge of my bed, my legs still around him, him still kissing me hard. I could feel him straining against his boxers and I pushed my hips against his, eliciting a low groan from his lips. He slipped his hands under my t-shirt and slowly slid his hands up my back, pushing my t-shirt up as he went. We broke apart long enough for him to tug it over my head, and his eyes flashed hungrily when he realised I wasn't wearing a bra. I grinned and leaned in, my stiff nipples brushing lightly across the hard plains of his chest as I kissed him again. His ice blue eyes darkened, and without warning, he flipped us around so I was flat on my back and he was above me, staring down as my chest rose and fell. My lips curved into a smirk as I trailed a hand across my breasts, my nipples peaking further from the touch. I couldn't help myself; the way he looked at me fuelled me to tease him and I gently rolled my nipples between my fingers, my eyes not leaving his.

Radleigh lowered himself onto me, snatching up my hands and pinning them above my head in a fierce grip, his face inches from mine. He leaned down, his mouth close to my ear and his breath hot on my neck. My own breath came out in small bursts as my heart rate kicked up.

"Tell me, Leah," he whispered. "Tell me how much you want me."

His words, and the way his mouth was so close to my skin but not quite touching, made me shiver with expectation. I turned my head, trying to capture his lips with mine, but he pulled away slightly, a smirk crossing his own face.

"Tell me."

"Radleigh," I murmured, as every part of me screamed out to have his lips on me. I *needed* it. Needed to feel what I'd pretended I didn't want for so long.

I wriggled a hand free, pulling one of his hands down with mine and placing it between my damp thighs.

"That's how much I want you."

Again, his eyes flashed, and he pushed his hand inside my knickers and flicked a finger inside me, making me buck my hips to meet his touch. He freed my other hand to slide my knickers down my legs then slowly kissed his way back up, his lips soft, like butterfly wings against my skin. He pushed my thighs further apart, and again, I raised, my hips, needing to get some relief from the ache building between my legs. His tongue flicked out, dipping inside me. He held my hips firmly, maintaining total control over my movements as he found his way towards the sensitive bundle of nerves that screamed for attention. Just as I was about to fall over the edge, sweat beading my skin and my breath ragged, he pulled away.

"Radleigh," I moaned, my own hand moving between my legs, desperate for a release. Again, he caught my hand and moved it away, shaking his head.

"Patience," he said, kissing my stomach with those soft kisses again.

I was about to explode. I needed him inside me. My body was his to do with as he pleased – I was weak, melted down from his torture, and when his thick, full lips found my breasts and closed over my nipple, again using his tongue to torment me, I couldn't help crying out.

I ran my hands down his back and he sucked on the hardened bud, his length digging firmly into my thigh. I pushed against it, hoping he'd give me what I needed, but his low chuckle told me he wasn't done yet. I buried my hands in his hair pushing him against me, making him suck harder until I wanted to scream from the intensity of it all.

Radleigh had been my nemesis, my enemy, the most challenging man I'd ever met. He'd been a temptation, a surprise. We didn't know each other yet we *knew* each other in ways other people didn't know us. Whatever the hell this thing was between us, it was inevitable, primal.

It made my head spin.

His kisses trailed from my breasts, up my neck, until he finally claimed my mouth again, his tongue battling with mine. I reached down to the top of his boxers and began to push them down, my hands pausing to grip his firm ass before I pushed them out of my way so I could get to what I really wanted.

He growled as I wrapped my fingers around his cock, moving my hand lightly, just enough to show him he wasn't the only one who could tease. In response, he kissed me harder, his hands moving to my hips and pulling them up towards him.

With my free hand, I fumbled in my bag, locating a condom without taking my focus off Radleigh and the sounds he made from the way I worked him with my other hand. He was getting close, and I was so ready to take what I needed from him.

His eyes held mine as he carefully rolled the condom on, and my breath caught in my throat when he sank straight into me, causing me to let out a small cry of relief.

It wasn't enough. I wanted to scream with every thrust because nothing, no one, had ever felt so fucking perfect. I closed my eyes, gripping onto his back, digging my nails into his skin, making him push harder, deeper inside me.

"Fuck!" Radleigh growled then pressed his lips against mine, swallowing my moans as I reached a shuddering, spine-melting climax.

I literally saw stars, and when his limbs weakened and he sagged down on top of me, I had to fight for breath, trying desperately not to blackout from the sensations wracking my body from head to toe.

Radleigh shifted his weight off me just a little but he didn't break contact with me. He leaned over and softly kissed me, a huge contrast to the kisses he'd given me a short while ago. This one was soft… almost tender. When I finally opened my eyes and looked into his, I saw… someone different. It was just a flash, but the man I'd gotten to know in Phoenix, and the one I'd danced with earlier, was lying close to me, showing me another glimpse of the real him.

Chapter 12
Last Night Was Wonderful, I Love You

My head pounded.

As I opened my eyes, the light streaming in through the gap in the curtains made me squint. After blinking several times, I glanced at the clock. Eight forty-two. I calculated I'd only slept for about three and a half hours.

I squeezed my eyes closed again, trying to ease the banging in my skull, but it didn't work.

I wanted nothing more than to pull the duvet over my head and sleep for the rest of the day, and it was at precisely that moment I realised why it couldn't happen.

The ache in my temples had distracted me from the gentle breathing which originated, not from me, but from underneath me. For a second, I couldn't move.

I'd woken up after having spent a night sleeping on top of Radleigh McCoy.

His arms were still around me, one hand on my lower back, just underneath the t-shirt I'd hastily thrown back on – proving Brits truly are uptight about nudity.

After the things we'd done together, it was ridiculous that I felt the need to cover up.

He'd seen every part of me. Explored every part of me. Made my whole body tingle and shiver when his hands, his lips, had travelled over my skin.

"Oh God."

It was bad enough I'd slept with him, but the fact it had been so damn good made the situation a million times worse.

I needed to move.

Carefully, I unwound Radleigh's arms from around me and slid off him, standing up. My head throbbed as I made my way to the kitchen in search of something to drink.

After going to the fridge and pulling out a bottle of water, I had a flashback to the night before. On the living room floor was Radleigh's duvet and the discarded packet of cookies, not to mention the pile of clothes he'd removed before I'd even got my hands on him.

With a groan, I slunk over to the sofa and collapsed on to the cushions. I took a long swig of water, hoping a drink would clear my head a little but it didn't work. I wasn't hungover. Just tired and ashamed.

Oh crap, I need him out of my room before Billy and Stacey wake up!

The thought shook me out of my slump. There was no way I wanted them to find out what happened between Radleigh and I, especially after I'd made such a big deal out of how much I hated him. Although, knowing them as well as I did, I realised they wouldn't surface until at least noon.

A quiet bleeping noise caught my attention. Missed call on my phone. It must have been going off all night. I dragged myself up from the sofa and into the hallway where I'd left my phone on the table beside the door. Pulling out my mobile, I saw one missed call, and a text message from Miguel. My heart gave a jolt as I read his name.

Hi angel, hope you had a great time at the party. I love you. X

I love you.

My eyes remained fixed on those three little words with huge meaning. In all honesty, Miguel hadn't even crossed my mind once I got home. I'd been too busy, first trying to keep McCoy out, then giving into the temptation I'd been fighting for so long.

Guilt began to fill me and I sank down on the floor in the hallway – too laden with remorse to move.

144

I could still smell McCoy on me, on my t-shirt, on my skin. What the hell had I been thinking? How could I have let myself give in?

You're so weak. Weak and stupid, just like when you were younger. You had a good thing with Miguel, and instead of sticking with him, a guy who adores you, you threw it away for a night of meaningless sex.

I ran a hand through my hair and with a sinking feeling, I was transported back to my days as a teenager. The days when I'd been led by my hormones instead of my brain. That was precisely what happened with Radleigh.

I thought I was past all that.

My head ached with regret, and my stomach twinged with guilt. How would I ever look Miguel in the eye after this?

And Taylor?

How could I be on her side when I'd literally slept with the enemy?

"Leah?"

Breaking my thoughts, Radleigh stepped out into the hallway. "What are you doing down there?"

For a second, I wanted to let him wrap me up in his arms and block out the confusion for a while. Stupid. That would only make things worse.

Pull yourself together, lady!

"Leah, are you okay?"

"I've been better."

He gave a sigh, like he'd been expecting that kind of reaction from me. "Before you start giving me a hard time about last night, just remember, I didn't force you."

"What did you *think* I was going to say?" I asked, my voice dripping with sarcasm. "*'Last night was wonderful, I love you?'*"

He tilted his head to one side, a smirk taking over his face and I said, "Oh, go to hell."

"Leah, talk to me," he said, as I rose to my feet. He followed me into the kitchen.

"I don't want to talk. I want to have a cup of coffee, and take a long shower."

"That's it? You're not gonna tell me I had this whole weekend planned out, and that I knew exactly what I was doing when I came here?"

"Well, we both already know that's the truth, so what would be the point in going over it?"

I wasn't sure what I'd been expecting when I looked into his eyes, but I hadn't anticipated seeing annoyance. Smugness, perhaps. But not annoyance.

Perhaps we'd both misjudged each other's reactions.

I changed my mind about the coffee. Instead, I wanted to hop straight into the shower to get away from him. When I attempted to walk past him, he stood in front of me, blocking my way.

"Radleigh -"

"You can't pretend last night didn't happen."

"Don't tell me what I can't do." I attempted to shove him out of the way. He grabbed my wrists but I continued to push, successfully moving him backwards into the living room; he didn't let go, though. He held firm until I stopped struggling.

"I know we can't pretend nothing happened. But that doesn't mean I don't regret it." I pushed him away and took a few steps back.

"Why? We both knew this would happen eventually."

He was absolutely right. But the realisation only made me angrier. With him, and even more with myself. In a fit of temper, I flung his clothes across the room towards him. As I did so, his wallet and mobile phone fell from the pockets of his trousers and onto the floor.

His wallet.

We both dashed forwards to grab the item he claimed to have lost, but I got there first, flipping it open to reveal the key card to his hotel room tucked into one of the pockets.

I dropped the wallet back to the floor and sank on to the sofa, full of self-loathing.

"I'm not sorry," Radleigh said matter-of-factly. "Not at all."

"I wish I could say the same."

"Would it have made a difference?" he asked. "If I hadn't lied about losing my wallet, would you really have sent me back to the hotel?"

I hated the question. Hated that I didn't want to allow myself to consider the answer because I was too scared of what it might reveal.

"I don't know." I sighed. "Maybe. Maybe not. I was drunk, and ..."

"And we were having a good time."

"A good time? You mean, me insulting you?"

"You were different. You were honest. I was, too."

I turned my head to look at him. For all the bad things he'd done, even he'd managed to give me some truthful answers last night. Didn't he deserve the same?

"What do you want to hear? That last night, I wanted you? Well, I did. But today, knowing I gave in makes me feel like hell."

"Why? Why is this such a big deal to you?"

I could have launched into the whole story of my teenage years, and told him the very idea I'd gone back to the way I used to be made me want to vomit. But that was far more than he needed to know.

You haven't reverted back to anything. It was a slip-up, the only one you've made in years.

"I've never cheated on anyone before," I said. "Never. I never thought I would. It makes me feel cheap, and-"

147

"I made you feel cheap? Thanks."

Cheap was the last thing he made me feel. His selfish demeanour and unbearable arrogance didn't extend to the bedroom. He wasn't all about instant gratification and satisfying his own needs. He read every signal I gave him, to do more, or to slow down without question, without me saying a word.

"No." I sighed. "Radleigh, *you* didn't make me feel cheap. The situation made me feel that way. The fact that I cheated on Miguel made me feel that way. Granted, your smugness didn't help matters, but-"

"You thought I'd leave quietly, after you spent so long telling me you weren't interested in me?"

"I didn't think anything! That's how I ended up in bed with you."

"Look on the bright side. At least the sex was good."

"What?"

"Imagine how much worse it'd be if you cheated on Miguel and all you got was a lousy lay and a bad hangover."

The corners of his mouth twitched but I refused to be amused by him when I was so angry with myself. Fantastic sex wouldn't make up for everything I stood to lose if anyone ever found out.

****

I arrived back home a little after seven in the evening on Sunday, to the unwelcome news that Richard wanted to see me first thing in the morning because he had something important to discuss. If I hadn't extensively searched every newspaper and website, just in case someone had seen me and Radleigh together, I would have been paranoid.

Miguel had called me almost as soon as I got home, too. He wanted to hear all about my weekend, and his enthusiasm made me want to cry. I knew how much he'd missed me, and how much pain he was still in from McCoy's beating. And while he'd been missing me, I'd been... I'd made an unforgivable mistake. I took the coward's way out, telling Miguel I was tired, and I'd talk to him at work. It would be harder face to face, but I needed some time. Time to think. Time to figure out why I'd allowed myself to make such a bad decision.

I said a quick goodnight to Freya, and curled up in bed for an early night.

When I arrived at work the next morning, I made my way straight to Richard's office before even stopping off at my own. It was clear from the smile Richard gave me that I wasn't in any trouble, but his face grew serious again when he started to speak.

"I got a call from Taylor over the weekend. She called me, hysterical, at eight o'clock yesterday morning. She said she was staying at Jesse's apartment while we were in Minnesota and McCoy was parked outside, watching her."

I felt the colour drain from my face.

"She didn't know how long he'd been there," Richard went on. "But she said he'd gone by nine-thirty. Obviously, I couldn't check for myself, but I tried to call McCoy and his phone was turned off."

Yes. Yes it was. It was also in Boston. Where he was with me. It was almost nine when I woke up the morning before, and McCoy was underneath me. My body betrayed me by giving a small shiver of pleasure at the memory.

"McCoy says he was at home alone. But I have it on good authority his car wasn't in his drive. I just need to verify that someone else noticed him outside Jesse's apartment and we've got him."

Every word Richard said hit me hard.

Taylor lied. She lied about Radleigh being outside Jesse's apartment.

I was his alibi.

Radleigh hadn't told the truth about his whereabouts. *Why?*

Overwhelmed with confusion, I stood up. "Well, erm … thanks for keeping me updated. I need to get to work."

"Leah, wait." Richard's eyes filled with concern. "Are you okay?"

I forced a smile. "I'm fine. I just have a lot to do this morning."

I practically ran out of his office to my own, my brain running a million miles a minute.

Why hadn't Radleigh dropped me in it?

I wasn't stupid enough to believe that just because he'd put so much effort into sleeping with me, he actually cared. Bedding me had been a challenge for him but once he'd got what he wanted, he could easily have put an end to my career, ready to make room for his next conquest.

"Leah?"

A deep voice uttered my name from somewhere behind me and I saw Bryce Warren peering out of the locker room.

"Leah, have you got a minute?"

"Sure," I answered. "Do you want to come into the office?"

He'd never attempted to talk to me alone before. From the seriousness in his tone, I figured he wasn't about to ask me for a morning of debauchery, so really, it could only be about one thing.

We stepped into my office and closed the door, both of us standing awkwardly, unsure where to begin.

"You know, don't you?"

Bryce nodded and I let out a groan, burying my face in my hands.

"It's okay," he said. "I won't tell anyone. But … I think you need to tell Richard."

"I know." I sighed. "How much do *you* know?"

"Everything. The party, the sleeping arrangements. Including how they changed in the middle of the night."

If Radleigh had told Bryce everything, I knew that would include details. Whether Bryce wanted to hear them or not, Radleigh wouldn't have been able to stop himself from telling him … Oh God.

Quickly steering the conversation in a different direction to save me from complete embarrassment, Bryce said, "It might not be so bad. You don't need to tell Richard the full story. It's fine if you exclude the sex."

I hadn't really considered that as an option. Not a serious one, anyway. Faced with Richard's unfaltering stare, I'd cave in and confess everything. And it wasn't fine, either way. Radleigh was still with me when he shouldn't have been.

"Why did Radleigh lie about it?" I asked. "Why didn't *he* tell Richard he was with me? He could easily have told him everything apart from us sleeping together. The fact he didn't makes it look even more suspicious."

I raised my head, waiting for Bryce's response.

"Simple. He didn't want to get you into trouble."

"Oh come on! We're talking about the man who reported me for things I hadn't done. Are you telling me he's grown a conscience in the last few weeks?"

"He didn't know you then, and I know that's no excuse, but maybe this is his way of making up for it."

He didn't know me then, and he doesn't know me now. Was I supposed to believe he'd leave his career hanging in the balance for me?

"He's not as bad as you think," Bryce said. "It's obvious Taylor made the whole thing up and if you're on his side-"

"On his side?" I repeated. "But-"

"You don't still believe her?"

In all honesty, I hadn't even thought about Taylor's original accusation. I'd been too caught up in recent events. Of course the story she told over the weekend threw doubt over her, but I couldn't quite bring myself to believe she'd lied from the start.

"I don't know." I sighed. "I wouldn't put it past him."

"He didn't do it, Leah. I admit he can be a sleaze but he'd never do anything like that."

Not knowing Bryce particularly well, it would have been easy to assume he was covering up for his friend, but there was something about him I trusted.

Not good news for you.

If Taylor made up the whole story, I'd been well and truly fooled. All of her tears and conflict over doing the right thing was a con.

"Okay," I said. "I'll talk to Richard, but I need to speak to Miguel first. I can't lie to him."

I didn't *want* to lie to him, and I clutched my stomach as a stab of pain hit me. The thought of losing him was a thousand times worse than the prospect of being fired but he deserved to be with someone a hell of a lot less messed up than me.

For the first time, the seriousness of what I'd done hit me full force. I'd thought about it only in separate pieces. How I could lose my job, how I'd hurt Miguel, how my vendetta against McCoy had fuelled Taylor to make up a further lie, unwittingly putting me in a position where I was the only one who could get him out of trouble.

Potentially, I could lose everything.

I'd have to go home. Back to Cornwall. Back to reality.

If I'd been a weaker person, I would've cried at my own stupidity. But I'd brought the whole situation on myself, and wallowing in self-pity wouldn't change that.

I stood up. "Well, wish me luck."

"Good luck, Leah. I hope everything works out."

"Me too."

Chapter 13
Don't Say A Word

I knew the earliest I would get to talk to Miguel would be during lunch, but there was no way I could confess at the training ground with so many people around. Instead, I went for a guilty bite to eat with him at noon and decided I'd tell him everything after work.

We planned to meet in the café across the street. As the minutes slowly ticked by, my stomach wound itself into a tight knot of guilt and anxiousness. But I had to be honest with him and deal with whatever the consequences might be.

My gut flip-flopped with shame when Miguel greeted me with a huge smile. He was still slow on his feet, and my hatred for myself multiplied because I was about to strike him another painful blow. When I looked into his brown, puppy-dog eyes, my resolve to be truthful almost broke.

"Hey, angel," he said, kissing me on the cheek. "You wanna order some food?"

I wanted to. Anything so I didn't have to tell him. Instead of backing out, I took a deep breath.

"There's something I need to talk to you about first."

First. Like he's going to stay once you've ripped out his heart.

Concern crossed his face as he sat down. "What's wrong?"

I spoke quickly to ensure I didn't back out. "Last weekend in Boston, McCoy showed up. He said he wanted to talk to me about Taylor."

"He didn't hurt you, did he?" Miguel asked, taking my hand in his and intensifying the feeling of sickness creeping over me.

"No," I assured him. "No. He didn't hurt me. But Stacey's boyfriend invited him to the party. I tried to make up reasons why he couldn't come but Billy insisted," rolling my eyes I added, "Billy thinks McCoy is God."

Miguel chuckled. "That must have made your weekend."

I didn't know what to say. I couldn't say I'd hated Radleigh's presence when I was about to make a full confession, but it was sort of the truth. I *had* hated his presence. I'd hated him being in the flat and at the party.

And I'd really hated the morning after.

"Anyway," I went on, choosing to brush past his comment, "when we got back from the party, McCoy couldn't find his wallet and... he asked to stay the night."

Far from looking horrified, Miguel seemed a little amused. I knew he thought I'd been oh-so-kind for letting the man I hated stay in my flat for the night. For the briefest moment, I thought I might leave it at that. Why ruin everything because of one stupid mistake?

You cannot go on lying to him. Not only is it unfair, it will eat away at you until you confess.

"Probably wasn't the smartest move," he said. "I mean, with his suspension and all, but it's not that big a deal."

My insides began to squirm. How could I tell him? It would break his heart and that was the last thing I wanted to do. But there wasn't any other option. At least not one I'd be happy to live with. I had enough secrets in my past already.

"It is a big deal." My voice beginning to tremble.

"Are you afraid he might tell Richard? Because if he does-"

"No. *I* need to tell Richard. The night McCoy stayed with me, Taylor told Richard he was outside her house, which means-"

"You're McCoy's alibi."

"Right."

"Wow." Miguel let out a breath. "She lied."

"Yes. She lied."

"You're worried about what everybody might think, aren't you? You shouldn't. People may never find out and Richard will believe you."

He sounded so calm, so understanding and I didn't want to burst the bubble of faith he had in me.

Well done, Leah. You've really fucked up this time.

"Miguel, I need to tell you something," I said, shakily. "When Radleigh showed up at my place and got invited to the party, I got drunk. I was drunk before I even left the flat."

That confession alone was shameful enough, without having to top it off by ruining our relationship. Miguel's eyes watched me.

"At the party, I had a few more drinks and -" I trailed off as I saw the realisation of the truth seep into Miguel's brain.

"Oh," he said, almost mechanically. "You slept with him, didn't you?"

Slowly, I nodded and Miguel dropped my hand.

"I'm sorry," I told him, my voice breaking. "I'm so sorry."

My words were so weak. How could a simple apology ever be enough?

"But… you hate him."

"I was so, so drunk. I don't even-" I paused for a moment, reminding myself I had vowed to be completely honest with him. "There's no excuse for what I did. None."

A few long moments passed, during which I didn't move and Miguel continued to stare at me in shock. After a while, I couldn't take it any longer.

"Please say something."

"You slept with Radleigh McCoy," he said, slowly. "You had sex with Radleigh McCoy."

"Miguel-"

"I don't understand, Leah. How could you … I thought …" he stopped, unable to fuse together the numerous questions circulating inside his head.

"I'm not going to do the cliché thing of saying I hope you can forgive me," I said, as a tear slipped down my cheek, "because I don't deserve it. I don't deserve it at all."

He shook his head. "Don't you dare cry. You made this mess. You have no right to sit there crying."

"I know," I said, wiping my eyes.

It was no use though, the tears wouldn't stop. His words sounded angry but his eyes were full of pain. I wished I could turn back the clock, to take back the action that had caused all of this, and more than anything I wished I could erase his hurt and make him smile again.

"I'm gonna go home," he said.

"Just like that? You don't want to talk?"

"I don't even want to *think* about it. There is nothing you can say to make this better."

I'd never been more ashamed of myself – and I'd done a *lot* of things I was ashamed of. Miguel was right. There wasn't a thing I could say to change the situation and if he sat there any longer, with me watching as his heart broke in front of me, I would break down completely.

"Goodbye, Leah."

With one last lingering look, he stood and walked away from me. My tears began to fall faster as I watched him cross the street to his car. He didn't drive away immediately. He rested his head on the steering wheel, and my heart ached. Ached for the pain I'd caused him, and for the huge mess I'd made. He didn't deserve to hurt because of me.

And I still had one more thing to do before I went home.

Heavy with nausea, I headed back to the training ground to find Richard. Thankfully, he was still in his office. If he hadn't been there, I felt sure I'd have wimped out of confessing.

"Leah," he said, then noticing my tear-stained cheeks added, "are you okay?"

"There are some things I need to tell you."

I took a seat and told him the story of my weekend, minus the inclusion of the sex, not that that made it any easier. He remained poker-faced, yet somehow, I still felt rising tension in the room with every word I spoke.

"Let me get this straight," Richard said with the kind of dangerous calmness that comes before explosive yelling. "You not only went out partying with a suspended team member, you also let him spend the night in your apartment?"

I couldn't do anything more than nod.

"Would you care to explain why?"

"I told you. He lost his wallet and-"

"Leah, come on!" he snapped. "You knew how much trouble this would cause if anyone found out! You should've sent him away!"

"I tried," I said, my voice rising a little. "But he wouldn't go."

"Then you should have called me!"

The anger and disappointment on Richard's face made me avert my eyes. He'd never looked at me that way before and it was hard to take when I'd only ever had encouragement and praise from him. Letting him down was almost as gut-wrenching as what I'd done to Miguel.

"That look of guilt speaks volumes," he said and as I glanced up at him, I knew he saw the truth.

"Richard -"

"Don't say a word," he interrupted, fiercely. "I don't want to have to fire you."

A brief rush of relief ran through me, even though I was about to be severely reprimanded. At least my job was safe.

"You know, I wondered if there was something going on between you and McCoy. When I found the two of you fighting in the locker room, I thought maybe -"

"Nothing was going on. Nothing *is* going on."

"And yet he was worth jeopardising your career? By getting him off the hook, you're risking your own job."

"It's not about him. He's done some shitty things, things he should have been fired for long ago, but he didn't do this. He didn't touch Taylor, and if he lost everything because I didn't tell the truth, I'd never forgive myself. So, if you have to fire me, I'll deal with it," I told him with more certainty than I possessed.

"I won't fire you, Leah. In spite of the amount of stupidity you've shown this weekend, you are damn good at your job. I won't lose you."

"So what's going to happen now?"

"I need you to stay here. I'll call Taylor and McCoy in so we can sort this out once and for all."

Richard immediately contacted Radleigh and Taylor, and they were told to be in the training ground restaurant in an hour. Seemed like a slightly weird meeting place to me, returning to the scene of the non-existent crime. It was definitely bigger than Richard's office though, which was a good thing. I wanted to be as far away from all of them as possible.

My head had ached almost constantly for twenty-four hours. First it was a hangover, then guilt, panic, shame and anger. Exhausted with all the emotion, I waited in the restaurant for everyone to arrive and tried to ready myself for my last huge hurdle of the day.

I hadn't thought about Taylor much. My mind had been too occupied with Miguel. Just thinking about the expression on his face when I told him about Radleigh made me want to curl up in a ball and cry. I planned to do just that as soon as I reached the privacy of home.

"Hey."

I jumped at the sound of Radleigh's voice. I'd been so immersed in my thoughts, I hadn't heard him come in.

"Hi. It's not like you to be early for a meeting."

"Well, it's very rare for me to be called to a meeting where I'm the victim."

I smiled at the truth of his statement.

"Leah, I want to thank you for … for telling the truth."

I looked up at him. "You knew I would."

"No I didn't. I wouldn't have blamed you if you didn't after the way I've treated you."

"Quit trying to butter me up," I told him, sharply. "I've already confessed. There's nothing more I can do for you."

"I'm trying to apologise."

"For what? For making my job harder than it should be? For trying to land me in trouble? What *exactly* are you sorry about?"

He rested his hands down on the table and leaned forward slightly.

"I'm sorry for everything I did to you before. But I'm not sorry we slept together."

As much as I'd tried to block out the events of that night, I knew Radleigh would never let it drop.

"I'm not buying this new, thoughtful you," I told him. "At least when you were being devious, it was real."

"You bought it on Friday night."

"On Friday night you weren't putting on an act."

"Wasn't I?"

"No,"

"Well, if that eases your conscience…"

His uncharacteristic openness *was* the only thing that stopped me completely hating myself. What he'd said about wanting to spend the night with someone who wouldn't sell him out was the most sincere thing he'd ever said to me, and I refused to allow him to take it away by trying to pass it off as a trick.

I narrowed my eyes. "Let's not speak until the meeting starts."

We sat silently until six o'clock when Richard and Taylor entered the restaurant.

She had her bowed and to my utter shock she still seemed to be playing the victim.

"Okay," Richard began once they were seated. "I met with Taylor a few minutes ago because I wanted to explain the situation to her and hear her side of the story."

My eyes shifted to her but she kept her head down.

"Now," he went on, addressing me, "I need you to go over your side of things again now we're all here. This has gone on for long enough and I want to get to the bottom of it today."

I realised he was trying to be professional but I knew there was little doubt in his mind that Taylor was the liar. I would never have provided McCoy with an alibi otherwise.

Richard met my eye. "Leah?"

"Radleigh arrived in Boston on Saturday afternoon," I said. "My former flatmate's boyfriend invited him to the party we were going to and when we got back, Radleigh realised he'd lost his hotel room key, so he slept on the sofa at my friend's house. He was still there when I woke up, so he can't have been outside Jesse's house when she called you."

I didn't even falter at the lie I told.

"Radleigh." Richard turned to him. "Is this what happened?"

Radleigh nodded. "That's what happened."

"Why are you lying?" Taylor finally looked up from the table to speak.

"Maybe a better question would be, why are *you* lying?" I said bluntly. "I believed you. You made me believe you, and all the time you were lying."

Taylor let out a laugh. "Funny how keen you are to defend him now. When I told you he'd forced himself on me, you couldn't wait to report him."

I felt McCoy's eyes on me but I didn't turn my head.

"That's not true. You said you didn't want to make trouble, so I offered to talk to Radleigh first."

"And did you?" Richard asked me.

"Yes, I did. He said he hadn't done anything wrong. The next thing I knew, Taylor had reported the whole thing to you."

"Only because I thought if I left it to you, he'd use his charm to win you over, like the slimy lech he is!"

"For someone who thinks I'm a 'slimy lech,' you sure spent a lot of time following me around," Radleigh said.

"I didn't follow you anywhere. I've no idea what you're talking about."

This girl deserves an Oscar.

"Let's focus on what we do know, shall we?" Richard suggested.

"What we know," Radleigh said, "is that I was with Leah when Taylor said I was outside Jesse's apartment."

"What I'm curious about," I began, "is why you even started this. What did you hope to achieve?"

"I hoped he'd get fired," Taylor answered, glowering. "If I had you on my side, I thought we could get rid of him. I saw him with you, Leah. I saw him outside your apartment. He pushed you up against the doors and trapped you so you couldn't move."

Goosebumps crept over my skin. That was almost exactly what she said he'd done to her. She'd been watching. Months ago, she'd been there, watching his every move.

"So… you used that as a way to make me believe you," I said, but it was more a realisation than a question.

"It worked, didn't it?"

Oh yeah. It worked. I couldn't bring myself to look at Richard. I didn't want to see disappointment again. I hadn't lied when he questioned me about whether Radleigh had ever done anything to me. I'd answered honestly, I'd just… left out a few details.

"Why did you want him fired?" I asked, trying to change the direction of the conversation.

"Look at him." She jerked her head in Radleigh's direction. "So fucking high and mighty. Even after I accused him, he didn't wipe that smug look off his face!"

I'd always thought Taylor to be an attractive girl, but with her face contorted in anger, her beauty was lost. She just looked bitter and nuts.

"Maybe that's because he had nothing to worry about," I said. "Clever as you were, you still got caught out. I think he's allowed to be a little smug."

Richard had been watching the three of us closely, and I viewed the situation through his eyes. I'd abandoned all sense professionalism to defend McCoy. In light of what Richard knew about the weekend's events, I just knew he thought there was more between Radleigh and I than we'd told him. The truth of the matter was simple. Taylor was a scheming witch. I wouldn't have wished the way she treated him on anyone.

"I think we've established the facts now," I said. "Taylor has made her confession, I am Radleigh's alibi and if you need any more proof there are about two hundred people in Boston who saw him at the party with me."

Slowly, Richard nodded. "Leah, Radleigh. You're free to go, but I'd like a word with you both outside first."

As the three of us stood up, Richard looked down at Taylor. "Excuse me for a moment."

Outside the restaurant, I waited nervously for whatever Richard had to say. Chancing a glance at Radleigh I saw he looked pretty much the same way.

"I don't know what's going on between the two of you," Richard began, "but it stops right now. I want you to quit behaving like adolescents and do the jobs you're paid to do. If you want to hang out together outside of work, that's one thing, but if you're in a relationship-"

"We're not," I interrupted. "Nor will we ever be."

Richard shook his head. "Well, whatever is – or *isn't* – going on, I don't want any more of your crap dragged in to work. I want you doing your jobs, not disrupting my team with your soap opera."

McCoy and I both nodded, but it was further agony for me knowing I'd let Richard down so badly. I already missed the man who'd helped me settle in at Westberg, and taken the time every day during my first few weeks to ask me if there was anything he could do for me. No more would Richard and I share a joke while discussing our daily tasks. From now on, it would be strictly business.

"We'll keep out of trouble," I assured him.

"I'm glad to hear it. Now, if you'll excuse me."

He turned and re-entered the restaurant, leaving me feeling like a schoolgirl who'd got a rollocking from the headmaster.

"Thanks," Radleigh said. "Thanks for everything you said in there."

"I didn't have any other choices."

He shook his head. "Not true. What you did was way more than was necessary."

I shrugged. "I don't like liars. And before you start getting all smug about how I said all that because I secretly have feelings for you, I don't. I still think you're a complete arse for the way you've treated me. So don't waste your breath."

"If you say so."

If we had been somewhere else, I would have yelled.

I glared at him. "Don't. We had sex, and now it's over. I don't want to talk about this anymore. You got what you wanted, and I ruined my relationship. Just... leave me alone."

For once, I was pleased Freya wasn't home when I got in. Most days, I loved talking to her after work, but that day, everything was still too raw to discuss.

Throwing myself down on my bed, I allowed myself to cry for a while, letting all of the day's tension drain away.

The mess that had suddenly become my life was self-inflicted and I had nobody to turn to. Freya would never understand what I'd done. Usually when things got rough, I turned to Richard. Since I first started my job he'd been like a surrogate father. But his disappointment in me was clear so that bridge had been burned too. In L.A, I'd found the best friends I'd ever had, but at that moment, I'd never felt more alone.

I had nobody to blame but myself.

Chapter 14
You're The Latest Gossip

I was rudely awakened in the morning by the slamming of my bedroom door. I blinked to clear the haze from my eyes and saw Freya standing over me.

"What the hell is going on, Leah?" she demanded, without even waiting for me to sit up.

"Good morning to you too," I muttered, sarcastically.

"Please tell me you didn't have sex with Radleigh McCoy. Please."

Wow. Gossip really does travel fast.

"Where did you hear that?"

"Will called me! He said Miguel went round to his place last night and told him you've broken up because you and McCoy slept together in Boston!"

"Why are you asking?" I pulled myself out of bed. "You already seem to have all the answers."

I began to head for the kitchen and Freya yelped, "Leah!"

"What?" I asked, turning to face her. Her eyes were wide with unspoken questions. "What do you want me to say?"

"I want you to say you didn't sleep with McCoy, and Will is wrong!"

"When has he ever lied to you before?"

As I started to walk away again, she grabbed my arm, forcing me to look at her. "You slept with him?"

"Yes, and no amount of repeating those words will stop it being true. If you don't mind, I'd like to have breakfast and crack on with what will probably be the worst day ever."

Urgh. I'd turned into "hard Leah" – donning my protective outer shell, ready to face the masses of people who were clearly already talking about me. I shouldn't have used that tone with Freya, but it was too late.

Besides, she's never going to forgive me anyway.

"Don't you even care how Miguel feels? Will said he was devastated!"

My protective shell crumbled at her words, causing me to take a sharp intake of breath as I remembered Miguel's expression the last time I saw him.

"I care."

Freya gently took my arm and led me back to my bed where she sat me down.

"Stay there. I'll make you a cup of tea."

The day had only just begun, and already I was getting abuse. From my best friend. If this was the way *Freya* reacted, I was in for a rough ride from everyone else.

After a few minutes, Freya returned, handing me a steaming mug of tea. "I'm sorry."

"Me too. I'm a little defensive this morning. I don't want to talk about it, Freya. Not at all."

"At least answer me this. If these rumours are true, how did you keep hold of your job?"

I glanced at her over my cup. "Richard. He knows the truth, but he said as long as I don't actually tell him, he won't fire me."

I took a sip of the hot, sweet tea, even though my shaking hands threatened to jolt it all over me. The taste was comforting, even if the atmosphere wasn't.

"I can't pretend the idea of you and McCoy doesn't make me feel a bit… sick," Freya said. "Or that I'm not completely shocked. Because I am."

"Well, that makes two of us."

"Was I even right?" she asked, dryly.

"About what?"

"*Did* he call out his own name when he reached orgasm?"

I stared at her for a moment, in shock but as her words registered in my brain, we both burst out laughing. The tension drained away and I knew everything would be okay between us. I was relieved she'd chosen to stand by me instead of grilling me about it. The questions were there behind her eyes, but she chose to let them be.

My morning was… interesting to say the least. I stayed in my office as much as possible, only venturing out when I had to. It seemed as though almost everyone had heard the rumours. Nobody said anything, but I got some unusually hostile glares, mostly from the small amount of female staff members and the guys who were closest to Miguel. Presumably they'd realised my alibi for McCoy and my break-up with Miguel were linked in a way that made me as much of a bad guy as Taylor. Her accusation had brought the whole team to a halt. Richard had allowed Jesse to take a few days off to cope with the shock, and there seemed to be a respectful silence amongst the team for him and what he was going through. Their show of support warmed my heart, but not a single ounce of compassion was directed at me, even though my confession had stopped Taylor ruining the career of their number one player.

By lunchtime I was frazzled from it all but Freya and Will dragged me to the restaurant with them. Well, Freya dragged me. Will couldn't have cared less whether I was there or not.

"Jesus," I said after ten minutes of awkward silence. "Can one of you please say something? The silence is driving me mad!"

"Sorry," Freya said. "It's… this is a weird day."

"No kidding. Apparently, sleeping with McCoy makes me a slut of the highest degree."

"You say that like it surprises you," Will muttered, not looking up from his food.

Both Freya and I stared at him. I felt like I'd been slapped.

"What did you expect?" Will asked. "You're the latest gossip."

"Nobody even knows the full story."

"Sounds like they do."

"Will, stop," Freya told him. "Everything they're saying is based purely on speculation."

"Doesn't change the fact that it's true."

"What's it to you anyway?"

"Miguel is my friend."

"In that case, don't you think it might be better for you to try and stop the gossip instead of fuelling it? You may be enjoying that Leah is getting hurt by all this, but Miguel is too. If you cared about him you'd tell them to keep their mouths shut!"

Will looked at her through narrowed eyes. "I can't believe you're okay with all this."

"I don't agree with Leah's decision, but I'm not judgmental enough to stop being her friend."

"Freya. She slept with Radleigh McCoy."

"Stop talking about me as if I'm not here!" I snapped. "I made a mistake, okay? Will, if you can't deal with it, that's fine, but treating me like I've murdered someone is not going to take it back!"

I stood up and strode out of the restaurant, keen to get as far away from Will as possible until he'd calmed down. *If* he calmed down. In my rush to reach the sanctuary of my office, I wasn't paying attention to where I was going and I collided forcefully with someone on the stairs.

"Oh, sorry," I stammered, looking up.

My face turned red as I realised the person I'd walked into was Miguel. He was technically still on sick leave, and with everything that went down the day before, I hadn't expected to see him.

"Leah," he said, softly.

"Hey. Sorry."

"It's okay."

I wanted to run. The ache of what I'd done to him coursed through my veins so fast I could hardly stand it. But my feet rooted to the spot. I stared at him, those big brown eyes expressing no hint of malice. Just pain.

"You seemed to be in a hurry," he said, breaking the silence.

"I was," I answered. "I had a fight with-"

I trailed off, realising Miguel was not the best person to tell.

"Will?" he finished. "He'll get over it."

I shrugged, unwilling to debate my unfaithfulness with the man I'd cheated on.

It felt unnatural to be near to him and not touching him. We were always holding hands or hugging and the distance felt wrong. His hand twitched involuntarily, like he thought the same thing.

"Leah," he began, but his eyes darkened.

It wasn't until I felt electricity surge through me as two warm hands rested on my waist that I realised why.

"Excuse me." Radleigh stepped around me, his hands lingering on me for a moment longer than necessary.

I shot him a glare. His timing was unbelievable. As I turned to look at Miguel again, I saw him walking away.

"Sorry," Radleigh said. "Did I interrupt something?"

His tone wasn't entirely genuine, but I was too disheartened to yell at him. "Go to hell."

I took one last glance at the retreating figure of Miguel, then turned and began to walk down the steps.

"Leah, wait." Radleigh placed his hands on my shoulders. "Come with me."

He led me downstairs to the locker room and sat me down on one of the benches.

"What are you doing?" I asked.

"Saving you from sitting alone in your office feeling guilty," he replied, taking a seat beside me.

"Unless you can turn back the clock, you can't help me."

"Even if I could, I wouldn't."

Funny how two people can view the exact same event in different ways.

"Everyone's talking about us. They all think we slept together."

He smiled. "We did."

"This is all so funny for you, isn't it?" I snapped. "Everyone thinks I'm a slut!"

"Who said that?"

"That's just it, nobody says anything! They just give me looks, like I'm the most horrible person in the world. Although, Will wasn't shy about making his thoughts clear."

"Will acts like he has a pole shoved up his ass. This isn't a big deal."

"You really believe that?"

"I do. I'm used to causing scandal."

"Well, I'm not. This is a complete mess. I don't... I don't know how to fix it."

"You can't. You just have to wait until everything blows over."

"And how long will that take?"

Radleigh grinned again. "Well, I could always sleep with someone else to speed things up," he suggested. "Or maybe we should sleep together again and *really* give them something to talk about."

"Oh, sod off." I stood up. "This isn't a joke. It's okay for you, people expect you to sleep around. For me, this is torture. I almost lost my job!"

"Still blaming me?"

"I'm not blaming you! I…" I trailed off, and turned my back on him, trying to get a grip on my frustration. When I was more composed, I turned to him again. "I just want this to be over."

He fixed his eyes on me. "When we were in Phoenix, I said you and Miguel are nothing alike, do you remember?"

I nodded, wondering where this was going.

"I know you think I'm the Devil," he said. "But can't you see I was right? You were bored with Miguel. I've seen it a thousand times before and you're no exception, Leah. You're feisty, and independent. I'm sure Miguel was very nice and all, but he wasn't right for you. You need someone who challenges and excites you. Miguel could never give you that."

I stared at McCoy in shock. He'd summed up exactly what type of person I was and, to my displeasure, what type of guy I needed. But I'd thought Miguel gave me that. *More* than that.

"And I suppose you think *you* could give me what I want?" I asked.

"I thought I did."

Memories of that night flooded into my brain. The way his hands knew where I wanted them to go, the way he'd kissed me like he couldn't get enough, the way he'd looked at me as if there was nowhere else he wanted to be. He made me forget everything, made me focus only on him until we were both so exhausted, we fell into a shag-happy coma.

And it was exactly what I wanted.

I couldn't stand the intensity with which he was watching me, I had to turn away. His blue eyes were burning into me.

"Someone who is good in bed is not the only thing I need," I told him.

"But it's important. You got on my case because I said I haven't found anyone who's good enough in bed to make me want to stick around, but you're not so different."

A protest formed on my lips, but what was the point in arguing? I didn't agree that we were alike, but considering the way I used to be, telling him great sex wasn't high on my list of vital ingredients in a relationship would have been a blatant lie.

After leaving Radleigh in his dressing room I had difficulty shaking the conversation from my mind. The truth he'd spoken about what I looked for in a man had got to me. The problem was, the only men I'd ever known who challenged and excited me were the ones who didn't want to be in a relationship. They wanted to challenge and excite multiple women, with no concern for who they hurt. Miguel was the closest I'd ever got to having everything I wanted, and somehow, it still wasn't enough.

When the end of the day rolled around, I was relieved. The easiest part of my afternoon was my session with Bryce. Aside from Freya, he was the only person who didn't think I deserved to be treated so harshly. He assured me there were only a handful of people who were looking at me differently. Most of the guys on the team didn't care for gossip and those who did would forget about it soon enough.

I couldn't wait to knock back a few glasses of vodka when I got home, but someone was waiting for me outside my apartment building.

Jesse.

His face, usually radiating happiness, was drawn and confused. I didn't know how he was going to react to me in light of the fact I'd found out about Taylor's accusations way before he did, and I was part of the reason she got caught out.

"Hi," I said.

Jesse's eyes filled with tears. I rushed towards him, letting him collapse against me. The sound of his sobs broke my heart and I wrapped my arms around him and held him tightly for a long time. When he'd released enough of his grief to speak, he looked up, red-eyed. "Can we take a walk?"

I nodded. "Sure. Let's go to the beach."

I linked my arm through his, and we took the shortcut beside my building until our feet reached the hot sand.

I could tell Jesse had a lot of questions and I wanted so much to apologise to him for not telling him everything Taylor had done but the words wouldn't come. My heart was heavy because of the stupid things I'd done, but it weighed so much heavier when I thought about what Jesse was going through.

We kept walking until we reached Genie's, a small bar situated on the beach which was often the haunt of surfers relaxing after a day of riding the waves. We went inside and ordered some soft drinks before sitting down in one of the booths.

"Jesse, I'm so sorry," I said, finally breaking the silence. "I should've... I didn't..."

"I'm not mad at you. If I was, I wouldn't be here. I wanted to apologise."

"What? Why?"

"Because I think what Taylor did is partly my fault. I've been thinking about it, and I knew she always had a thing for McCoy, even before the night at the club. I had no idea she was crazy but I think she was kind of... jealous of you."

It was an insane notion that a gorgeous eighteen-year-old with a hot boyfriend and a bright future as a soccer wife might be jealous of a twenty-six year old who spent a large proportion of her time fending off a horny sportsman.

"She never admitted to it," Jesse went on. "But I think she'd been following McCoy for months. She didn't like how much attention he paid to you. She used to make little digs about you, saying stupid stuff like how she didn't understand what he saw in you."

"Wow. A girl can never hear that enough."

"No, come on, it was all jealousy. I just didn't realise until now."

"That doesn't make it your fault." Jesse shrugged, and I said, "Have you spoken to her today?"

He shook his head but his jaw clenched as if the idea of talking to her ripped his heart out all over again.

"Last night after Richard told me what happened, I called her and asked her to come to my apartment. I needed to hear it from her. She cried and said you'd all made it up. How stupid does she think I am? There was a lot of yelling, and eventually she broke down and told me the truth. You know the worst part? She didn't even say she was sorry. Not to me, not to you, not to McCoy. She walked out like I didn't matter at all. I guess I didn't. I was just easy access to what she really wanted."

I'd seen some crazy fangirls in my time, but I'd never known anyone to stoop so low to get close to another person. McCoy wasn't worth that level of scheming, and Jesse didn't deserve to have his heart broken by a girl with a hidden agenda.

I reached out across the table and held his hand. "It would be so easy for me to patronise you and tell you you're young, you'll get over it. Those things are true, but you're not a kid. And I'm not going to treat you like one. I made mistakes here too, Jesse. I should have made her tell you what was happening, or I should have told you myself. I thought I was helping her to protect you because I believed what she said."

"I would have believed her too."

"You loved her. I should have seen through her but I was so angry with McCoy, I didn't even stop to question her."

"He called me."

My eyes widened. "McCoy?"

"Yeah, this morning. I thought he'd be mad about everything she did, but he said he was sorry for what happened. He said he shouldn't have flirted with her, and maybe he made things worse. He wanted to make sure there were no hard feelings between us."

As much as I hated to admit it, Radleigh scored huge points with me for talking to Jesse. He was as aware as anyone of how much Jesse idolised him, and while he could easily have said nothing and hoped the situation would go away, he stepped up and took a little responsibility.

Who would have thought it?

"You know, everyone was worried about you today," I said. "Between what Taylor did to you and what I did to Miguel, the atmosphere was pretty sombre at work."

"I'm coming back tomorrow. I want to be back, keeping my mind off everything."

His green eyes flashed with determination but I could see the doubt behind them. He wasn't ready. Not at all. He was holding it together but it wouldn't take much to knock him off his feet again.

"You should take the time off," I told him. "You don't need to rush back."

"I don't want people to think I'm a wimp. I got hurt, it happens, right? I should get on with my life."

I smiled and squeezed his hand. "I admire your efforts, but at least give it one or two more days. If you want to play the game, your head really needs to be in it and it's not at the moment. And that's okay."

Jesse nodded. "You're probably right. But I feel like an idiot for caring so much."

My mind flicked to Miguel. In my lifelong search for the ideal man, I'd found a string of unsuitable, un-feeling, and un-caring ones. Since I'd been in L.A, I'd met two guys who were both the kind any woman would be lucky to have. I threw away something special with Miguel, and Taylor threw away something special with Jesse.

"Do me a favour, Jesse. Don't ever stop caring. I'd hate to see you turn into an asshole like McCoy because you got hurt by some girl who wasn't clever enough to realise what she had."

"Is that what happened to McCoy?"

I shrugged. "I don't know. I think *he* might just be an asshole."

Chapter 15
Is Spiderman Here?

The next few weeks passed by in a blur. I threw myself into my work even more deeply than before, at first as a way of keeping my mind off the seemingly endless gossiping, and then to prove to Richard that I was still up to the job. Things were not right between my boss and me, and I knew they never would be.

That seemed to be the story almost everywhere. Freya, Jesse, Bryce and Bree were the only people who still treated me the way they always had. Will had got a little better but we were nowhere near as close as we used to be. Even Jude, who I'd always got on well with, wanted to keep Bree away from me in case I led her astray.

Ironically, Miguel was amongst the few who'd softened towards me. Whenever we saw each other things got a bit less awkward and a bit easier to handle. The hurt I'd caused him hadn't gone away. It wouldn't for a while but day by day the rift was healing. Having him as a friend was more than I ever dared to hope for.

And Radleigh? Nothing ever changed there.

****

The time between my brother calling to tell me he was coming to America and the time he actually arrived seemed to stretch on forever. They flew into Tampa, Florida, a few days before I was due to meet them, giving them a chance to settle in and recover from the jet lag.

The rest of the team weren't scheduled to arrive in Tampa until late afternoon but I woke up early that Friday morning in order to be there by noon. I slept most of the way, and when I landed, I felt sick with excitement.

I was lucky enough to get to the hotel, check-in and shower before meeting my family in the hotel lobby. They'd checked into the same hotel as me so we could squeeze in as much extra time together as possible – a feat which had taken a lot of organisation on my part. Thankfully, things went exactly as planned and when I stepped out of the lift into the lobby at twelve-thirty, my heart did a gigantic leap of joy.

"Auntie Leah!" Jamie squealed, launching into a run to greet me.

My nephew threw himself at me and I squeezed him tightly. "Hello my darling!" I kissed the top of his head. "It's so good to see you!"

"I missed you, Auntie Leah!"

"I missed you too!"

"Let her breathe," I heard Josh say as he, Christina and Grace came towards me.

Jamie took a step back and Christina hugged me, and handed Grace to me for a cuddle. She had grown so much since I'd last seen her. I knew she didn't really know who I was, but she grinned at me. "Hi hi!"

"Hi hi, Gracie," I said, giving her a kiss on the cheek. "Look how big you've got!"

"Getting bigger every day!" Christina laughed. "It's great to see you Leah."

"You too!" I hugged her again as I passed Grace back to her.

I finally turned to Josh who grinned at me.

"Got a hug for your big brother?"

I flung my arms around him and Josh squeezed me even more tightly than I'd squeezed Jamie.

The moment was perfect.

We found a trendy little café nearby and sat outside in the sunshine while we ate. Jamie didn't stop chattering, telling me about school and his friends. Hearing about Jamie's accomplishments was one of the things I'd missed most. When I lived in Zellor, Jamie always came to me when something had upset him, and I was the first to hear when he'd achieved something new. Being so far away made that difficult. It was the same with Grace. I hadn't been around when she learned to walk or said her first words, and it bothered me sometimes. They were growing up so fast and all the small but important milestones in their lives were passing me by.

Jamie seemed so grown-up. His brown hair was a little darker and he'd grown several inches, making him closer to my height than I'd expected. Clearly he'd inherited Josh's tall genes, not my tiny ones.

I loved that our bonds hadn't weakened. We were all as close as ever, and Jamie never left my side for a second.

It wasn't until we had finished eating that Jamie finally asked the inevitable question.

"Auntie Leah," he said, seriously, "please may I have my birthday present soon?"

"Jamie," Christina said, "it's rude to ask for presents!"

"But I already know I've got one! Daddy told me."

I laughed. "Don't worry, Jamie. I haven't forgotten, but I have to give it to Daddy to look after."

His eyes widened. "What is it?"

Leaning down to pick up my handbag, I pulled out two tickets for the upcoming Warriors match.

"Tomorrow night," I told him, "you and Daddy are coming to watch Westberg's match. You'll see all of your favourite players up close because you'll be sitting right at the front of the stands."

His mouth dropped open and he looked from me to Josh, then back to me again.

"No way."

I nodded. He pounced on me, wrapping his arms tightly around my neck.

"That's the best present anyone's ever given me! Thank you!"

"You're very welcome," I told him, smiling at how happy I'd made him.

"Will Radleigh McCoy be there?"

"Yes," I answered trying not to gag. "He'll be there."

The high from seeing my family somehow made the stress of the last few weeks fall away. Work didn't feel like a chore because I knew that later, I'd see them again so we could spend more time catching up. We all had an early night on Friday, and I managed to grab a few hours with them in between training and the game on Saturday.

The match between Westberg and Tampa seemed extra exciting knowing Josh and Jamie were in the crowd. Before the game began I chatted to them over the barriers a little way away from my seat with the coaches and reserves. Jamie jumped up and down wearing his Westberg team shirt. I couldn't recall ever seeing him so energised. Mid-conversation Jamie let out a yelp, signalling that the players were coming out of the tunnel. As the Warriors lined up on the field, McCoy spotted me. Surprise crossed his face. I was supposed to be in the technical area, not chatting to the crowd. I think my moment of rebellion amused him because he winked at me, making my stomach flip over.

What the hell?

I hadn't felt anything other than irritation for him in a long time, mostly because I'd made "Avoiding McCoy" my new favourite work game.

It must have been the adrenaline.

"Leah, did Radleigh McCoy just wink at you?" Josh laughed. "I thought you said you hated each other?"

"We do. He's just trying to bother me."

"Looks like it worked."

"Shut up. I need to get to work, but have fun. I'll meet you outside afterwards."

Before my brother could tease me any further, I ran back to my seat and flicked my brain into work mode.

It was a miracle. There wasn't a single injury and the game was one of the most intense of the season. Westberg secured a 4-3 victory in the final minutes, with McCoy scoring the winning goal. I knew Jamie would be ecstatic because he'd got to see his favourite team win, and when we finally got out of the stadium, he proved me right. Even Josh had caught the buzz.

"That was amazing," Josh said. "I haven't been to a football game in years but that made me want to go out and buy a season ticket!"

"I saw Radleigh McCoy!" Jamie squealed. "He is the best footballer in the whole wide world!"

"Blasphemy," I said. "An insult to football legends worldwide."

"Blasphemy?" Jamie asked, looking up at me curiously. "What does that mean?"

"It means Auntie Leah has a crush on Radleigh McCoy and won't admit it!"

Jamie's gaze flicked between me and his father, utter confusion on his face and I said, "Point one, that is not an accurate explanation of the word blasphemy, and point two, your father is deluded."

"Stop using long words!" Jamie whined, and Josh laughed.

"It's not funny," I told him. "Next you'll be telling him McCoy's going to be his uncle."

"Oh, don't tell me it hasn't crossed your mind!"

While Jamie was in what can only be described as a trance of overexcited bliss, I dragged Josh closer to me.

"Will you stop!" I snapped. "This isn't funny, okay? Sure, there is something between McCoy and me but it's not what you think. You have no idea what I've been through because of him so before you start telling everyone I fancy him, check your facts!"

I hadn't meant to explode, but with the constant battle of not knowing what I felt for McCoy from one minute to the next, I didn't want to dissect the situation, and certainly not with my brother.

"Leah, come on. I was only messing around."

"Well, don't. I don't have a sense of humour where McCoy is concerned."

Josh stopped me. "What did he do to you?"

"It doesn't matter."

"Tell me," Josh insisted.

"We just don't get on. He spends his days trying to anger me, and I spend mine plotting ways to kill him. That's just the way things are."

The three of us took a cab back to the hotel, with Jamie still chattering enthusiastically the whole way. He didn't stop until we reached the hotel lobby. I peered into the bar quickly to see if Freya and Will were in there. They weren't.

"Come on then, soldier." Josh placed his hands on Jamie's shoulders. "Time for bed."

"Daddy, I'm not tired!"

"It's very late, Jamie. If you don't go to bed now, you'll be tired out tomorrow."

"No I won't, I promise! Daddy, pleeeeeeease?"

I grinned. "Go on, Josh. Let him stay up and have a glass of Coke. He's too wound up to sleep yet."

"And you think Coke is the answer?"

"Please?" Jamie fixed his father with puppy dog eyes.

"Okay," Josh agreed. "One drink. Then bed."

"Yay!"

The three of us went into the bar and I took Jamie to sit down while Josh bought the drinks. The team hadn't yet returned from the stadium and I hoped by the time they got back, Jamie would be in bed. I didn't think he could take any more excitement.

When Josh returned, he was smiling.

"Do you always stay in hotels this expensive?" he asked, placing the drinks on the table.

I nodded. "Always. I don't know what I'd do in a hotel with less than five stars now!"

"Snob," he teased. "When you come home I'll make you stay in a B&B, see how you like that!"

"I could do it. But I'd rather not. You get used to all this expensive stuff."

"I bet." He glanced around at the plush décor of the hotel bar. "You've done well for yourself. I'm proud of you."

"Thanks. I'm happy here. Travelling is tiring sometimes, but I'm getting paid to travel around America which is amazing."

Josh glanced at Jamie who was looking around with interest. "We were worried about you, you know? When you left."

"I know."

My decision to leave England had been sudden, to my family, anyway. I didn't tell them what I was planning until it had all been arranged. I was two months from leaving when I sprung the news. They tried to talk me out of it, telling me America is a long way from home, that I'd be away from everyone I knew. They didn't understand that was exactly the point.

My parents suggested I was suffering from some kind of depression or something. In some respects, they were probably right. I'd never fully dealt with the repercussions of my bad decisions. Whenever I returned to Cornwall, my guilt intensified. The memories of all the mistakes I'd made, of the pain I'd suffered. I couldn't erase them. Even though so many years had passed, seeing the places I used to go to always reminded me.

Leaving the country had seemed like, and indeed had been, the solution.

"I think you did the right thing," Josh said, eventually. "I really do."

"Leaving you all behind broke my heart, but the alternative was being miserable for the rest of my life. I needed to get out."

We hadn't ever had this conversation before, not even when I left. He hadn't wanted me to go but he never said a word. He told our parents to back off and let me go, even though he wanted me to stay close.

"We miss you," he said, as he saw tears forming in my eyes. "But you being happy is more important."

"Thank you. I thought maybe Mum and Dad would never get over it."

Josh laughed. "They still haven't. They miss their baby girl."

"I miss them too but this is where I need to be right now."

Jamie had almost finished his drink when the team began arriving in the bar. The sight of Jude Collinson perked Jamie up again.

Then it happened.

"Oh my God!" Jamie squeaked. "Radleigh McCoy!"

My eyes swivelled towards the door where Radleigh and Bryce were entering, followed closely by Cody Rivera.

"No," Josh said, before Jamie even opened his mouth. "It's bed time."

"One more Coke? Please?"

Josh looked to me for support but I said, "Don't involve me in this!"

"Some sister you are." He turned to Jamie. "This is your last drink. I mean it."

Jamie and I high-fived each other, laughing.

"I'll get the next round." I took out my purse. "I'll be right back."

"Leah," Bryce said as I approached. "Can I buy you a drink?"

As I looked up to meet his eye, I noticed Radleigh and Cody gazing down at me too. I had to take a moment to cope with the gorgeousness surrounding me.

"It's okay," I answered. "I'm getting a round in for my brother and my nephew."

"Then perhaps you'd like to sit on my shoulders," Cody offered. "The bartender will never see you otherwise!"

The guys laughed and I said, "Two vodka and cokes, and one straight coke, please."

Bryce winked at me then turned back to the bar to place my order.

"Your brother's here?" Radleigh asked.

"Yeah, and my sister-in-law and my niece and nephew."

"So *that's* who you were with tonight."

"Who did you think they were? My secret husband and son?"

"Very funny. How long are they here?"

"Two weeks. I'm not going to get much time with them, but we've got the whole day tomorrow."

"That sounds cool," Cody said. "It must have been a while since you've seen them."

"Yeah, it has. Too long. Tomorrow's going to be brilliant though. Well," I added, "if we can get my nephew to calm down. He hasn't stopped bouncing since the moment he got here. He nearly died from the joy of seeing Radleigh earlier."

Radleigh smiled. "He likes me? Must run in the family."

"Deflate your head, McCoy."

"Too late," Cody said. "There is no denting an ego that size."

"Well, I do my best!"

As Cody laughed, Radleigh said, "You're in a good mood tonight."

"Yes, I am. Please don't ruin it."

"I don't intend to. I like it."

"Well, try and remember that next time you get the urge to make me angry." I gave a sarcastic flutter of my eyelashes.

"But," he began, leaning in closer to me, "you are *so* hot when you're angry."

"Get lost," I laughed, placing my hands on his chest and pushing him away. I let my fingertips lurk there for a second longer than I needed to. His eyes locked onto mine. This was the closest we'd been since Boston, and my body tingled a little at the memory. *Dammit, wasn't once enough?*

"Here you go, Leah." Bryce handed me my tray of drinks.

I jumped in surprise. Radleigh had me mesmerised. Again.

"Thanks," I said, as I took the drinks. "I guess I'd better get back. Have a good evening, guys."

"Wait," Radleigh said. "Don't you wanna introduce your nephew to his hero?"

I glanced around the room. "Is Spiderman here?"

Bryce and Cody cracked up, and McCoy glared at me.

"Just kidding," I told him, giggling. "I'm sure he'd love to meet you but-"

I trailed off, not sure whether to finish the sentence. The truth was, I didn't want to give people anything more to talk about. If I took Radleigh to meet my nephew, however innocent the motive, people were bound to start gossiping again.

"Screw them," he said, reading my mind.

"If anyone says anything we'll set them straight," Bryce added, and that was enough for me.

As we approached, Jamie watched, his eyes glued on McCoy. Jamie surveyed him, open-mouthed and when we reached the table, I said, "Radleigh wanted to come and meet you, Jamie."

Suddenly shy, my nephew snuggled into his father.

"Hi. I'm Josh, Leah's brother."

Radleigh shook his hand and we sat down.

"My son is having difficulty taking in everything that happened today," Josh laughed. "It's been quite an experience."

"I bet." Radleigh smiled. "Did you enjoy the match?"

"It was incredible."

"Even I enjoyed myself," I said.

"Yeah, I heard you," Radleigh teased.

Josh watched as we went off into our usual passive aggressive banter, and I knew his mind was ticking over. My behaviour towards McCoy didn't back up the way I'd said I felt about him, but this was precisely how things worked. For a while Radleigh and I got on fine then everything would flip and we'd be fighting again.

While we'd been talking, Jamie slowly peeled himself away from Josh and towards me. He looked exhausted as he sat down on my lap. I wrapped my arms around him, and with one hand, gently stroked his hair.

"Bedtime for you soon," I told him.

"I'm not tired," he answered as a yawn escaped his lips.

"I guess you'll have to stay down here by yourself, then. I want to go to sleep so I'm ready for tomorrow."

"Where are you going tomorrow?" Radleigh asked.

"Aquarium," Jamie answered, addressing him directly for the first time.

"The Florida Aquarium is awesome. I went a couple of years ago when my parents were in town. My mom dragged me and my dad there."

"Yeah, we're only going because of Leah and Christina," Josh laughed. "Although my wife says it will be educational for the children."

"It is educational. It's surprising what you learn when you're... looking at fish."

"Daddy told me there are sharks at the Aquarium."

Radleigh nodded. "There are. I heard people can even go swimming with them now."

Jamie's eyes lit up at the prospect. "Maybe a shark will eat Grace!"

"Jamie!" Josh said. "That's a terrible thing to say about your sister!"

"I didn't mean it." He grinned mischievously.

I tapped him on the leg for being so mean but I had to laugh. Josh used to say the same kind of things about me when we were younger.

"Daddy, can Radleigh come with us tomorrow?"

Josh, Radleigh and I fell silent. It was an innocent request from Jamie's point of view. To the rest of us, it held huge implications.

"Oh, Jamie, I don't know," Josh said. "I'm sure Radleigh has other things to do tomorrow."

Jamie looked at Radleigh, his eyes wide with hope. I glanced at Josh, and he shrugged.

Did I want Radleigh with me when I was trying to enjoy being with my family? No. Did I want to disappoint Jamie by saying Radleigh couldn't come? Not at all.

If Radleigh had been a decent human being, he would have made up an excuse to save me from this awkward position I'd been put in. He said nothing.

Oh, I see. You're gonna make me *make this decision.*

"Are you busy?" I asked, stiffly.

Radleigh smiled. "I'm not busy. But I'll only come if you're sure it's okay."

You shit. You know we're never going to say no. Firstly out of politeness, and secondly so as not to disappoint Jamie who will sulk all day if we say you can't come.

"It's fine."

"Yay!" Jamie said as enthusiastically as his tired body would let him.

"And on that note," Josh said, standing up, "we'd better go to bed."

Jamie let out another whine but Josh gave him the 'look' so he reluctantly climbed off my lap. He gave me a hug and a kiss before taking Josh's hand.

"Goodnight, Jamie," I said. "Night, Josh."

"Night. Leah. Radleigh," Josh answered, eyeing me a little warily. I smiled reassuringly and he nodded in understanding.

"We'll see you tomorrow."

Once they were gone, I turned to Radleigh, fixing him with a poisonous stare, though I wasn't sure I pulled it off. I didn't *want* him hanging out with my family, but I'd had enough practice being around him and not completely loathing his presence to know it might not be as bad as I anticipated.

Maybe.

"You could have said no," he said, before I had a chance to open my mouth.

"No I couldn't and you know it. If you must come with us tomorrow, can you at least do me a favour?"

He smirked, and catching his train of thought, I said, "Don't be a pervert."

"What *can* I do for you?"

"Just behave yourself, okay? Don't annoy me, don't make me angry, just … don't be yourself. Can you do that?"

"I can, but don't blame me if your family fall in love with me."

"And don't blame me if I feed you to the sharks."

Chapter 16
Sex Would Be A Bonus

The morning of the trip to the aquarium got off to a surprising start when I went to meet my family in the lobby, and Radleigh was already with them.

Wow. Can't make it to work on time, but offer him a day out, and he's right there.

Jamie, in spite of his late night, was once again jumping up and down with glee – his shyness around Radleigh long forgotten.

"Good morning," I said as I approached.

"Hello," Jamie answered, grinning but not leaving Radleigh's side.

Grace was already settled in her stroller, but she waved to me and I leaned down to give her a kiss.

"Did you sleep well?" I asked Josh and Christina.

"I did," Christina answered. "I didn't even hear the boys come in."

"I, on the other hand," Josh said, "had to handle a hyped up eight-year-old for another hour after we got up to our room."

"How can that be?" I laughed. "He was almost asleep when you left the bar!"

Josh shook his head. "I have no idea. He wouldn't keep still long enough to actually fall asleep. I had to, very quietly, read Harry Potter for an hour."

I winked at Jamie. "Good choice."

"So." I turned to Radleigh. "Found your alarm clock, did you?"

"I did. I didn't want to get into trouble for being late." I rolled my eyes, and he added, "Can you guys excuse me for a minute? I need to go find out if I can stay here for another night or I'll be sleeping in the parking lot."

"Oh, we wouldn't make you do that. Josh hired a car. I'm sure he'd let you sleep in there."

"Funny. Will you come with me?"

"You need me to hold your hand while you talk to the hot woman at the reception desk?"

He turned to check out the petite redhead who was speaking on the phone. "On second thoughts..."

"Maybe she'll let you share *her* room?"

Before Radleigh could respond, Josh grabbed Jamie, and laughing, covered his son's ears.

"There are children present."

"Sorry." I grimaced. I grabbed Radleigh's arm. "Come on, let's go."

As I hauled him towards the desk, I said, "I probably should have mentioned there should be no innuendo in front of the kids."

"You started it!"

"I know," I admitted, my cheeks flushing.

The receptionist really was attractive, even more so close up. I tried not to glare as her eyes drifted up and down Radleigh's body.

Easy tiger, he's not yours. Even so, there was a difference between a woman appreciating a good-looking man, and blatantly undressing him with her eyes. She was not subtle at all.

"Good morning, sir," she said politely, in spite of her blatant leering. "How may I help you?"

Radleigh leaned down on the desk, and fixed her with a charming smile. "I was wondering if I would be able to extend my stay for another night."

He gave the receptionist his room number and she tore her eyes away from him to check her computer.

"I'm sorry," she said. "That room has been reserved."

"Is anything else available?"

The redhead looked back to her computer and after tapping away for a moment or two, she said, "I'm afraid we're fully booked, but I'd be happy to recommend some other hotels in the area."

Radleigh turned to me and raised an eyebrow.

"No," I said before he could even ask. "You're not staying in my room."

"Oh come on, Leah. You've been sharing with Freya so I know your room has two beds. Let me share."

I shook my head. "It's bad enough I have to spend the day with you."

"Please?"

The receptionist stared at me as if I were insane for even contemplating rejecting him. On a purely physical level I totally understood, but she hadn't been subjected to months of his crap. On the flip side, the way she was ogling him was bugging the hell out of me, so I smiled up at him. "Okay. You've won me over."

Once she'd stomped away, I hissed, "If I catch you even thinking about trying something-"

He grinned. "I wouldn't dare."

****

Radleigh was right. The Florida Aquarium was *awesome*. Jamie was, of course, hyper as we walked around. He was completely fascinated by the sharks, while I loved the coral reefs. There was a huge panoramic window where we stood watching the colourful fish swim by. It was so relaxing I could have stayed there all day.

I was so chilled out that Radleigh's presence didn't even bother me. I was enjoying myself too much. Besides, he didn't have a chance to irritate me. Jamie kept him occupied, talking a mile a minute.

When lunchtime arrived we went to the restaurant and ordered two huge pizzas for us to share. While we waited for our food, Christina let Grace out of her stroller so she could have some freedom. She toddled over to me, and with a grin, I hoisted her up on to my lap.

"Hello, Gracie," I said as she bounced up and down.

"Hi hi. Fishies!"

"That's right. We've seen lots of fishies today, haven't we?"

"Fishies. Pretty."

Grace smiled at me again then noticed Radleigh, who was sitting next to me. She stared at him curiously for a second then wriggled, signalling that she wanted to get down. It took her three steps to reach Radleigh and she placed both of her hands on his leg, making him jump. Her arms lifted out for him to pick her up and he looked at me for a clue to what he was meant to do.

"You can pick her up," I laughed. "She won't bite."

"Well, that's not true," Christina teased. "She *may* bite!"

"That's okay." Radleigh lifted Grace on to his lap. "I've had worse injuries."

Grace stood up on his lap, Radleigh holding her gently so she didn't topple over. She put her arms around his neck and rested her head on his shoulder, her dark curls tumbling into her eyes.

The sight of someone with as much physical strength as McCoy being so gentle with my niece made me dizzy with lust. Men who are good with children were right at the top of my hot list.

"Leah?"

"Huh?" I shook my head. "What?"

Radleigh grinned. "Are you okay?"

Busted.

"I... I don't," I stammered, "I forgot what I was going to say."

I took a long swig of my Coke as my heart rate re-adjusted, then joined in the conversation as if I hadn't had a fangirl attack. What made it most surprising was that for once, he wasn't even aware of what he was doing. Holding Grace hadn't been some pre-conceived plan to make me lose my mind.

It just happened naturally.

Once we'd eaten and Grace was back where she belonged, away from Radleigh to save me from having another seizure, we took a walk around the rest of the aquarium. Jamie wanted another look at the sharks, so Josh and Radleigh took him, and Christina, Grace and I wandered back to the restaurant to grab a coffee and a chat without the boys.

"Finally!" Christina said as I placed our drinks down on the table. "Time to talk at last!"

We truly were on our own, as Grace had fallen asleep in her stroller so even she didn't need attention. Christina stood up and hugged me. "Oh, Leah. We've missed you so much!"

"I've missed you too. Do you know, not a single person I've met here can make a decent cup of tea? I had to train my roommate to do it right!"

Christina burst out laughing. "Damn yanks!"

Giggling, I took a sip of my coffee and Christina said, "So, what's going on with Radleigh McCoy? Josh said today might be awkward because the two of you don't get on very well."

"Well," I sighed, "today has been one of our better days but it could have gone either way. He thinks he was put on Earth to sexually satisfy as many women as possible and when I told him I wasn't going to be one of them, he tried to get me in trouble with my boss."

"What?" Christina choked. "That man who let Jamie drag him around all day and helped me carry Grace's buggy up and down the stairs did that?"

I nodded. "He's only here today to annoy me."

"I don't know, Leah. I don't know him but I certainly don't think he's only here to bug you. Think about it. He could be at home with his own family but instead he's here with yours. Nobody does that purely to irritate someone."

"You don't know what he's like."

This is a guy who followed me to Boston in the hope of getting laid.

"Are you telling me you've never once considered that Radleigh might actually like you?" Christina asked.

"No, I haven't. Sure, he may be attracted to me but that doesn't make me special. He's attracted to most women with tits and a pulse. He's purely about one night stands. Lots of them."

"You don't think -" Christina began, but I held up my hand to stop her.

"He is *not* misunderstood," I told her. "He's not just looking for the right woman. He's an over-confident, self-obsessed pain in the arse."

"Okay," Christina said, sensing my rising animosity. "I'll take your word for it."

"Sorry." I gave a sheepish grin. "I don't hate him or anything. It's a personality clash."

"Weren't you seeing someone a while ago? What happened there, because it seemed as though you liked him a lot."

"I did. I still do. But… it's complicated."

Christina didn't push me, she just waited silently. Her patience was one of the things I loved the most about her. She knew when to ask questions and when to hold back. It took me a few minutes to prepare myself but I wanted to tell her what happened. I *needed* to.

"A few weeks ago, when I was back in Boston, McCoy showed up. He was in trouble with work and he wanted me to help him. I told him there was no way but in true McCoy style he wormed his way in and got himself an invite to the party I was going to. I got absolutely smashed. I... well, we..." Christina nodded in understanding and I continued, "After that, I couldn't stay with Miguel. I really hurt him. You think I'm a terrible person, don't you?"

"No, not at all. Everyone makes mistakes, and I can see how you'd be tempted by him. I would never have thought he was the type to sleep around, though, not based on how he's been today. I guess he's a good liar."

"He's not being fake today," I said, a little alarmed that I'd learned to tell the difference. "And he doesn't lie about relationships. He doesn't promise the world to the women he sleeps with, and most of them don't want it anyway. All they want is to say that they slept with Radleigh McCoy."

"What did you want when you slept with him?"

I drew in a deep breath. Honestly, I'd never asked myself that question. The answer wasn't complicated, just... disappointing. It made me disappointed in myself.

"I wanted to end the tension. I wanted it to be out of the way so I'd stop wanting him. That was the worst part for me. I loved being with Miguel but it still wasn't enough to stop me-" I trailed off with a sigh. "I don't know if anyone will ever be enough, and that scares the hell out of me."

Christina rested her hand on my arm. "I'm sorry. I didn't mean to bring you down by talking about this. But you shouldn't be so hard on yourself. You got it wrong with

Miguel, but it doesn't mean you'll never find someone who has everything you're looking for."

"Or maybe I'm looking for something that doesn't exist."

"It exists. Trust me."

She smiled, but I didn't get the chance to respond. Josh, Jamie and Radleigh approached and the sound of Jamie's giggles woke Grace up.

We left the aquarium at four and went back to the hotel so we could change before dinner.

After dinner, the kids were exhausted. I was pretty tired myself but being the kind, generous sister I am, I offered to watch Jamie and Grace so Josh and Christina could have some time to themselves. They leapt at the opportunity, and after putting Grace to bed in their huge two bedroom hotel suite they went down to the bar. Naturally, Jamie wanted Radleigh to be his babysitter so he joined us. Jamie snuggled in between Radleigh and me on his parents' bed. A kids' movie played on the TV and while the colourful cartoon characters caused mischief, I zoned out, allowing myself to absorb the events of the day.

Cuddled up with Jamie and Radleigh was not quite how I'd expected the day to end. The more likely scenario saw me in bed in my room and Radleigh in the hotel bar searching for alternative sleeping arrangements. I liked the reality a lot more. For a day I'd been dreading, it had turned out pretty well. I'd never forget the joy on Jamie's face when he watched the sharks with awe, and the shriek he let out as Josh snuck up on him while he was engrossed causing him to run to me for comfort from his dad's prank. The image of Radleigh holding Grace, and the way Christina had listened while I explained the stupid mistakes I'd made were all memories I'd hold on to forever.

I should have hated that Radleigh had wangled an invite, but how could I be angry when his presence made Jamie's smile so big? 'Rebel' pushed his reputation aside and allowed my nephew to hold his hand, sit on his shoulders and play like they'd known each other forever.

"Leah," Radleigh whispered. "Jamie's asleep."

I glanced down at him. His head rested against Radleigh's arm, his hair falling across his closed eyes.

"Well that didn't take long." I laughed. "Can you carry him into the other room?"

"Sure."

Carefully, Radleigh shuffled to the edge of the bed and I held the back of Jamie's head to stop it thudding against the mattress. When he was up, Radleigh gently lifted Jamie and took him into the second bedroom. My heart did another flip as I watched Radleigh tuck him in to bed, and brush Jamie's hair out of his eyes. To distract myself from having another lame girly moment, I checked on Grace who was still sleeping soundly.

"Back to the movie?" Radleigh asked.

"Sure, why not?"

It felt weird sitting on Josh and Christina's bed without having Jamie between us as a buffer. Everything in me wanted to touch him. To hold his hand, to move closer and rest my head on his chest. We'd never held hands before. Any time we'd touched each other, it was always leading to something more. Something that would make me giddy with lust, but wouldn't mean anything beyond the desperate fumbling of two people who had no plans for anything more serious than hot sex. I knew if I turned my head in his direction, I wouldn't be able to stop myself reaching for him, so I forced myself to stare at the television instead.

You're tired. You had a good day and it's making you think and feel things that aren't really there. In the morning, you'll wake up and you'll go back to remembering all the reasons you despise him.

No matter how hard I tried to believe that, the same question kept returning to me. *Why did McCoy come to the aquarium with us?* I still didn't buy Christina's theory that he'd wanted to be with me but doubts were beginning to bubble in my brain. I had to let them out.

"Radleigh, can I ask you something?" I said, before I had chance to wimp out.

"Sure."

"Why did you come out with us today?"

I hadn't expected to see surprise on his face, and for a second or two he looked as though he genuinely didn't know the answer.

"Well," he said after a while, "I didn't want to disappoint anyone."

"You could have made an excuse. Sure, Jamie would have been a little upset but he'd have got over it."

"Maybe Jamie wasn't the person I was worried about disappointing."

I watched for a sign that he was joking. His face stayed serious.

Round One to McCoy.

"You arrogant berk. You don't think I would have cried myself to sleep because you said you couldn't come?"

"Oh, you wouldn't have cared?"

"No," I answered, honestly. "You were never involved in my plans today, you just got invited along. Strange as this may seem to you, I don't spend every minute of the day wishing you were with me."

He smirked at my insult. "Okay, I'm sorry. I came because I wanted to. I thought it would be fun. And it was. Your family's really nice, Leah."

"You sound surprised," I teased. "What would you expect relatives of mine to be like?"

"I knew they'd be nice but I didn't expect your nephew would want to hold my hand all day, and I didn't expect your brother to be so laid back."

"Why not? I'm laid back."

"Right." Radleigh laughed. "Sure you are."

"I am!" I punctuated my point by whipping a pillow from behind my head and hitting him with it. "You just don't know because you're the one who winds me up!"

Radleigh laughed harder, taking the pillow from my hands. "You were laid back today."

"Well I knew you wouldn't try to bug me today. You wouldn't want to look bad in front of your adoring fans."

"Leah, come on, cut me some slack. I know how much you missed them. I didn't want to ruin your day."

He smoothed the pillowcase out before handing it back to me. "Can I ask *you* something?"

"Go ahead."

"A few times you've mentioned your past relationships. And once you said you'd had one night stands."

Amazed he ever listened, and not only listened but remembered, I said, "What's the question?"

"I was wondering… how you changed so much."

"Why do you ask?" I said, buying myself some more time while debating whether or not to tell him the truth.

"I'm interested. You said you've met men like me before, and you fell for some of them."

"Are you looking for tips?"

"I don't need tips. I just want to know."

"Okay. I grew up in a town where the entertainment level was zero. It's the stereotypical English village. It's beautiful, but for a teenager, it's dull. As soon as I was old enough to be let into pubs, my friends and I started hanging out in them at the weekends. I was young, confident, horny and stupid. Not necessarily in that order."

"And you had one night stands."

I nodded. "Yeah. A lot. Having sex was my favourite way of easing the boredom."

"Why did you stop?"

"I met a guy I liked. Luke. He didn't feel the same way, though. He was using me, but I thought we'd eventually get together so I stopped seeing other people. I turned into one of those idiotic girls who thought great sex equalled love."

"Did you get together?"

"No. I got pregnant."

I'd never told anyone that before. Not my friends, not my boyfriends. No one. Maybe Radleigh wasn't the right person to confess to but he was the first person who'd attempted to delve so far into my past. I couldn't look at him, but his silence seemed to be asking me to continue so I did.

"When I told him I was pregnant, he said I wasn't pinning it on him. That I'd slept with so many men the baby could be anyone's. In the past that was true. But since I met him, he was the only one. I had an abortion, and it made me realise how stupid I'd been."

I didn't need to tell him the whole truth. But I wanted to. The memory made tears prick my eyes. Having an abortion had changed everything in the world as I knew it. The disappointment from my parents had crippled me almost as much as my decision to end my pregnancy. I couldn't have a baby, not at eighteen. I didn't want to be the girl with the illegitimate child, and I didn't want any reminders of the way Luke treated me. It was a horrible time in my life, one I never let myself think about. From then on, I never slept with another man before getting to know him first.

Not until I moved to Westberg anyway.

"Wow." Radleigh let out a breath. "I wasn't expecting that."

"I'm full of surprises," I answered with a weak smile. "One of the reasons I'm here in America is because the memories of my hometown are not exactly fond ones."

"I'm sorry, Leah."

"Thanks. You know," I said, thoughtfully, "when I first met you, you reminded me of him a bit. That's probably why I was so tense around you. Maybe I owe you an apology."

Radleigh shook his head. "You don't. I don't think I'm much like him though. Would he have spent the whole day with you and your family?"

"He would if he thought he'd get sex at the end of it."

"I wasn't thinking about sex."

"I know. If I thought you were, I would never have agreed to you being with us today."

"I'm thinking about sex now though." He grinned.

"I suppose it was too much to ask that you lasted the whole day."

"It's still different, though. He would have gone out for the day with you for sex. I went out with you and had fun. Sex would just be... a bonus."

I burst out laughing. "A bonus?"

"Yeah. Not an expectation."

"Radleigh," I said, with a slight tone of teasing in my voice. "Was this an example of you being genuine?"

"Yes. Make the most of it, it doesn't happen very often."

"I know."

There was a long silence between us, then eventually, Radleigh said, "My last relationship, the one that lasted for two years, ended when my woman cheated on me with one of the guys on the team."

I turned my head to look at him. "What?"

He shrugged. "It was a long time ago. Jen was... she was gorgeous. Everyone wanted her. I was stupid enough to think her flirting with other guys was harmless, but she was screwing... I don't even know how many people. But I caught her with James Winters. He was our team goalkeeper before Jude. We were friends, but he was messing around with Jen behind my back for at least six months of our relationship. James quit the team at the end of the season, and they moved to New York. Last I heard, they're still together, and they've got two kids now, so I guess it worked out for them."

Oh. That's why Bree was so sure he'd never hit on a teammate's girl.

Radleigh gave a small smile, and I felt it, unexpectedly. Just as I didn't open up too often, I knew he didn't either, and knowing he wanted me to hear what he'd been through, to show me more of his genuine side made me brave enough to reach for his hand.

"How long have you been single, Radleigh?"

"Four years."

"And you've never wanted to get serious with anyone in all that time?"

"No. Being in a relationship is too much hassle. It's easier not to get attached."

His eyes softened, the way they did in Boston before he asked me to dance and I'd subsequently lost my mind, but the moment passed quickly.

"Well... I'm still not going to have sex with you," I told him, breaking the bubble of tension around us.

Radleigh laughed out loud, stroking the back of my hand with his thumb. "Damn."

Chapter 17
A Tacky Souvenir From Florida

The next morning, Radleigh had to leave for the airport at eight-thirty to catch his plane home. Staying an extra night meant he'd had to book an early flight to get back to L.A for training. We'd debated whether or not he should have taken an overnight flight but he insisted on staying which made Monday morning one gigantic rush.

It had been worthwhile, though. Delving into Radleigh's mind had been a revelation, and I'd actually enjoyed spending time with him. We talked a lot overnight. Sharing a room with him meant we didn't have to stop, and we fell asleep chatting. It was so strange. He'd gone out of his way to make me uncomfortable when we first met, and while I hadn't forgotten any of the things he did, I was finally getting a real glimpse of who he was underneath his well-practiced persona. It was the side of him he'd shown me in Phoenix, and then a little more in Boston. I didn't know why I was the one allowed access to such privileged information, but I knew this wasn't part of any game. It was, well, the real McCoy.

My plane wasn't due for a couple of hours after Radleigh's. Richard had, generously considering recent events, allowed me to arrive at training a little later than normal to allow me to enjoy a long breakfast with my family before heading home.

Naturally, Jamie wanted to say goodbye to Radleigh so everyone got up super early to make it happen.

In the lobby, Christina combed Grace's hair. Josh set down his newspaper when Radleigh and I arrived, and Jamie was sulking.

"Do you have to go already?" Jamie asked Radleigh, sticking out his lower lip into a pout.

Radleigh crouched down to be at eye level with Jamie. "Yeah, I need to catch my flight home so I'm not late for work. But you still get to spend a couple more hours with Auntie Leah."

The look on Jamie's face said he would happily have swapped me for Radleigh. I should have been offended, but I saw his point. Compared to his hero, I was a nobody. At his age, if someone had dangled He-Man in front of me and said it was him or my aunt, I know which one I would have chosen.

"I don't want you to go!" Jamie wailed.

Radleigh glanced up at me, not knowing what to do so I knelt down beside him and drew Jamie closer to me, giving him a hug.

"It's not fair!" he sobbed, clinging to me with one arm and wrapping the other around Radleigh. "I want to come with you."

"You can't, J," I told him. "You're going to have lots of fun with Mummy and Daddy and Grace though!"

"And," Radleigh added, "we'll be coming to England in a few months. Your daddy said he might bring you to a match if you're good, and I'll take you to meet the rest of the team."

There was a scheduled trip to the UK at the end of the season which I'd completely blocked out because I didn't want to go. At least, not until I'd been reminded of how much I missed my family. The Warriors had a five match tour which would see them playing friendlies against some of Britain's top teams, as well as doing several television appearances.

"Really?" Jamie asked.

"Really."

Jamie's tears began to fall more slowly, and a surge of warmth rushed through me at Radleigh's promise. Anyone who made my nephew smile like that deserved a little credit.

We stood up, and Radleigh said goodbye to Josh, Christina and Grace, then ruffling Jamie's hair, he picked up his bag and the two of us headed outside to find him a cab. As we stood at the top of the steps to the hotel, I said, "That was sweet of you."

Radleigh nodded, his face breaking into a smile. "You owe me now."

I rolled my eyes. "Okay, you can go now. I've had enough of you anyway."

"Sure you have."

"Seriously. Thank you. Jamie will never forget this."

"It was no trouble at all."

An awkwardness hung between us, one that had never, ever been there before and for once, I had no witty insults to toss at him.

"Well," Radleigh said, breaking the silence, "I should go. I'll see you in a few hours."

"Yeah."

We stood for a moment or two longer, and I wished I was eight years old so I could legitimately break down and ask him to stay.

Jesus, Leah! What's wrong with you? He was nice for one day. That does not make him a reformed character. Stop acting like such a girl!

He smiled. "See ya."

He started to walk down the steps, then stopped and turned back. "Oh yeah, I almost forgot."

Trying not to blush at the fact I'd intended to watch him walk away instead of going back inside, I said, "What?"

Resting his bag down on the steps, he tugged the zipper open. As he straightened up he pulled out a rectangular box.

"I bought you this yesterday," he said, and I walked towards him as he held it out to me.

He grinned again as I lifted the lid. I put my hand inside and took out its contents. In my hand was a small plastic dome filled with clear liquid, with a black top hat and tiny carrot floating inside. Along the edging at the bottom were the words 'Florida Snowman'.

I laughed out loud and Radleigh said, "A tacky souvenir from Florida."

Looking up at him, I smiled. "Perfect. Supreme tackiness."

"I thought you'd like it."

"I do. Thank you."

With the snowman in one hand and the box in the other, I reached up and gave him a hug. The warmth of his arms around me was a little more than I could handle but I didn't want to let go. He'd remembered, all that time ago, I'd told him about my love for tacky keepsakes.

"I guess I really do owe you now." I smiled as I reluctantly released him.

He kept his hands on my waist, his eyes glistening with mischief. "I'll try to think of a fitting way for you to pay me back."

My body shuddered a little, remembering what those hands had the power to do to me but I kept my face as lust-free as possible. "Get out of here, McCoy."

Saying goodbye to my family was awful. We'd had so little time together and although I was grateful for what we'd had, I wished it could have been more. Jamie cried again as I said goodbye to him, asking me to stay, which obviously, I couldn't. I hated leaving him.

I cried all the way to the airport, and most of the way home.

I entered the training ground weighted down with unhappiness. I wanted to be with Josh, Christina, Jamie and Grace. I thought I'd be all light and happy after being with them, but the reality was, I hated having to be away from them when they were still in the country. If they'd gone home again it would have been marginally easier.

Ironically, I was looking forward to seeing Radleigh. I never thought *that* day would come. But he'd been there with me and my family. It made me want to be around him, if only to help me hold on to the memories for a bit longer.

He spotted me as I walked around the edge of the pitch on my way to check in with Richard, and he jogged over to me. Had he been waiting for me? No, of course not, why would he? However, he smiled as he approached and my bleakness lifted a little.

"Hey," he said. "You're back. How was the rest of your morning?"

"Good, thanks. Jamie talked about you non-stop."

"That must've been annoying for you."

I nodded. "It was."

"Did you miss me, Leah?"

"You wish," I laughed. "How about you? Did you get here on time?"

"Only just. I'd rather have had the extra couple of hours in Florida, though."

"Jamie would have loved that."

I would have loved it.

I wasn't sure where all the soppiness came from, but it startled me. My over-emotional state was messing with my head.

"Are you okay?" Radleigh asked.

Clearly my inner turmoil showed on my face.

"Yeah. I just don't want to be here today. If you thought Jamie reacted badly when you left, it was nothing compared to how he reacted when I had to go."

"I can imagine. He really misses you, huh?"

"Leah!" I heard Bree's voice, and turned to see her bounding towards me, followed by Freya.

My girls distracted me from my confused thoughts about Radleigh, and I smiled as they bundled me into a hug as if I'd been gone for years instead of days.

"Hi." I hugged them back.

"We figured you'd be sad after leaving your peeps behind in Florida," Bree said. "So I'm here to cheer you up!"

"Aww, that's sweet, but you do know I have to work now I'm here?"

"Yes, but first, a coffee break!"

As they dragged me towards the restaurant, I paused for a second to glance back at Radleigh. An unreadable expression crossed his face but he smiled when I turned to him. I gave him a quick wave, then let my friends do what they intended to do.

The happiness of my break lasted precisely thirty minutes. On my way to the office to find out who my first patient of the day would be, Jesse stopped me and yanked me back up the steps, and into the spa's male changing rooms.

"Bloody hell, Jesse," I said, catching my breath from the speed he'd dragged me up the two flights of stairs. "What are you doing?"

"I'm sorry, but there's something you need to see and I didn't think you'd want to do it with too many people around."

I'd never seen him so worried and my heart began to thud in my chest as he handed me his mobile phone. My eyes widened in shock. A text message from Taylor read: ***"You still think your precious Leah is so innocent?"***

Underneath was a black and white photo of me and Radleigh. It had been taken early that morning, when Radleigh handed me my gift. The photographer had obviously taken full advantage of their zoom lens because both of our expressions could be seen clearly.

If anyone who didn't know better saw the photographthey would think something was going on between us. For the briefest moment a look had passed between Radleigh and I. We looked like… a couple.

There was a link to a website underneath the photo. I didn't want to see, but I clicked anyway to find out exactly what I was dealing with. The link took me to a soccer fan site, and listed on the main page were the top ten topics being discussed in the site's forum. One of the headings read, *"McCoy's mystery woman."* I clicked again, and found the same photo had been posted as the introduction to the topic, along with a photo of us hugging. Underneath it said, *"Who do you think she is? Secret girlfriend or quick fling? Post your thoughts here."*

As I read on, some of the replies shocked me. Some wished him luck, some said I was 'obviously' a one night stand, and several said I looked like a whore and was probably using him. With each response, sickness churned faster in my stomach.

"I'm sorry," Jesse said again, and my head snapped up in surprise. I'd forgotten he was there.

"Where did she find this stuff?" I asked, my hands shaking.

He shrugged. "I guess she did some kind of internet search for McCoy and this came up."

"You don't think … I mean, she couldn't have taken these herself, right? This happened this morning. In Florida."

Jesse's eyebrows knitted in confusion. "Wait, *that's* why he was late this morning? Because he was with you in Florida?"

"Yes, but… not in the way these pictures make it look."

"Man, what *is* it with that guy?"

If the situation hadn't been so serious I'd have laughed at his expression. Seemed like every woman he knew had a link to McCoy in some way.

"Jesse. Focus."

He shook his head. "I don't think Taylor took them but she won't waste any time making sure people see them. Even if she doesn't, the photos will be all over the news tomorrow."

He was right. Those photos had been published on the fan site several hours ago, and with the speed of social media, they had probably found their way to several news sites already.

"Oh hell."

Still holding Jesse's phone, I walked as fast as my wobbly legs would carry me, in search of Radleigh. I needed to find out if he already knew about the photos, and if he did, how we were going to stomp out the rumours. I found him in my office reading a newspaper.

"Surprise." He closed the newspaper and placing it on my desk. "I'm booked in for a… you okay?"

Without a word, I thrust Jesse's phone at him and watched as he looked at the pictures.

"Where did these come from?" he asked.

"Taylor sent this to Jesse. Someone posted them on a website and now they're all over the place."

"Huh. I should think about getting a restraining order for her."

His calmness only served to make my temper flare, and I snapped, "You should see what people are saying about me, Radleigh! There are comments from strangers who think I'm a prostitute you hired for the night!"

"Precisely. Strangers. Who cares what they say?"

"I do! My family might see this. I don't want anyone thinking those things about me! Half the people who work here have still got it in for me after the last incident, and we didn't even do anything this time!"

Radleigh stopped staring at the photos and surveyed my face. The intensity with which he was looking at me made my heart race again.

He really was beautiful. Those ice blue eyes, and perfect, full lips…

"Is it so bad if people think we're dating?" he asked, breaking my internal swoon. *Now is not the time.*

"Yes, it's bad! I'll get fired! And we're not dating!"

"Do you wanna?" He grinned.

"What? You… I… No, I don't wanna! Do you?"

"No," he answered, after a slight hesitation. "I like things as they are."

I hadn't expected to feel his words so strongly, and more than that, I hadn't expected them to hurt.

"Fine," I said, somehow functioning even though my heart sank into my stomach. "So what are we going to do?"

"The same as always. We wait it out. And if anyone says anything, tell me. I'll set them straight."

Slowly, I nodded. "Okay."

How could that have hurt?

After we slept together, everything had changed. Actually, things began to change in Phoenix. We still fought and annoyed each other, but the more time we spent away from the watchful eyes of the team, the more I felt something between us. Despite my denial, I felt *something.* My mistake was thinking he felt it too.

"I thought I might find you two together."

Richard's voice made me jump and I looked up at him in surprise. Even though Radleigh had been about to tell me I was supposed to treat him for... something, the last thing I needed was to be found with him by Richard.

"Leah, I want to see you in my office. Now."

I didn't even look back at Radleigh, I followed Richard, the ache in my chest getting worse with every step. There wasn't enough time to process my feelings. I wanted to freeze the world for a while so my brain could catch up. I barely even noticed when I'd reached Richard's office.

"Sit down." Richard took his place behind the desk.

I sat and waited for him to begin.

"Is there anything you want to tell me, Leah?"

"Actually, no."

"So, you don't want to explain this?" he asked, placing his phone in front of me, the image of McCoy and me piercing another hole in my chest.

"Again, no."

"Are you dating him?"

"No. I don't think there's anything more to say."

"How about telling me how you came to be photographed with him early this morning."

"We stayed in the same hotel last night. This morning, when that photo was taken, he'd just said goodbye to my family."

Richard's eyebrows almost shot off his forehead. "You introduced him to your family?"

"My nephew is a fan."

"A big enough fan that McCoy had to spend the whole weekend with you?"

I sighed, running my hands through my hair. "I know how it looks, okay? But what you and everyone else is thinking is not true. Nothing happened."

Well, if you don't count staying up all night swapping life stories. The memory caused a sharp pain to shoot through my veins because it clearly didn't mean as much to him as it did to me. How did this happen? How did I go from hating him to being hurt by him?

"Leah, if you and McCoy are-"

"We're not. We're not a couple, we aren't anything!"

"But based on what happened before-"

"What? I deserve *this*? Richard, I've been labelled the team slut and I haven't even done anything wrong. I'm tired, okay? I'm tired of fighting to get people to respect me, and I'm tired of wondering how long it will take before people forgive me for making one mistake. It's like being back in high school! I'm sick of it!"

All the anger and pain flooded out of me. I couldn't seem to stop it. I didn't want to. As the tears began to fall from my eyes, I said, "I didn't deserve any of this."

Richard watched me for a moment and I wiped my eyes as he stood up and walked around the desk towards me. "You knew how people viewed McCoy before you started hanging out with him. Whatever kind of relationship you have with him, people were always going to talk."

"How they view him is one thing. Making rash judgements about me based only on circumstance and rumours is quite another."

There was a long, desperately uncomfortable pause then Richard said, "We need to talk about your future here. I understand you didn't ask to be placed in a situation that made you sacrifice your own reputation to get McCoy out of trouble, and as angry and disappointed as I was with your actions, I always respected the way you saved his career. But this can't keep happening. I don't care that McCoy's photo is all over the internet because he gets photographed with women all the time. It's the fact that it's you, the team physiotherapist that's the problem."

"You know what," I said, my eyes burning with tears. "I can save you the trouble of firing me. First thing tomorrow morning, I'll be handing in my notice."

Chapter 18
Numb

The decision to leave the Warriors was a spur of the moment one, made while over-emotional and angry. After leaving Richard's office and getting on with the rest of my day, I knew I'd made the right choice. Everywhere I went filthy looks followed me around, and everyone I treated refused to engage in a real conversation with me.

I just wanted to be away from all the drama. Working at Westberg seemed like the perfect job on the surface, but I hadn't signed on to deal with media speculation and psychotic stalkers.

As predicted, the photographs of me with Radleigh made it to the newspapers, and I was only saved from the gossip-hungry journalists outside the stadium by Freya, who parked directly by the stadium entrance and bundled me into her car in a blur of flashing lights.

She drove me home in silence. We hadn't had a chance to talk much that afternoon but I knew she'd seen the photos too. I could tell by the disappointment in her eyes. Like everyone else, she assumed the worst without bothering to ask me for the truth.

It wasn't until we got into the apartment that she threw her bag down on the floor in the hallway and shouted, "When were you going to tell me, Leah?"

I stopped in my tracks. Her words were tinged with hurt that I hadn't told her I'd been with Radleigh. I was so used to the stabbing guilt pains, I should have been prepared, but I wasn't. Not at all.

"Freya," I began as I turned to her, and she held up her hands to stop me.

"Didn't I deserve to hear it from you? You had the whole weekend to tell me! We talked on the phone and you still said nothing!"

"It's not what you think."

"No? You didn't see Radleigh yesterday? You didn't wake up with him this morning in Florida?"

"Yeah, both of those things happened. We spent yesterday with my family, and we stayed in the same hotel room last night. What people don't seem to understand is those things can happen and still be completely innocent."

"Innocent? You already slept with him once and now you're introducing him to your family? How is that innocent?"

It's innocent because he doesn't want me!

"I didn't expect to go through this with you," I said, more calmly than I felt. "I thought you'd believe me."

"I believed you before. Now... I don't know."

I shrugged. "Then I guess there's nothing else to say."

"There's one more thing." Her voice wobbled. "I went to see Richard this afternoon. I told him whatever is happening between you and Radleigh is nothing more than friendship because I thought he was on the verge of firing you. He told me you're handing in your notice."

It was like I'd knocked her to the ground then kicked her in the gut. Tears glistened in her eyes, and suddenly, I understood.

Her outburst wasn't about Radleigh at all.

"Freya."

"You should have told me."

"I know, but it's been a hell of a day. I was hoping to get some rest before dropping that bombshell."

Freya sighed. "I'm sorry for yelling. But all of this stuff with Radleigh, it'll blow over soon and everything will be okay again."

"No. According to everyone here, I committed the ultimate sin by sleeping with him. They won't forget. I can't change their opinions of me, Freya. They've labelled me as something I'm not. I won't put up with being treated that way. I'm going home."

"Home," she repeated. "To England?"

The words slipped out of my mouth before I'd thought them through, but I knew they were right.

"Yeah. If being with my brother this weekend taught me anything, it's how much I miss my family."

Freya took a moment to process what I'd said, and I felt bad for springing it on her so abruptly.

"I don't want you to go."

"I'm sorry. I didn't want things to end up this way."

"Have you told Radleigh you're leaving?"

I shook my head, my stomach clenching at the sound of his name. "Not yet. I don't think he'll care."

"He spent the weekend with you. I don't think he'd do that if he didn't care."

Her words almost exactly echoed Christina's, but I knew better. He didn't want me. We were friends at best. Even that seemed like an exaggeration.

It took less than two hours for the news of my resignation to become public knowledge once I'd given my official resignation letter to Richard. I knew he was disappointed but he didn't try to change my mind. The team always came first, and I understood. That didn't stop it hurting, though.

On my walk back to my office I nearly jumped out of my skin when a hand grabbed my arm, stopping me in my tracks. Whipping around, I came face to face with an angry-looking McCoy. He must have been lurking outside Richard's office waiting for me. I hadn't expected him to appear out of nowhere and seeing him knocked the breath out of me.

"You're leaving?"

Even in my state of numbness, the first tingling of pain began to seep into my consciousness. I didn't want to talk to him, I wasn't ready. I'd spent most of the night before trying to figure out how I'd ended up feeling so much for him after despising him so much. My conclusion? Radleigh was right all along. We were more alike than I wanted to admit, but not just in the ways he was thinking of. It *wasn't* only about wanting amazing sex. We'd both been screwed over by people we loved, we'd both made mistakes, we'd both been afraid to get serious with anyone new. There was a connection between us. Or so I'd thought.

Looking at him through narrowed eyes, I released myself from his grip. "Yes. I am."

"Why?"

"Because I've had more than I can take from gossips and people who think I'm a slapper."

He watched me intently, his blue eyes staring straight into mine. "I never thought you were the type who cared what others think about you."

Stop. Stop trying to get into my head.

He was right, though. Usually I wouldn't have worried about what people's opinions of me, but it was much more than that.

It was *him*.

That was more pathetic than I cared for and I said, "It's not only the gossip. I miss my family. What's left here for me now?"

"How about your job and your friends?"

For one minute I thought, *hoped*, he was going to say what about him.

"My friends? Will can barely stand the sight of me, Jude hasn't forgiven me since I broke up with Miguel, Richard still has difficulty looking me in the eye, and my job is becoming so unbearable I'd rather stick needles in my eyes than come here and face so much judgement every day."

His face hardened. "I never thought you'd be so weak, Leah."

Weak? Was being weak providing an alibi for someone I hated, even when it almost cost me my job? Was it weak when I ruined my reputation and my relationship with Miguel to save his ass?

"I'm not being weak. I'm cutting my losses." I told him, before turning to walk away.

I hadn't taken more than a few steps before he grabbed me again. "Don't you think running away now will make you look more guilty?"

"Honestly, I don't care what people say about me once I'm gone. I won't be here to listen to it."

"You want to go back to the place you hated so much?" he asked in an almost taunting way. "The place with all the bad memories?"

I used all the strength I could muster to hold back the tears. I hadn't thought it was possible for him to hurt me any more.

"I can't believe you used that against me."

"I'm not using it against you, I'm just asking you if that's really what you want to do. I can't believe you're going to throw your life here away because a few people said crappy things about you. They say things about me all the time and I haven't run away yet."

"That's because most of the things they say about you are true. What does it matter to you anyway? I thought you'd be glad to be rid of me so you can move on to your next conquest."

An unreadable look crossed his face, then his jaw clenched in anger.

"You're right. You shouldn't be too difficult to replace. There are a million pretty girls who could easily fill your shoes."

"I'm sure," I said, keeping my voice steady, even though his words sliced at my insides. "And I'm sure you'll have a great time getting to know them. After all, that's what you're about, right? The thrill of the chase?"

"That's right. No point in letting things get boring."

His stared right at me as he used the word "boring" and the knife twisted a little further.

I'd handed him the power to hurt me when I told him about my past. I'd been stupid enough to think he would understand, and maybe even care. Instead, I'd given him another way to break my heart.

Without waiting for him to say anything else, I stalked along the corridor, and back to my office.

****

How I managed to stop myself from bursting into tears during the afternoon, I had no idea. The numbness returned, and I immersed myself in it, blocking Radleigh out of my head. I couldn't believe the way he'd reacted to the news of me leaving, and his confirmation I was nothing more than another notch on his bedpost was more than I could stand.

Freya put my emotional mood down to the stress I'd been dealing with. I couldn't bring myself to tell her the truth. In order to cheer me up, she decided to hold a mini party for me at our apartment that night. What I really wanted to do was drown in my own depression but she was too good a friend to let me.

There was one more thing I had to do before I attempted to pretend to enjoy myself. I had to call home.

It took me a full hour to prepare myself to pick up the phone. I had no idea how to break the news to my parents, and my reluctance to do so wasn't helped by knowing how my mum would react. She was, predictably, ecstatic when I told her, before adding she knew I'd "come to my senses" eventually. As much as I loved her, I hated that turn of phrase. It made me feel like a failure.

I didn't have too much time to wallow in my sadness. I took a quick shower and changed my clothes, ready for my friends to attempt to break me out of my funk.

Will, Jesse, Bree and Miguel showed up at seven, bringing with them a feast of Chinese food; they knew it was my favourite. It was a strange mix of people. Will, who still hadn't quite got over the fact I slept with Radleigh, Jesse, who was still nursing a broken heart, Miguel, the man whose heart I'd stomped on, and Bree, who... well she barely noticed anything had changed. Collectively though, they were my friends and it was hard to be unhappy in their company.

"I think," Bree announced, when we were all stuffed with food and sprawled all over the living room, "I should be allowed to drink wine tonight."

"And why do you think that?" Will asked from his spot on the sofa. "You are underage, little lady!"

"Because," she went on, "Leah won't be here for my big 21st birthday party, and that means she won't see me the first time I get drunk!"

I'd forgotten about Bree's party. The invites hadn't gone out yet because it wasn't until the end of the year but she hadn't wasted any time making sure everyone saved the date.

Giggles echoed around the room. "I appreciate you thinking of me but I'm not sure if I want to see you getting pissed and embarrassing yourself in the name of celebration!"

"Bree embarrasses herself even without alcohol," Jesse teased, sitting up straighter. "But she has a point. Leah won't be here for my 21st either so I think I should have a beer… you know… because I don't want her to miss out."

"Ha! Your 21st is years away kiddo," I laughed. "No beer for you! Anyway, it's not like either of you have never had alcohol before!"

Jesse and Bree both faked an identical look of mock horror, causing everyone to burst out laughing again.

"She's right." Freya looked at Bree. "We were there the night you demanded to try vodka after our first, and last, Zumba class."

"Oh my God!" Bree squealed. "I thought I was going to die from the dizziness!"

"Well you're not meant to neck the whole glass when you're not used to it."

"You could have told me!"

"You didn't give us the chance!"

"Okay." Miguel grinned. "Bree has earned a glass of wine because we've been picking on her."

Bree saluted him and poured herself a gigantic glass of red, sipping it slowly and licking her lips.

225

"Mmm, delish!"

I reached over to the cooler beside me and handed Jesse a beer. "Don't tell anyone I'm leading you astray, okay?"

"Wouldn't dream of it."

"Where I come from, people can drink from the age of eighteen so let's pretend we're in England tonight."

Jesse smiled when I winked at him, then as everyone began to break off into their own little conversations, I turned around to Will.

"You okay? You're pretty quiet tonight."

He nodded. "Yeah. I'm okay. I broke up with Heather a couple hours ago."

I heaved myself around to fully face him. "You what? Why?"

Will shrugged. "She was too clingy. I couldn't even leave my apartment without her asking where I was going and how long I'd be."

"I'm sorry. But you don't look too upset."

"I'm not. I don't think it was ever going to work. The more needy she got, the more I wanted to get away. Maybe now it's over I can get my friendship with Freya back on track. I mean… that was one of the problems, right? She felt left out."

Shaking my head, I lifted myself up to my knees to whisper in his ear. "She didn't feel left out. She's in love with you."

Alcohol wasn't the motivator for my revelation. Even though it wasn't my place to tell him, I couldn't stand the idea of him wasting any more time when it was so obvious how much they cared for each other.

Will's eyes widened and he sat bolt upright, then sprang to his feet and dragged me across the room and out to the balcony, closing the doors behind us.

"Well, luckily nobody noticed," I said, sarcastically. Everyone inside was staring, probably because we'd trampled over them as he'd pulled me outside.

"Sorry, sorry. But… what?"

"Your inability to see the bigger picture is astonishing. Freya is in love with you. She has been for years and you are the only person who hasn't realised."

He stared at me for a moment, processing the information.

"That's impossible. If she… I would know if she… if she felt that way about me, right?"

"You'd think so but, no."

He leaned back against the railings and let out a sigh. "Wow. Why didn't she tell me?"

"Why didn't *you* tell *her*?"

Will's mouth opened to protest, but he changed his mind and sighed. "Because it didn't occur to me that she would ever have feelings for me. I'm Will, her buddy, her co-worker."

"I'm starting to think I'm in high school again. It shouldn't take me saying, '*Hey, guess what, my friend fancies you,*' to get you to see what's obvious."

"I'm a guy. We're notoriously dumb when it comes to women."

"You're thirty-two. You should have learned something by now, especially when that something is that your best friend has spent the last few weeks wanting to die because she didn't know how to cope with her feelings for you."

Probably more information than he needed, but I was on a roll. Will's eyes glistened. "What do I do now?"

"Once you've recovered from the shock, you should talk to her."

He nodded. "I guess I have to. Thank you, Leah. I don't think I deserve this much help after the way I've been since, well, you know."

Will stood awkwardly, fidgeting a little on the spot.

"We don't need to talk about that," I told him.

"I am sorry, though," Will said. "I should have listened instead of writing you off."

"It doesn't matter. You're here now. You're supporting me now. Let's leave the past behind us."

Chapter 19
Do I Want A Drink?

My last four weeks at work were like hell on Earth. Once news of my resignation spread, it was only natural more rumours began circulating to replace the old ones. The most popular was that Radleigh had dumped me, breaking my heart and causing me to quit. I suppose it wasn't so far from the truth. He hadn't "dumped" me but he'd made it clear he didn't want me.

And it hurt in ways I never expected.

In spite of my endless protests that I'd never fall for an arrogant prick again, and Radleigh McCoy would never mean anything to me, I'd fallen hard. Seeing him every day was torture, especially since he wouldn't speak to me unless absolutely necessary.

I'd decided that, rather than prolong my stay in America, I would leave as soon as possible, so I packed up all of my things right away and had them shipped back to my parents' house. I couldn't believe how much stuff I'd accumulated. My time with the Warriors was only a tiny proportion of the time I'd been in America, and when I'd first arrived I had almost nothing, ready to start afresh.

I could barely believe that at the age of twenty-six I was going backwards.

When my final weekend in America arrived, I'd reached that weird stage of numbness again. In some ways, it was welcome. It meant I didn't have to deal with the pain of leaving. But it also meant I couldn't fully appreciate the time I had left.

I was due to return to England on a Sunday morning in early July. My last working day was in Iowa, where the team had a match that weekend. I had to fly from Iowa back to L.A to collect my things and then catch my flight to London. From London I had to fly to Newquay, where my parents would be waiting to collect me for the last part of my journey home, by which time it would be the early hours of Monday morning, and I would be comatose.

But before the nightmare journey I had a few final days with my friends, and my leaving party, which was to take place on Saturday night. It was really just an excuse for everyone to go to a club and drink too much but that was fine with me.

Getting ready to go out is always both exciting and nerve-wracking. The buzz of a night out, versus the stress of making sure you look good is overwhelming. When you threw in the fact it was my last night out with the team and the last time I'd see Radleigh, there was an added pressure I didn't need.

"What if nobody comes?" I asked Freya, as I walked out of the bathroom. I'd chosen to wear the blue dress I wore to Alison's wedding. Somewhere in the depths of my brain, I thought maybe the memory of that night might trigger Radleigh to… I don't know… say something, anything to me that was more than the occasional grunt in passing.

Freya turned to look at me. "Don't be ridiculous. It's your last night!"

"Yeah, so? Most people here still hate me."

"No, they don't. You can count on me, Bree, Will, Jesse and Miguel as definites. Even if nobody else shows, isn't it more important that you spend the evening with the people who love you rather than a bunch of strangers?"

I nodded. "You're right. I guess I'm just nervous."

"Nervous? Why?"

With a deep sigh I said, "After tonight, it will all be over. This whole experience will have been like a long dream and when I wake up I'll be at home, as if I never left."

It was too Wizard of Oz for words.

"Oh, Leah." She walked over to hug me. "It won't be that way. We won't forget you."

"I know. I'm just going to miss you so much."

"Hey," she said, firmly, although there was the slightest wobble in her voice. "Let's save the tearful goodbyes for tomorrow, okay? Tonight we're having fun!"

When we arrived at the club I was surprised to find it was already jam packed with people. Scanning the room, I took note of who had turned up – as well as trying to spot Radleigh in the crowd.

Freya immediately led me to the bar where a clamour of people offered to buy me drinks. I took a cocktail from Will then he, Freya, Bree and I found an available table and sat chatting for a while. My eyes kept drifting around the room, fully expecting to spot Radleigh dancing with someone younger and infinitely less trouble than me. But as the evening wore on it became more and more obvious he wasn't there.

He's not coming.

Whenever he popped into my mind, I danced. I spent the majority of the evening on my feet, drinking, and accepting the good wishes of almost everyone on the team. Despite the gossip that had been circulating about me for weeks, a decent number of people seemed sad I was leaving, and wished me all the best for the future. If they had been so supportive a few weeks ago, I may not have made the same decisions.

Don't fool yourself. All the support in the world means nothing if you can't get it from the one person you want it from.

Obviously, it was time for another drink.

I excused myself from the dance floor in search of another Cosmopolitan. Bryce Warren stood at the far end of the bar and as I approached he gave me a warm grin.

"Hey, Leah. I hoped I'd catch you tonight. I wanted to say I'm sorry you're leaving. I hope you find whatever you're looking for back home."

"Thanks, Bryce," I replied, his dark eyes penetrating me. His gaze left me wondering if he was making a vague reference to my relationship with McCoy.

He didn't push the issue, and instead said, "So, are you enjoying yourself?"

I nodded and gave him a small smile. "Yeah, I am. How about you?"

"Oh, I don't know. I think I'm a bit old for all this clubbing."

He may have been significantly older than the likes of Jesse and Jude, but by no means was he old.

"Rubbish!" I told him, "I saw you on the dance floor giving those hormone filled teenagers a run for their money!"

"Well, I try." He laughed.

The bartender handed me my drink, and I decided to ask Bryce the question that had been plaguing me all evening.

"Bryce, where's Radleigh?"

His shoulders sank. I'd obviously uttered the one question he hoped I wouldn't ask. "He told me he didn't feel like going out tonight."

"Right," I said with a hint of sarcasm. "I understand."

He just didn't care enough.

"Leah, come on. It's not like that."

"It's okay, I get it."

"I don't think you do."

"Well, by all means enlighten me. Because I would love to know what goes on inside that head of his."

I'd tried so hard to get through the night without making a big deal out of Radleigh's absence, but I was leaving in less than twenty-four hours and it was becoming more and more apparent he wasn't going to swoop in and beg me to stay. Not that I genuinely expected him to.

"Have you even talked to him lately?" Bryce asked.

"No. But he hasn't spoken to me either."

Bryce rolled his eyes. "You're both as bad as each other."

"He made it quite clear he doesn't care whether I leave or not. Why would I approach him?"

"Because his enormous ego prevents him from making the first move."

"All he had to do was show up here tonight, say goodbye, and that would be the end of it."

"Would it?"

"Yes," I said firmly, not wanting to confess my feelings to Radleigh's closest friend. "It would."

As I walked away from Bryce, that horrible ache began to fill me again and I sat down at the nearest table, not bothering to check whether it was already taken. The weight of the pain I'd been carrying around had become too much. I needed to let it pass. Not that it ever fully went away. Talking about Radleigh instead of just thinking about him had made it more real again.

I couldn't stand it. I hadn't left America yet and I missed him already. I missed his smile, and the sound of his voice. God, I even missed him annoying the hell out of me while I was trying to work. I missed the man I thought I'd gotten to know. The one who opened up to me, and listened when I told him things I never told anyone.

"Leah, come dance with me."

Miguel offered me his hand and I let him lead me down to the throng of clubbers, where he gently pulled me close to him.

It felt kind of nice to be in his arms again. He was comfortable, familiar. And, as always, he had come along at the right moment to save me.

Everything that had happened between us seemed to have been brushed under the carpet. We never mentioned it at all. Not just me cheating on him, but the whole relationship. It was sad that it had to be that way because the time I'd been with him was something I'd never forget. But if pretending we had never happened was what it took for us to have a friendship, I was happy enough with it.

"So, where is he?" Miguel asked.

"Where is who?"

He raised his eyebrows in a *'don't pretend you don't know who I mean'* kind of way.

"Let's not go there."

I hadn't yet recovered from the last mention of Radleigh.

"I thought he'd be here," Miguel pressed on.

"I thought he'd be here too. But he's not."

"He really is a dick."

"You won't hear any arguments from me. I'm looking forward to the day when I won't ever have to see him again."

"Right. Now tell me the truth. I don't doubt that you think he's an idiot. But that's not all you're thinking. You've been looking around for him all night."

I was ready to protest but the only thing that came out of my mouth was a tiny squeak, followed by a lone tear sliding down my cheek.

"I'm sorry," he said. "I'll shut up now."

"I'm sorry too." I rested my head on his shoulder and tried to stop the flow of tears that had been threatening to fall all evening. "Apparently I'm over-emotional tonight."

"Well maybe if you were honest about what's upsetting you, it might be easier."

"I thought he'd be here. For one last petty argument if nothing else."

Miguel leaned away from me a little, forcing me to look at him. "Leah, what really happened between you two in Florida?"

"Nothing," I told him. "He didn't lay a finger on me. I mean, apart from the hug that ended up in all the papers."

He shook his head. "I don't mean physically. Something was different when you got back. I saw you and Radleigh together when you came in to work the day you got home. You looked at each other differently. And-" he began, then stopped.

"What?"

"I don't think… I don't think you slept with him just because you were drunk."

My heart stilled because we'd never talked about this.

"Miguel, I didn't…I… when I was with you, you were what I wanted. I don't want you to think I wanted to be with him when I was with you."

He smiled, a little sadly. "I know. But thank you for saying that. Leah, do you love Radleigh?"

My stomach dropped at his question.

"Is it possible to fall in love with someone you used to hate? Someone who challenges you to the point of rage, and then puts your head in a spin by showing a side of himself he maybe doesn't show anyone else?"

Miguel nodded.

"Then yes. I love him."

If my confirmation hurt Miguel, he didn't let it show. Instead, he gently placed his hand on my cheek and brushed away my tears with his thumb. "Go find him, angel."

At his use of the nickname he gave me, I hugged him tightly, so grateful to have his support.

"I'm scared, Miguel."

"I know you are, but you can't leave without seeing him. You have to go."

He took my shaking hands in his and I said, "Thank you."

"I just want you to be happy. Now go and talk to him before I change my mind and tell you it's a bad idea."

With a small laugh, I kissed him on the cheek. "You're amazing."

"Right back at ya. Want me to come with you to find a cab?"

Ishook my head. "No thanks, I'll be fine. Will I see you in the morning before I go?"

"Yeah, what time do you have to leave?"

"I have to be at the airport for nine-thirty. I'm meeting Will, Freya and Bree in the hotel lobby at eight thirty."

"I'll be there."

I gave him one final hug before darting through the crowds to grab my bag then made my way out of the club without a word to anyone.

All the way back to the hotel, my stomach churned.

What will I say to him? What if he asks me to stay? What if he doesn't? What if he won't even talk to me?

I almost told the taxi driver to turn around and take me back to the club. I didn't have the slightest idea what my opening line would be when I saw Radleigh.

After paying the cabbie I stepped nervously out of the cab and made my way inside. I decided to check the bar before going to his room. It was a good thing I did too, because that's precisely where he was. He was sitting on a stool at the bar, a bottle of beer in his hand.

Wearing the blue shirt. The one he wore to the wedding.

Great minds, indeed.

My heart stopped as a woman sidled over to him and sat at the stool next to his. He looked up at her as she began to make her play for him, but much to my amazement, he glared at her and said something which clearly caused offence. She scurried back to her friends looking completely mortified.

I didn't much fancy being rejected the same way.

Oh, come on. What have you got left to lose at this point?

Steadying myself I walked into the bar, head held high to convey a confidence I wasn't feeling.

"Drowning your sorrows?"

Radleigh looked up from his beer bottle, his face set as if he were about to rip someone's head off. When he saw me his expression didn't change much.

"Aren't you supposed to be at your leaving party?" he sneered.

He was clearly drunk but I took a seat beside him anyway. "Aren't *you* supposed to be at my leaving party?"

"Why would I be there?"

"A decent night out? Hundreds of scantily clad women for you to get your claws into?"

"What do you want?"

"I have no idea," I answered. "I don't know what possessed me to leave my own party where I was having fun to come all the way back here to find you drunk in a bar."

"You wanted to see me?" he asked, the first glimmer of something more positive in his voice.

I nodded. "I guess I did."

The air seemed to crackle around us, and he reached forwards to rest his hand on my thigh. Warmth spread through me at his touch, along with a tingle of pleasure. He had made only the tiniest movement but it made everything slide out of focus.

Everything except him.

"Why did you want to see me?"

"Would you really have let me go without saying goodbye?" I asked softly. "Because that's all I wanted. To say goodbye."

Our eyes connected in a silent conversation, an understanding.

"Excuse me, Miss," I heard a voice say. "Can I get you a drink?"

Without taking my eyes off him I said, "Do I want a drink, Radleigh?"

He shook his head, and in one fluid movement the two of us stood up and headed for his room.

Chapter 20
This Is It

I didn't even have time to breathe.

The second we got into Radleigh's room he slammed me up against the door, crushing his mouth against mine.

He smelled incredible. The strange combination of beer and the scent of his aftershave made me a little lightheaded and I wrapped my arms around his neck, drawing him in closer as his hands moved from my waist to unzip my dress and slide it down over my shoulders.

I unbuttoned his shirt and let it drop to the floor, my hands gripping his back. He let out a low growl and lifted me up, kissing me hard as his hands began to slide underneath my dress. He carried me over to his bed and we fell on to it. I didn't care that for a moment he was crushing me, I couldn't breathe anyway.

A soft moan escaped my lips as he pushed my dress up, his fingers digging into my hips as his tongue danced with mine.

A thousand emotions ran through me at once, from fear to excitement, but none of it compared to how much I wanted him. I couldn't think about what had happened before — all that mattered was the moment we were caught up in, my hands clawing at his back and his kisses on my neck.

I loved the feeling of his muscles beneath my fingertips, tracing his tattooed arms with my tongue, the tautness of his stomach.

He was perfect.

Tell him. Tell him now.

My words were lost as his hand slipped inside my knickers. I raised my hips a little, willing him to go further but he remained in control causing me to let out another moan, this time of frustration.

I raked my hands through his hair as his lips found their way to the swell of my breast, but before I even had the chance to enjoy the sensation his weight lifted off of me and he rolled away, sitting on the edge of the bed, his head down.

Not entirely sure what just happened, I didn't move for a moment. I hadn't been ready to stop and I certainly hadn't expected him to. When he made no move to come back I sat up, my head still spinning.

"Radleigh?"

"You have to go."

Surely I'd misheard him.

I shuffled across the bed, pulling my dress up. "What?"

"You have to go," he repeated.

"Why? I thought... I mean..."

I actually had no idea what I meant. Less than a minute ago, we'd been about to engage in some wild, frantic sex, and then everything stopped.

"What?" he asked, his blue eyes looking at me coldly. "What did you think?"

Resisting the strong urge to pull him back on top of me so I could show him, I said, "Why don't you tell me what *you're* thinking?"

"I just want you to go. Get out of my room and go back to your party."

I refused to move, still reeling. With the strength of my feelings for him and the emotion of knowing I was leaving in the morning, being rejected by him – again – caused angry tears to spring to my eyes.

"What is this? Your final attempt to drive me crazy? You couldn't have asked me to leave you alone when we were in the bar instead of bringing me up here and-" I stopped abruptly, my words sticking in my throat.

"You said you wanted to say goodbye. What did you think would happen?"

"I didn't have a thought in my head, actually. I just wanted to see you."

"Now you have. So you can go."

I stood up to straighten my clothes but he didn't even look at me. He kept his back turned and stared straight ahead at the wall as if I wasn't even there.

Without another word I left his room, pausing for a second to glance back at him, willing him to turn around and say something. When he didn't move I closed the door and went to my room.

The night was long and sleepless. My head ached and my eyes were sore and puffy.

And it was time to go home.

Freya greeted me with the usual strong cup of coffee, which I really needed having only managed one measly hour of sleep. All night I kept seeing Radleigh's face when he told me to leave. The coldness.

Freya perched herself on the edge of my bed. "What happened with McCoy last night?"

I didn't look up from my coffee cup because I didn't want to discuss it, and I especially didn't need a lecture. Things were hard enough already.

"We were worried about you," Freya went on. "Miguel said you'd gone back to the hotel. I wanted to come back to be with you, but... he told me you'd gone to find Radleigh."

I would have been angry with Miguel for confessing my secret but he'd done me a favour. If Freya had come to the hotel to find me I would have been in no mood to talk to her.

I nodded. "I did."

"Why?"

"I needed to see him," I said, my voice quivering already.

"Oh, Leah." She moved closer to me to put her arm around my shoulders. "What did he do now?"

"It doesn't matter. I'm going home today, so it just doesn't matter."

"So why are you crying?"

I let my head flop on to her shoulder, too tired and broken to stop the tears. "I'm such an idiot. I thought… I thought he'd be happy to see me."

"And he wasn't?"

Cringing at my patheticness, I confessed what had happened in Radleigh's room. Freya listened carefully while I told her he'd thrown me out after things got heavy between us.

"How could he do that to you?"

"I don't know. It was so humiliating."

Maybe he never intended to sleep with me at all. Maybe he meant to make me feel the way I did.

Stupid, unwanted and desperate.

"Why should you be humiliated, honey? He was the one who started it. You didn't throw yourself at him."

"That doesn't change how completely embarrassing it is to be kicked out of a room by someone you…" I trailed off again. "Being rejected by Radleigh McCoy has to be the ultimate slap in the face. He never turns anyone down."

"Did you want something to happen between you?"

"As soon as I saw him I did. But that isn't why I went to see him. It wasn't about sex."

She didn't answer and I looked up, seeing the realisation hit her. Her mouth dropped open.

"You love him, don't you?"

I nodded. "How stupid can you get?"

"It's not stupid. You can't help how you feel."

A look of sadness crossed her face, forcing me out of my own self-pity.

"I guess you know how that goes."

"Yep." She sighed. "I do."

It wasn't the same, not when Will loved her too. I was done revealing the truths of their relationship though. They had to do some of the work on their own.

"Can you at least tell me it gets easier?" I asked, hopefully.

She shook her head. "I wish I could. It's not always unbearable but it's never easy."

I made a face. "Well, you're a great help."

The two of us began to giggle.

"Leah, what will I do without you?"

"You'll be fine," I told her. "You'll still have all your friends around you. I'll be at home on my own."

"Then don't go. Stay here."

I shook my head. "I won't find another job as good as the one I had, and even if I did, it wouldn't be the same as working with you every day. I need to go home. Besides, with the way things are with Radleigh, I just want to be as far away from here as I can."

Freya nodded. "I understand. I do. I just wish things were different."

"Me too."

An hour later my bags were packed and it was time to say a final goodbye to my friends. Both Freya and I were trying to hold it together as we stepped into the lobby to meet Will, Bree, Jesse and Miguel. We both failed.

The tiredness, the grief at having to leave them all behind seeped into every part of me, and I still couldn't stop myself sweeping my eyes around the room for Radleigh.

Will was the first of my friends to wish me good luck, and make me swear to keep in touch. I assured him he wouldn't get rid of me just because I wasn't in the same country as him anymore. There was still unfinished business regarding him and Freya. Even if I wasn't right there to guide them, I hadn't finished hoping they'd figure things out.

Bree was next. She gave me the tightest hug I'd ever received. "I'm going to miss you so much."

"I'll miss you too," I told her, trying to control my tears. "I can't believe I won't be able to steal clothes from you anymore."

She laughed through her own tears. "I'll come and visit and we can swap. I hear the shopping in London is great!"

I nodded, and laughed. "Yeah, it is."

"Then we have something to look forward to," she said, in her usual sunny way. "I'm going to call you every day to make sure you don't forget!"

Smiling, I wiped a tear from her cheek. "That *is* something to look forward to."

Jesse was waiting patiently for his turn to say goodbye, and my heart broke a little more as I looked into his eyes.

"Don't you look at me like that," I said. "You have a whole lifetime to make girls cry, don't start with me!"

He managed to flash me his familiar, laddish grin even though he was visibly upset. He wrapped his arms around me. "I don't think it's very cool for me to cry so I'll try not to. But you were my first real friend on the team. And you helped me so many times, with so many things. Thank you."

"Ha, you better remember that when you're super rich and even more famous!"

"I will. My mom always tells me I should remember everyone who helps me on my way up. I don't usually listen to her, but she happens to be right about this."

I hugged him tighter, overwhelmed by how much I felt for this young man who I'd struck up an unexpected friendship with.

"Stay in touch, okay?"

"You can count on it, kiddo."

Finally, it was Freya's turn. She was crying even more than me, but seeing her so upset made me break down further.

Freya had been the closest thing I'd ever had to a sister, and to leave her was like leaving behind a part of myself.

"Is it worth me begging you to stay one more time?" she asked, pulling me into a hug.

"It never hurts to try," I told her. "But you know I can't."

"I know. I just don't want you to go."

"I wish I didn't have to. But it'll be okay. We'll talk every day. I won't give you a chance to miss me!"

She laughed. "I'll miss you as soon as you've gone."

"I'll miss you too. So much."

"Call me when you get home?"

"I will."

We hugged once more and finally I turned to Miguel.

If I'd thought saying goodbye to Freya was hard, Miguel was going to be even worse.

He seemed to read my mind and he smiled. "Don't worry, we can delay this for a little longer."

"We can?"

"Yeah. I'm coming to the airport with you."

My eyes widened. "Really?"

"Really. We drew straws to see who would have to put up with you while you waited for your plane and, well, I drew the short straw."

I punched him playfully but gave him a grateful smile and he said, "You ready?"

"I guess so.

I gave everyone one last hug, then Miguel picked up my bags and we left the hotel and got into a cab.

'This is it,' I thought as the door closed and we began to drive away from the hotel. *'Now I begin my journey home.'*

There was a solid knot of gloom in my stomach as I thought, not only about the friends I was leaving behind, but about Radleigh.

As I broke into tears again, Miguel wrapped his arm around my shoulders and let me cry.

My flight wasn't due to leave for two and a half hours, and I was severely dehydrated and exhausted from crying so much so Miguel took me into one of the airport cafés and supplied me with what looked like a bucket of coffee.

I barely had the energy to lift the cup.

Across the table, Miguel watched me but didn't say a word, until I got tired of him looking at me. "What?"

"What happened last night?"

"Well," I began with a sigh, "let's just say Radleigh made it clear he didn't want me."

"He really said that?"

Again, Radleigh's icy expression filled my mind, making me ache.

"Please," I begged softly, "don't make me talk about it."

He reached over and held my hand. "I'm sorry, Leah."

"It's my own fault. I should have taken the hint when he didn't show up at the party. I never should have gone to see him. It made things worse. And that's saying something. I didn't think things could *get* worse."

"The fact that he turned you away proves what a complete loser he is. He doesn't deserve you. He never did. He never will."

I looked up at him, his beautiful brown eyes completely genuine. I squeezed his hand. "Miguel, I'm so sorry. I don't know how you can even stand to look at me after what I did to you."

"It's simple. What we had was important to me. You're important to me. If I held a grudge I wouldn't get to have you in my life at all."

As I squeezed my eyes shut against the pain, the kindness of Miguel's words washed over me and the emotion was too much. Moving my coffee cup aside, I rested my head on the table as a huge out-pouring of grief and regret came flooding out of me.

I heard him move and felt him as he wrapped his arms around me again, holding me tightly, gently stroking my hair with one hand.

Chapter 21
Mullets and Shell Suits

My journey home was long and exhausting. My mum and dad greeted me just after one a.m on Monday morning at Newquay airport. Even though I'd slept a lot on the journey from Los Angeles to London, I still felt tired.

My parents were thrilled to see me, but my enthusiasm was stilted to say the least. On the plane, whenever I hadn't been asleep, I'd been crying. Physically I was in England but my mind and my heart were still very much in America.

Arriving back in my parents' house and going back to my old room filled me with a mixture of comfort and sadness. I loved the familiarity of it, the way the rooms smelled, and how everything looked the same as when I left.

Bur they weren't my surroundings. Not anymore.

I didn't wake up until well past noon on Monday afternoon. As far as my body was concerned, it was still early morning so I didn't feel like I'd woken up at the wrong time. Even so, when I traipsed down to the kitchen in my dressing gown at two-thirty, my mum looked a little amused.

"Hi," I said, rubbing my eyes.

"Good afternoon. Can I get you anything?"

I shook my head. "It's okay, I can manage."

She sat at the kitchen table with a cup of tea, reading one of those women's magazines full of quizzes and depressing real life stories. I felt like I'd been teleported back to my teenage years.

As I put the kettle on and popped some bread into the toaster, Mum said, "How are you?"

"I'm okay." I turned to her. "A little tired."

She looked at me closely, the way mothers do when they're trying to decide if their child is telling the truth.

"Leah," she began, "you still haven't told us why you left America. If you want to talk-"

"I don't," I interrupted. "I'm fine. I'll just need a bit of time to settle in."

"But something did happen?"

"Mum, I really don't want to talk about it. At least not yet. I want to put it out of my mind for a while."

Turning away from her so I could make my breakfast, I realised moving back with my parents was going to be every bit as hard as I'd thought.

Once breakfast was over and I'd showered and dressed, I called Freya, as promised. Hearing her voice brightened my mood and I had an inkling I'd need to call her a lot over the coming weeks in order to retain my sanity. I hoped it was just the enormous change of scenery that was making me so miserable, and it would all settle down soon, but at that moment I couldn't imagine not feeling the emptiness inside me.

Freya and I chatted for half an hour, by which time some of my grogginess had lifted, so I decided I should start unpacking some of the boxes that were taking up valuable floor space.

With a sigh, I lifted the first box on to the bed and began emptying its contents. It was full of clothes. Clothes I would probably never even wear again. Exactly where in Cornwall would I go to wear the black lacy corset Bree had persuaded me to buy, or the outrageous short pleated skirt Freya thought would look cute on me? Sure, there were clubs in Cornwall, but I didn't have anyone to go out with anymore.

Never mind. At least you'll be the trendiest person in town.

That wasn't saying much. There were still people sporting mullets and wearing shell suits in Zellor.

249

I hadn't realised how many clothes I owned. It didn't seem as many when I'd packed but as I hung them up in my wardrobe I ran out of hangers.

"Unbelievable."

I dumped a pile of t-shirts back into the box they came out of, making a note to myself to buy some more clothes hangers when I went into town.

God, what a change. A week ago, shopping meant Rodeo Drive. Now it means picking up hangers in an everything-for-a-pound shop.

The next box I came across was the one I'd least looked forward to opening. When I'd packed, I'd been too angry and frustrated to appreciate everything it held. I'd thrown everything in, hating every item that had a memory attached.

It was the box in which I'd packed everything that was special to me. Inside were masses of photos I'd taken in places I'd visited with work, of my friends, of nights out. I flipped through one of the albums, needing to see Freya, Will and Bree.

It wasn't only the four of us, though. There were many photos that had been taken the first time we'd gone clubbing, the infamous night when I made my debut as a pole dancer and had my first kiss with Miguel. There were several photos of him, a couple of the two of us together and numerous pictures of soccer players freaking out on the dance floor.

There didn't appear to be a single photo of Radleigh, though. If I hadn't been so suddenly desperate to get a look at him I'd have laughed. How much had I despised him back then that I didn't even take one picture of him? I even had a photo of Taylor. But not one tiny glimpse of Radleigh.

I knew there was a simple way to fix my problem. Josh and Christina. When we went to the aquarium, a lot of photos had been taken I hadn't seen yet. Also, Jamie's bedroom was full of Westberg merchandise so if I ever got completely overcome with the need to see Radleigh, I could always go there.

Groaning at my own lameness I slumped onto my bed, the memory of him still too painful to dwell on.

The one thing Josh knew I'd missed about England was a traditional English breakfast, so he suggested taking me out for my long awaited greasy fry-up the next morning. I intended to spend the whole day with him, Christina and Grace, even if it was just hanging out at their house. I was dying to see Jamie, and I couldn't stand another second cooped up in my room to avoid my mother's worried glances.

I met up with my brother, sister-in-law and niece at ten-thirty on Tuesday morning, in the same café my mum used to take us to when we were younger. It was our "local" for want of a better term.

After all of the formalities of hugging and ordering our food we sat at a table by the window with our cups of coffee. I waited as the inevitable topic of conversation lurked in the background. I was certainly not going to be the first to mention Radleigh, and Josh knew me well enough to know that so it was no big surprise when he approached the subject first.

"So," he began, "now we're away from Mum and Dad, do you want to tell us what's going on?"

I sighed. "Not really. But I guess I ought to tell someone instead of stewing in my own misery."

"What happened?" Christina asked. "All you said was that people were talking about you and Radleigh because of some photos. You're not the type of person who is bothered by that kind of thing usually."

251

"How about when you realise you're in love with the guy you're being linked to, only to find out he's not interested?" I played with a sachet of sugar so I wouldn't have to look at them.

"Okay," Josh said. "Start from the beginning."

With another sigh, I explained to them what had happened with the photographs and how, on confronting Radleigh, he'd made it plain he didn't want a relationship with me. I told them how he had reacted badly to the news I was leaving, and finally most, but not all, of the events of Saturday night.

When I'd finished, I started to realise how stupid it sounded. Who runs away from a job because of one rejection, from one guy?

He wasn't one guy. He was THE guy. The guy who made you feel things you haven't felt in years, and more than that, who made you feel things you hadn't ever felt before.

The knot in my stomach tightened but I was starting to get used to it. I barely even flinched.

"Leah, are you sure you aren't getting your wires crossed?" Josh asked. "Because he seemed genuine to me. And when I say genuine I mean it seemed like he was interested."

Christina rolled her eyes and I knew why. She had a few important pieces of information Josh didn't have. One being that Radleigh was unable to keep it in his trousers for longer than five minutes, and the other being that I slept with him.

"Well," she said, "all men seem genuine when they want something."

"What's that supposed to mean?"

"It means he thought by being nice to me he could get me into bed," I answered, dryly.

Christina looked at me closely for a minute. "Leah, come on. Think about this for a second. You can spot men who are just trying their luck a mile away. I don't believe for a second you were wrong about him."

"I've been wrong before. If he felt anything at all for me he wouldn't have treated me the way he did. He didn't even... he didn't even say goodbye."

Across the table, Josh put his hand over mine. "If I'd known what an idiot he'd turn out to be, I'd never have let him spend so much time with us. I'm sorry."

"Not your fault. I always knew he was an idiot. Just my type, huh?"

"You certainly know how to pick 'em."

Josh and Christina were both looking at me with concern and I said, "Please quit staring at me. I get enough of that at home."

"Sorry," Josh said, again. "But I've seen that look on your face before. It's your *'I want to die but I'm pretending everything's okay'* look."

"There's no fooling you, is there?"

"No. So don't even try. I've seen you go through something like this before and I don't want-"

"Josh," I interrupted. "It's not the same as with Luke. I was young and stupid back then. This is different. Well. I'm still stupid."

"You're not stupid, and don't pretend you don't care as much about McCoy as you did about Luke. It's not so different – except McCoy at least managed to treat you with a little bit of respect."

If he knew the full details of what had happened on Saturday night he would have retracted that statement.

I ran my hand through my hair, trying to keep control of my wavering emotions. It seemed the more I tried to make sense of my relationship with Radleigh, the more confused I became.

"I'll be okay. I'm far away from him now and I don't have to deal with him, or with people talking about me behind my back. I want to move on."

"Okay. But can you promise me you won't pretend everything's fine if it isn't? I don't want you to bottle everything up. I'm worried about you."

"Josh, please. I'm a big girl now. I'm fine."

"I'm sorry. I will stop being so big brother-ish now. Let's just have breakfast and talk about something else."

Thankfully, that was what we did. After breakfast we went to Josh and Christina's new house. It was beautiful with its four large bedrooms, the most enormous kitchen I'd ever set foot in and a huge back garden for the kids to play in, complete with swings and a slide.

We spent the rest of the day catching up and for the first time in weeks I relaxed. When Christina asked me to stay for the night I jumped at the offer. Anything to put off going home for a bit longer. It felt claustrophobic at my house with my mum's eyes constantly following me around. I was close to my parents but they never understood my desperate desire to get as far away from Cornwall as possible. They'd both lived there all their lives and believed everyone else should do the same.

When Josh brought Jamie home from school, my nephew launched himself at me and hugged me tightly.

"Hello, sweetheart."

"Auntie Leah! You're really home!"

"I am," I laughed. "How are you?"

"I'm okay. School was boring!"

"Have you got any homework?"

"Nope. I don't have homework on Tuesdays so I'm allowed to watch football now."

I looked over the top of Jamie's head at Josh, who said, "I have to record it for him because he can't stay up to watch it."

Of course, international football *would* be on at unsociable hours.

"Auntie Leah," Jamie said. "Will you watch it with me?"

I gave Josh a panicked look. I didn't want to disappoint Jamie but I wasn't ready to see the people I'd only just left behind. It was far too soon.

"You'll have to watch on your own for a while, buddy," Josh answered. "Auntie Leah is sleeping here tonight so I have to take her home to grab some clean clothes for tomorrow."

Jamie was so thrilled by the prospect of me staying over, he wasn't too disappointed about me missing the game.

As soon as he'd settled in front of the television, Josh drove me home. I let him deal with mum and dad while I threw some clean clothes into a bag. I knew he wanted to tell them to back off and give me some space, and rather than be in the room while he did it, I decided to keep out of the way. Whatever he said worked because when I went into say goodbye to them, they smiled which was a welcome change from the looks of concern I'd been getting since my return.

Back at Josh and Christina's I managed to avoid watching the match by helping Christina with both the cooking and the washing up, then giving Grace a bath and putting her to bed. After watching TV for a while with Jamie curled up on my lap, it was finally time to put him to bed, too.

Jamie's bedroom was like a shrine to the Warriors and it was entirely my fault because I'd sent most of the stuff to him. Posters of the players adorned the walls, and his duvet, curtains, and lampshade were emblazoned with the Westberg logo.

"Wow." I looked around in amusement.

"Do you like it?" Jamie asked enthusiastically.

"It's… interesting."

Jamie smiled and dived into his bed, wrapping himself in his duvet in much the same way I was partial to doing.

I tucked him in then sat down beside him. I was about to say goodnight when a photograph beside Jamie's bed caught my attention.

I lifted the frame to look more closely. It was a photo of me, Radleigh and Jamie at the Aquarium. I remembered the exact moment it had been taken. It was right before we left, and Josh insisted we had our photo taken together. I'd grumbled but Radleigh had put his arm around me, and with Jamie in front of us, we'd been snapped.

The photo turned out great, unlike my relationship with Radleigh. It was a happy picture, we were laughing and the emotion shone through.

Tears prickled my eyes as I let my gaze linger on Radleigh's face.

God, when will this endless weeping be over?

"Mummy said I could keep this photo by my bed because you and Radleigh McCoy are my favourite people in the whole world."

Quickly wiping the tears from my eyes, I placed the photo back on the bedside table and smiled at my nephew. "I'm one of your favourite people, huh?"

Jamie nodded, looking at me seriously. "Mummy said I mustn't talk to you about him because he's not your friend anymore."

"Oh, Jamie, you can talk about him. It's okay."

I appreciated that Christina had been trying to ease any potential awkwardness but I didn't want Jamie to have to quell his soccer enthusiasm on my account.

"I don't want to make you upset," Jamie said.

"Don't worry about me. If I feel upset, it isn't your fault."

"Did Radleigh McCoy make you sad?"

"A little bit."

"Please don't cry, Auntie Leah." Jamie unravelled himself from his duvet and sat up to give me a hug. "If you don't want me to like him anymore, I won't."

The thoughtfulness of this little boy was overwhelming.

"You don't have to stop liking him. I still like him."

"Do you?"

I nodded. "Just because we're not friends anymore, doesn't mean I don't like him. And it certainly doesn't mean you should stop liking him."

"I like you the most, Auntie Leah, don't worry."

With a soft laugh I said, "I'm glad to hear it. Now, it's time you were asleep, young man!"

"Okay," Jamie agreed reluctantly.

He got back into bed and I kissed him on the cheek.

"Goodnight, J."

"Night night. I love you."

"I love you too."

I stood up and turned out his bedroom light, lingering a moment to watch as he turned over and closed his eyes. If one thing was going to make being at home worthwhile, it was watching how incredible Jamie was turning out to be. Eight years old and already he was more thoughtful than most fully grown men I'd ever met. How many children would offer to give up on their hero to make their aunt happy?

The memories of what I'd left behind crippled me, but at least with my family around me, I wouldn't have to deal with it alone.

Chapter 22
Don't Make This Difficult

"Leah, you have to come! Please?"

Those were some of the final words Freya said to me during the last phone conversation we'd had. I'd been back in England for five long uneventful weeks and in another three, Freya, Will, Jesse and Miguel were amongst the people coming over for the Westberg Warriors tour. It seemed like years since I'd seen them and passing up the chance to spend time with them wasn't something I'd ever imagined doing. However, Radleigh's inclusion on the tour was a factor I couldn't ignore. When Freya asked me to meet up with them in London, I'd been a little vague about my answer. She understood my reluctance, but throwing this opportunity away because of what happened with Radleigh seemed insane to her. I didn't have a good reason not to go. Josh was taking Jamie to one of the matches as promised, so I wouldn't even have difficulty getting there.

The real problem was facing Radleigh.

I wouldn't be able to avoid him. Bree had already told me to start finding good places to party in London, and I knew what that meant. It wouldn't only be my close friends, it would be everyone on the tour going out with us. On the one hand, a decent night out was exactly what I needed. On the other, an evening spent being ignored by the man I (still) loved was exactly what I didn't need.

Thinking about it gave me a headache. I needed to talk to someone.

After mulling things over for three straight hours while pretending to watch television with my parents, I decided to get an early night then talk to Christina the next morning.

"Do you really not want to see him?" Christina asked once I'd explained things to her.

The two of us sat in her conservatory, heavy rain pounding down on the glass roof. On the floor between us, Grace played contentedly with her toys as I stared out at the torrents of rain pouring from the sky.

"I really don't want to see him."

"Why not? Maybe a bit of closure will be good for you."

"Closure," I repeated. "Sure. But it won't happen. All that will happen is we'll exchange random glances but neither of us will actually say anything because there's nothing left to say."

"No? Leah, are you telling me there is nothing at all you want to say to him?"

"Like what?"

"You tell me. There's no point pretending you don't think about him, though. There must be *something* you want to say to him."

I missed you. I hate you. Why didn't you call? Did you even notice I left?

"I think about him but that doesn't matter," I said. "I'm not going to feed his ego by telling him I missed him. What would be the point when he made his feelings crystal clear before I left? Seeing him would bring it all back again and I don't know if I can stand it. I wish he wasn't coming at all, then everything would so much easier,"

With a small laugh Christina said, "Okay. Imagine Freya calls you back and tells you he isn't coming after all."

I actually clutched my stomach at the very scary prospect that he *wouldn't* be there. I looked up at Christina in surprise. She gave me a knowing smile. "You want to see him."

I closed my eyes. "I guess I do."

✳✳✳✳

Josh, Jamie and I drove up to London the day before the match. As an extra bribe to make sure I didn't back out, Josh bought us tickets to see *We Will Rock You* in the West End on Sunday night.

What can I say, I'm a Queen fan.

We decided to make the weekend a huge event. Theatre on Sunday, football on Monday.

In spite of my doubts, I was excited to be going, not only to see my friends, but to be back to London. The city gave me a real buzz and although I wouldn't have time to see much of it, knowing I was breaking free from the boredom of home was enough.

It was a six hour drive from Cornwall to London, so we set off early. I wasn't sure Jamie had slept the night before because he was so keyed up. In the car, he took his Nintendo DS to keep him quiet but he barely played with it. The three of us chatted and had a singalong to Josh's favourite Queen CD to put us in the mood for the show.

We arrived in London a little after one that afternoon. Our hotel was right in the heart of the city, and frighteningly expensive, too. It was the same hotel my friends would be staying in, which explained the price.

After we checked in and had lunch I went up to my room to relax for a while. As always, my mind drifted to Radleigh. In the three weeks I'd had to psych myself up, ready for the prospect of seeing him, I'd fluctuated between freaking out and wanting to see him. On some levels I couldn't wait to be in a room with him again, to see his face, to hear his voice. But I was terrified, too. I had no idea how he would react to me, and thinking about it made me feel sick.

Going to the theatre on Sunday night was a great distraction from the nerves. Jamie and I were still singing the songs in the cab back to the hotel. After one quick drink in the hotel bar, we decided to call it a night, and exhausted as I had been from the journey and the worrying, I fell asleep as soon as my head hit the pillow.

The following morning – despite how worn out I'd been the night before – I awoke exceptionally early. The nerves and anticipation of seeing my friends overwhelmed me. I couldn't keep still.

I knew Jamie would be equally as feverish, and would have woken Josh up at the ass crack of dawn so I showered, changed and headed down to meet them for breakfast.

True to my suspicions, when I arrived in the hotel restaurant my nephew was bouncing up and down in his seat as my brother tried to make him calm down and eat his Coco Pops.

"Morning." I slipped into my seat and helped myself to a cup of tea and a slice of toast.

"Hello." Josh smiled. "Looking forward to today?"

I contemplated my answer momentarily. Obviously, I was dying to see Freya, Will and the others. However Radleigh was at the forefront of my mind and I didn't know what to expect from him.

"Yeah, I am," I replied, before looking at Jamie and breaking into a grin. "I can see someone else is, too."

"Tell me about it. He's been up since five-thirty!"

"I don't want us to miss anything," Jamie said. "What if there's traffic on the way that makes us late?"

Freya and Will had promised we could take Jamie on a tour of the stadium and meet some more of the team. It was a generous offer but it had led to Jamie being even more hyped up than usual, which was fine for me because I didn't have to share a room with him. For Josh, it was like being caged up with a kangaroo with ADD.

"J, chill. Everything will be fine."

Thankfully, the day went smoothly and we arrived at the stadium at ten minutes to two. The ten minute wait seemed like a lifetime. I couldn't stop glancing at my watch every five seconds. The time moved so slowly I could have sworn it was going backwards.

Finally, the sound of Big Ben in the distance announced it was two o'clock and Freya and Will pulled up in a cab, dead on time, and clambered out to greet us.

"Freya!" I exclaimed, running down the steps and flinging myself into her arms. "It's so good to see you!"

"It's good to see you too!"

After embracing Freya once more, I turned to Will.

"I've missed you both so much," I said.

"We've missed you too," Will said. "Work isn't the same without you around. It's too quiet for starters."

We laughed, relishing being reunited again, and then I turned to introduce my friends to Jamie and Josh before we headed into the stadium, where Will and Freya signed in as Westberg employees. Josh, Jamie and I were presented with visitors passes. It felt a little odd for me to be entering as a visitor and not a worker, although I was pleased I wouldn't have the usual pre-match stress heaped on me when someone injured themselves at the last minute.

Once inside, Bree immediately descended on me, screaming my name.

"I can't believe you're really here!" she squealed.

I laughed. "Me neither, but I couldn't keep away!"

"I missed you so, so, so, so much!"

It was easy to fit back in with everyone, and after introducing Josh and Jamie to Bree and chatting for a while, it was as if I'd never been away. Jamie gazed at both Freya and Bree in turn, an adoring look on his face. He'd barely said a word since we'd met up with them, suddenly shy. He stayed close beside me, holding on to my hand.

"Where's Jesse?" I asked. "Is he late?"

"Oh!" Freya said. "I meant to call you but I was so busy yesterday, I completely forgot. Jesse took a fall during training and hurt his back. He'll be okay, but he was in too much pain to make the trip."

"Aw, I was looking forward to seeing him and legally buying him a beer!"

"He was looking forward to seeing you too."

"I'll give him a call in a few days and check how he's doing."

I jumped as something tickled my cheek and as I turned, I grinned, seeing Miguel's head peering over my shoulder. He'd crept up on me while I'd been talking.

"Hello, angel." He kissed me on the cheek. "How are you?"

"Better now I've seen you!"

"You look great, Leah. Really great."

I'd missed Miguel as much as I'd missed Freya. I'd missed those big brown eyes, and the wild hair, not to mention the warmth of his hugs and the soothing sound of his voice.

"Thanks, but I look like hell."

"You never look like hell, and I know you'll have made sure you looked perfect before coming here so quit being so hard on yourself."

I laughed because he was right. In the car, I'd checked my make-up and reapplied my lip gloss. Perfect was a bit of a stretch, though.

I hugged him again but our embrace was cut short as Jamie let out a yelp of excitement.

"Radleigh!"

Jamie let go of my hand and as I turned, my eyes were greeted with the sight of a surprised looking McCoy. Jamie flew at him and Radleigh recovered from the shock enough to smile at my nephew and lift him into the air.

"Hey, Jamie," he laughed. "How are you doing?"

Jamie hugged Radleigh. "I'm fine. Daddy and Auntie Leah brought me here and Auntie Leah's friend let us in early to meet everyone!"

The whole place seemed to stand still as Radleigh and I surveyed each other.

When you don't see someone for a while, sometimes the image of them changes in your mind. Maybe they get thinner, or the details of their face begin to fade. Not with Radleigh. Everything from the way his t-shirts clung to his muscles, to the colour of his eyes and the shape of his lips had never left my mind.

Taking a deep breath, I surprised everyone, including myself, by approaching him. If I had to speak to him, I may as well get it over with.

"Leah," he said with an uncertain smile. "I didn't know you were coming."

"There's a reason for that."

"You didn't want to see me?"

"Not particularly. I came to see Freya."

"And Miguel, by the looks of it." His tone was somewhere between teasing and mild discontent.

"I came to see my *friends*," I told him, emphasising the last word.

As his ice blue eyes gazed at me, he examined my face, like he was searching for a sign I'd missed him. I tried to keep my expression neutral. It wasn't easy with him looking at me that way.

"Leah, can we go somewhere to can talk?"

My heart leapt into my throat but I was very aware there were at least six people staring at us, so I needed to either accept his offer or quickly decline so as not to prolong the moment any longer.

The problem was, I didn't know what I wanted to do.

264

"I don't know. I've only just got here and-"

"Please?"

It was a simple plea. But that was exactly what it was. A plea.

I looked down at Jamie. "J, can you tell your dad I need to talk to Radleigh for a while? I won't be long."

Jamie swivelled his eyes from me to Radleigh with a serious expression. "You're not going to argue, are you?"

Perceptive kid.

"No," I told him. "We're not going to argue."

I couldn't be sure, but I'd have said anything to put his mind at rest.

Jamie turned to Radleigh. "Please don't make Auntie Leah cry. I don't like it when she cries."

I wasn't sure whether to hug him or throttle him. He'd spoken with such innocence, but strongly implied I'd been crying a lot, which was true. I just didn't want Radleigh to know.

Radleigh smiled down at Jamie. "I won't make her cry."

Jamie grinned at him. "Okay."

He bounded back over to Josh and the others.

Once Radleigh and I were away from prying eyes, in another unfamiliar locker room, I said, "What do you want?"

For a moment he looked as confused as I felt, so I sat down on a bench and waited for him to begin. I'd kind of missed the pungent smell of locker rooms. The very distinct aroma of football boots, clean team shirts, sweat and mud was strangely welcoming.

Radleigh's silence allowed me to take in every detail of him. His dark hair, the tattoos peeking out from the sleeves of his shirt, his strong arms that had held me close then pushed me away.

"I'm glad you're here, Leah."

His words released me from the bad memories.

"Why?" I asked.

"Why do you think?"

I shrugged. "Maybe you missed having me around to annoy. Maybe you haven't argued with anyone in a while so you thought you'd try me. Or perhaps you want to have another go at humiliating me. Am I close?"

"I missed you," he said, in a tone I'd never heard from him before.

"Right. Sure you did."

"Don't make this difficult. I'm trying to apologise."

"Well excuse me if I find that hard to believe." I stood up. "Is it any wonder I'm suspicious of you? You drag me in here after speaking to me for thirty seconds, and-"

"Shut up!" he shouted. "Stop talking and listen!"

Taken aback by his outburst, I took a step away from him and sat down again.

While I waited for him to speak, my eyes lingered on his. How could a man who had hurt me so much, who'd embarrassed me and let me down, still be so perfect to me? My mind was torn in two. I couldn't change the part of me that had wanted to talk to him every day since I'd left Los Angeles, but I also couldn't silence the animosity inside me for what he'd done.

"I… I wanted to tell you… I've missed you, Leah. I wasn't prepared to see you today and-"

"Jesus Christ," I muttered. "The fact you needed to 'prepare' to talk to me doesn't exactly fill me with confidence."

"I just don't want to say the wrong thing. This is important."

"What's this about, Radleigh?"

"You know what this is about."

His words were loaded with an unspoken confession. But was it the confession I'd been hoping for, or was this another one of his games where I thought he meant one thing when he meant something else?

"That's just it," I said. "I don't. You're not telling me anything and I'm not in to guessing games."

"I'm trying to tell you I'm sorry."

"You could have said this any time over the last two months, but you didn't."

"Right. Because this is really a conversation we could have had on the phone."

"Why the hell not? You had eight weeks to call and you didn't. If you weren't in the UK and I wasn't here you never would have, would you?"

"I would," he said quietly. "Why are you making this so awkward?"

"How hard did Valdez elbow you in the head? Did you honestly expect me to fall into your arms?"

His eyes shifted towards me and a smile crossed his face. "You've been watching?"

"Yes." I sighed. "Sometimes Jamie makes me. Last week Josh thought I might enjoy seeing you taking a bash to the skull."

"And did you?"

"No. Whenever I see someone smacking you in the head, I just wish I was the one doing it."

Instead of glaring at me, his smile widened. "You watch because you missed me."

"Wrong. Watching is like slow torture. Seeing everyone on television and not being there is horrible and I don't make a habit of it."

"But you missed me," he persisted.

"Don't push me, McCoy."

"Leah, come on." He took a step towards me. "What do I have to do?"

Much to my annoyance the single step he'd taken made me start to shake. It had been a long time since he'd been so close to me. I'd never forgotten how his nearness made me feel, but I was always surprised by the strength of it. Of having him right there, close enough to touch.

And what happened the last time you were alone together?

The second flashback to that night in the hotel forced me to move away from him.

"You can't make up for everything with one apology," I told him. "And you can't expect me to accept it when all you've given me is a half-arsed attempt at an explanation. It's not enough, not by a long way."

"What do you want? You want me to beg for forgiveness?"

"What I want is for you to experience even half of the pain I've been in since I left Los Angeles!"

Before he could respond, I stormed out of his dressing room, my chest aching with grief just as it had the last time I'd seen him.

I could have told him I'd missed him and accepted what he'd said to me. But he didn't deserve to be let off so easily. I meant what I'd said. Maybe it was cruel, but I didn't want to be the only one suffering.

Walking out on him, I knew, was the final nail in the coffin of our 'relationship'. He'd never come after me, he'd already proved that. But any man who was capable of inflicting so much pain on me didn't deserve anything more.

Chapter 23
British and Uncouth

As I frantically sifted through the shopping bags full of clothes I'd bought, Freya said, "It's not in there."

"What isn't?"

"The perfect outfit. The one that will make you confident, and take away the pain of having your heart shredded by a man."

I let out a small laugh. "Damn."

As soon as the Warriors match ended, Freya, Will and I said goodbye to Josh and Jamie and hurried back to the hotel. Just like the old days, I went to Freya's room to get ready but none of the outfits I had seemed like the right one.

Freya came to sit beside me. "I know you don't want to talk about Radleigh, and I understand, but I don't want him to ruin tonight."

"He probably won't even show up so it shouldn't be a problem."

"It doesn't matter whether he shows up or not. He's on your mind."

"I'm trying, Freya. I'm trying."

"I know you are." She took my hand. "I know seeing him today can't have been easy. But we haven't seen you for two months and I want us to have fun."

I nodded. "Me too. And we will. I'm sorry. I'll try to cheer up."

Freya gave me a much needed hug. "You don't need to apologise. I just want us to enjoy the time we have. Besides," she added, "I need to sample the British men. That'll be fun!"

"Yeah, wait until you see the beer-swilling losers we have here."

"British men are hot! Prince William, David Beckham, Daniel Craig. Tell me I'm wrong?"

She wasn't fooling me for a second with her talk of finding a man. The only William she was interested in was the one who still hadn't gotten around to making his move.

"Well, actually," I said, "you're right. At the club I'm taking you to there will be plenty of good looking men. At least, there always used to be. It can't have changed that much."

I was right, it hadn't.

Slinky's was more like an upmarket bar than a nightclub, with a huge dance floor and a karaoke bar upstairs. They didn't play the latest club tunes, they played current chart hits plus a few choice songs from other decades. Music created for dancing. When I lived in London I'd spent many weekends in Slinky's with my friends and we'd had some brilliant nights there. It was perfect because unlike a nightclub, the music didn't take over the entire place. There was a quieter end of the bar for people to socialise, and a noisier end where people could go to let loose. I had every intention of doing both.

I finally settled on the perfect outfit for the evening, a black, sleeveless top, which had a zip running down the left side. Such a daring top might have been asking for trouble, but I decided to risk it anyway. Coupled with the dark blue flared jeans I'd bought that morning, and my favourite pair of strappy heels I thought I looked pretty good.

"Wow, Leah, this place is great!" Will said as we walked through the doors.

It was pretty impressive with its modern décor, complete with a highly polished wooden floor and the world's longest bar, which was already filled with people.

"What do you guys drink over here?" Will asked.

"Tea," I answered, keeping a perfectly straight face. "All varieties. Instead of mixers and beer taps we just have a load of pretty coloured teapots lined up behind the bar."

Freya cracked up and Will rolled his eyes. "Very funny."

I smiled. "We drink pretty much the same as you but probably in larger quantities."

"What are you having? My treat."

"Why thank you. I will have a Smirnoff Ice, and as I am in my own country and don't have to worry about pleasantries, I'll drink it out of the bottle with a straw!"

"Me too," Freya added.

Will shook his head. "I've never seen you like this before, all British and uncouth!"

"I am not uncouth!" I insisted. "Now… let's get ratted!"

Freya and Will exchanged a look of confusion.

"It means drunk," I explained. "Short for 'rat-arsed.'"

"Rat-arsed?" Will repeated, sheer confusion on his face. "Some of your weird English phrases make sense but… rat-arsed? Unless you grow pointy teeth and a long tail when you're drunk?"

Freya giggled and I said, "Let's leave the dissection of that term for later. I'm thirsty, William!"

Getting all dressed up and hitting the town had helped me push my melancholy to the back of my mind. Freya was right – us getting together was a rare event and it was only right that we made the most of it. I would worry about Radleigh if and when I next saw him.

That time was just a few hours later. Radleigh, Bree, Miguel, Jude, Cody, and Bryce all arrived together. Will, Freya and I had moved closer to the dance floor by then. Not too many people took up the tables there, due to the fact they either wanted to be dancing, therefore not sitting down, or they wanted to talk, so they stayed at the other end of the room. Miguel and Bree were the first to join us. The others took seats nearby, so we were all in fairly close proximity.

Radleigh was, as usual, sitting with Bryce and Cody, and I tried not to take too much notice of him. It wasn't easy though. When he hadn't been there, not thinking about him was just about possible. But he was so close. I tried not to feel the ache that washed over me at being so near but so far from him. I needed a distraction.

Sensing my mood, Bree came to my rescue. She took my hand and dragged me to the dance floor.

"No moping," she said firmly. "You're supposed to be doing that thing."

"What thing?"

"That thing where you pretend nothing is bothering you."

"Oh. *That* thing!"

"Uh-huh. So what do you say we find you some nice guy to dance with?"

I laughed. "I don't think a man is what I need."

Not just any man, anyway.

"I need to keep dancing," I told her. "With my friends, not strange men."

"There are no poles in here." She looked around just in case she'd missed them.

"No poles. There is a karaoke bar upstairs though."

Bree's eyes widened. "Karaoke? Really?"

Her enthusiasm could only mean bad things.

"I love karaoke!"

"I bet you do." I giggled.

"Please, please, please, please can we go up there?" she begged, squeezing my hand and jumping up and down.

"Do you sing?" I asked.

"Not well, but that's not the point. It's fun!"

I had to agree. Karaoke was something I'd done in my youth as an extra way of attracting men. Apparently, nothing makes a man more horny than a girl singing suggestive songs. The added bonus of heading up to the karaoke bar was that Radleigh wouldn't be there.

"Okay," I agreed. "Let's go!"

We told Freya and Will where we were going, picked up our drinks, and made our way up the stairs. Because it was getting late, most people were drunk enough to sing things they never would have attempted sober. As we entered the room a woman was wailing out a horrific version of a classic rock song but everyone was up dancing and singing along.

Bree squealed excitedly. "I want to sing!"

"You're on your own. I'm not singing tonight."

"Oh, yes you are." She dragged me along to a vacant table to study the available choice of songs. "We'll sing together!"

"Bree, come on!" I wailed. "Don't make me. I promise to cheer up!"

Fixing me with puppy dog eyes, she smiled. It was impossible to resist her when she slipped into cutesy mode.

"I hate you," I groaned.

We trawled through the pages and pages of songs before we decided on *Brass In Pocket*. Bree scribbled our names and song choice down on a submission slip, and ran over to hand it to the DJ before I had chance change my mind.

It would be a while before we were called up so we got ourselves some more drinks and chatted, while being subjected to some of the worst singing I'd ever heard. After a while, Freya and Will came to join us, followed by Miguel, and to my horror, Bryce, Cody and Radleigh.

"I am *not* singing in front of him," I said firmly.

"It'll do him good to see you enjoying yourself," Will pointed out.

"Enjoying myself, yes. But public humiliation? That's different."

Clearly, my sense of bravery had gone out of the window since I was eighteen. Back then, this would have been a challenge I'd have relished but things were different now. Making an idiot of myself in front of Radleigh was not a pleasant thought.

Get a grip. What does it matter anyway? You pretty much ruined any chance you had this afternoon. You may as well complete the day with a final act of stupidity.

I was in the middle of a deep discussion about the guy who had taken over my job with Freya, Will and Miguel when I heard the DJ announce it was time for Bree and me to sing.

"Oh hell." I stood up. "Where's Bree?"

"She went to the bathroom," Freya answered. "Too much to drink."

"Can you go and get her? I'll delay the DJ, please just find her!"

"I'm on it." She stood and ran towards the bathroom as fast as possible in her enormous heels.

With a last look of fear at Miguel and Will, I slowly walked towards the stage. Butterflies began to flap around in my stomach. I walked up the steps to the stage and turned to see if Bree was coming. The DJ hadn't noticed me yet, he was clearly searching for our song and I didn't alert him to my presence in order to buy myself a couple more minutes. I noticed Freya returning to our table alone, and she shrugged at me, indicating that she couldn't find Bree.

"Ah, there you are," the DJ said, making me jump. "You ready?"

"Erm," I began, "my friend is in the bathroom. Is there any way we can wait?"

The DJ shook his head. "Sorry. No time."

Panic coursed through my veins as he grinned and handed me a microphone. Terrified, I turned to face the crowd. Some were looking expectantly at me, some weren't taking any notice at all, but my friends were cheering and whistling which made me even more scared.

Relax. Most of the people here are drunk, and if you're awful, people will assume you're drunk too and cheer for you anyway.

I knew this to be true. It wasn't the strangers in the room that bothered me, though.

I didn't have time to stress any longer as the opening bars of the song began. There was almost no introduction before the lyrics kicked. I just had to go for it.

The moment the first line was out in tune, I relaxed, allowing myself a quick glance at Radleigh. He was watching my every move and as the first chorus began, my confidence soared.

I stepped down from the stage and sashayed towards my friends. Without even needing to look at the words, I sat myself on Miguel's lap in time for the second chorus. He grinned as I stood up and winked at him. I moved over to Radleigh, Bryce and Cody for the next part of the song. Standing behind Bryce and seductively running my hand down his chest, I continued belting out the lyrics. He looked up at me shocked, but smiling before I went back on to the stage.

For the first time all night I felt free of the pain, if only for the duration of the song. I wanted to enjoy every second before it ended and Radleigh found a way to make me suffer for feeling up his friend.

Wild cheers, whistles and screams filled the room as I finished and I laughed at how much I'd enjoyed myself. Stepping down from the stage again, I went back to my friends who had been re-joined by Bree.

"I missed it!"

I gave her a hug. "Next time we meet up, we'll find a karaoke bar and stay there all night."

This satisfied her and as I reached for my drink, Will said, "Are there any other talents you're keeping from us?"

"Karaoke isn't really a talent."

"It was the performance." Freya grinned. "I thought McCoy might die from the shock!"

"Meh." I shrugged. "I was too busy molesting Bryce to worry about Radleigh."

Even as I said it, my eyes shifted to where he sat. He was still watching me, annoyance on his face. When he saw me looking, he glared and turned away.

I don't want to love you. You don't deserve it.

"Hey, over here," Will said, distracting me from my thoughts. I smiled as I turned to him, and he added, "Freya, go get Leah another drink. If she's drinking, she won't be thinking."

He and Freya high-fived each other, then Freya headed over to the bar.

"Is that your plan for me tonight?" I asked. "To drown my brain with alcohol?"

"If it keeps your mind off McCoy, yes."

"I'm probably too far gone for that to help, but thanks anyway."

Will gave me a sad smile. "He hasn't been the same since you left. He's been more of a dick than usual, but not in the same way he used to be. He's just been a moody bastard. You know how much I hate that guy, Leah. But I think he's missed you."

It was good to hear, especially from someone who thought Radleigh was a total prick. It wasn't enough, though. Not enough to force me to try and talk to him. One look at his face told me I'd be wasting my time. I didn't regret the things I'd said to him earlier, though. I was honest. The most honest I'd been with him in a long time.

"Anyway," I said, eager to steer the conversation away from Radleigh, "isn't it time you grew a pair and told Freya you love her?"

He smiled. "Yes. Actually, I've been thinking about telling here while we're here in London. Not tonight while we're... rat-arsed... but maybe while we're away from home it'll be easier to get the words out."

Short of Radleigh sweeping me off my feet, nothing could have made me happier than Will's words. I kissed him on the cheek. "That's what I like to hear!"

"Don't get too excited yet. I might still wimp out!"

"You won't. It's easy when you already know she feels the same way."

"Oh sure, why don't you go and tell Radleigh you love him?"

"He doesn't love me, Will."

Will looked over his shoulder to where Radleigh sat, staring miserably at his bottle of beer. "No? You could go tell him right now, and don't think he would turn you away, because he wouldn't."

"He would because he's an arse. Freya is a sweetheart and she deserves for you to tell her the truth."

He nodded. "I know. I will."

We left Slinky's at one-thirty; relatively early for us but everyone was pretty tired so we decided to call it a night. Both Bree - who took full advantage of the fact that she could legally drink - and Freya were smashed, so Will, Miguel, Jude and I took it upon ourselves to take them back to the hotel. Everyone else stayed at the bar, and after saying goodbye to them, we fell into a cab.

"I wish I was drunk," I said to Miguel as we got out of the taxi at the hotel.

"You could always go and attack the mini bar in your room."

"That's the plan."

Miguel put his arm around my shoulders. "There are better answers than drinking."

"I know, but look at them." I jerked my head in the direction of Freya and Bree who were giggling uncontrollably as they tried to make their way up the steps to the hotel. "I wish the only thing I had to think about was getting back to my room without falling over."

"You need some sleep. If having a drink is what it takes to help, than have one. But don't get drunk. It's not worth it."

I let out a groan and rested my head on his shoulder, more lonely and unhappy than I'd felt in a long while.

I'd faked having fun for the rest of the evening, and I'd tried to be enthusiastic but it was difficult when my mind was elsewhere. I kept thinking if being apart from Radleigh was so difficult, then I should just speak to him and put an end to it. But every time I looked at him he either glared or feigned disinterest and that only served to make me angry with him.

"I don't think I'll meet up with you guys next time you're here," I said. "If it's going to be like this, I… I'd rather be at home."

"No, no, no, no, no," Miguel insisted as we began to make our way up the steps. "There is no way in hell McCoy will come between you and your friends. Besides, in a few months, you might even be over him!"

As much as I wished Miguel's words were true, I knew my feelings wouldn't fade so quickly. It had already been a couple of months and Radleigh was still the last person I thought of every night, and the first person I thought of every morning.

Seeing him had set me back even further and my mind wouldn't relax. I tried watching TV, reading, staring at the ceiling, but nothing worked. A little after three a.m the sound of my mobile alerting me to a new text message startled me. I reached to pick it up with a grin, thinking it was probably Freya complaining she had thrown up in her hair.

Radleigh's name filled the screen and I clicked to open the message. *Are you awake?*

For a second, I contemplated ignoring it. After all, he'd been ignoring me all evening. I shook my head, telling myself to stop being so childish. One of us had to be the first to stop playing stupid mind games, so I simply typed back, *Yes.*

Good. I'm outside your room. Let me in?

He was outside my room? At three fifteen in the morning?

I heard a gentle knock and swore to myself under my breath as I climbed out of bed. Pulling on my bathrobe to cover my underwear, I ran to the door.

Chapter 24
Would You Like A Shovel?

"What are you doing here, Radleigh?"

It was the only question I could think of. His call had surprised me and his appearance hadn't given me time to think. I knew my hair was sticking out at weird angles from where I'd been tossing and turning, trying to fall asleep, but it was too late to worry about vanity.

"Are you going to let me in?"

I opened the door a little wider, allowing him to step inside. A shiver ran through me at being disturbed from the comfort of my bed, and I wrapped by dressing gown more tightly around me.

In spite of it being the early hours of the morning, Radleigh looked kind of... gorgeous. He wasn't groomed to within an inch of his life like usual. His jeans were crumpled, and his hair was tousled from being in bed. It made him look vulnerable.

"I want to show you something," he said.

He put his hand in his pocket, pulled out a small rectangular piece of paper and dropped it on the bed. I picked it up, and my mouth dropped open when I read the printed words.

It was a plane ticket from London to Newquay, departing on Friday morning.

I looked up at him, astounded. "You... you were coming to see me?"

"Yes," he answered coldly. "But like always, you were one step ahead of me."

Weird. I'd always felt like he was the one who was one step ahead.

"Why didn't you say so earlier?" I asked.

"Because you wouldn't stop yelling."

A blush began to creep over my cheeks. "I'm sorry."

He shrugged. "It doesn't matter. I just wanted you to know."

The idea that he, Radleigh McCoy, had intended to get on a plane to Cornwall and attempt to find me was huge. He *had* been thinking about me. My softer side wanted to go to him and erase the unhappiness on his face, but a meaner, more antagonistic part of me still didn't think he'd suffered enough. I hadn't decided which side of me would win.

"Leah, please say something."

"What do you want me to say, Radleigh?"

"I don't know... something, anything. Why are you making this so hard?"

"Because," I said, placing the ticket on the bed, "for the last eight weeks I've been tormenting myself over my feelings for you, thinking I was stupid for believing you cared about me, and trying to get you out of my head."

"What do you think *I've* been through over the last few weeks?"

"Knowing you, I'd say, several fan girls and any remaining staff members you hadn't already screwed!"

Something changed in his eyes, like he'd shut down from the conversation. "Forget it."

He turned to leave and I let out a mocking laugh. "How typical. I hit a nerve and you walk out on me!"

Turning back, he snarled, "I haven't so much as looked at another woman since you left! And that's not because of a lack of offers, it's because I wasn't interested!"

He started to walk away again and I knew if I let him go this time, it really would be over.

"I'm sorry," I said as he reached the door, and he stopped without turning around. "I don't want you to go, but if you stay you'll have to deal with my anger. I can't pretend not to be angry when I am."

He turned to face me again. I gave him an apologetic smile and sat down on the bed.

"I know I should have called," Radleigh said.

"What stopped you?"

"I didn't think you'd speak to me. I wanted to talk to you so much but the thought you might hang up on me stopped me from trying. I wanted to talk to you somewhere that couldn't happen."

"You didn't consider I might slam the door in your face?"

He nodded. "But I figured you'd take pity on me after I'd sat on your doorstep for a few hours."

I couldn't suppress a smile. "I suppose I would have."

"Leah, I'm sorry. I'm sorry about the last time I saw you in America. I have a lot to apologise for, but that was the worst."

At the mere thought, my chest began to ache with suppressed grief. Tears formed in my eyes as I remembered the humiliation of being undressed then rejected.

"You won't hear any arguments from me. I've never felt so used."

He hung his head, and the way his shoulders sagged told me it had been as painful for him. He came towards me, and sat beside me on the bed.

"I wasn't using you. If all I'd wanted was to sleep with you, I would have."

"If you weren't going to, why did you even…" I couldn't bring myself to finish the sentence.

"I don't know how to explain. I didn't want to be at your leaving party, so when you came into the bar and you looked so incredible, it surprised me. I didn't think you'd want to see me."

"You must've known I'd want to say goodbye."

"How? We weren't speaking."

I took a moment to process his words. For all his bravado, and his enormous ego, did he really not understand how I felt about him? I forced myself to look into his eyes for a second, but it was enough. Enough to tell me he hadn't understood.

"Why didn't you talk to me?" I asked. "You could have bought me a drink and talked to me."

"Leah, I was drunk out of my mind. I didn't know what the hell I was doing. I wanted you so much, but you were leaving the next morning and I-" he trailed off.

"What?"

"I didn't want to wake up and find you gone."

Slowly, I raised my head again and this time I didn't look away. I fixed my eyes on his as the first tear slid down my face. "You're so stupid. All this pain, and feeling so... empty. All you had to do was tell me the truth."

He shook his head. "That's not fair. You weren't so honest yourself. I asked you if you wanted to be with me and you said no."

"I didn't think you were serious!"

"I didn't know I was serious until you said no."

I furiously wiped the tears from my cheeks, angry with myself. Because of our own fears and stubbornness, we'd ruined anything we could have had before it had even begun.

He reached for my hand. "I don't wanna fight."

"Why not? That's what we do."

"But we're good at it. And we always make up afterwards."

"No, we don't." I pulled away from him and stood up. "We just brush it aside, because more often than not, another argument comes along to take its place."

"You wouldn't want me if all I ever did was agree with you."

That much was true, but I didn't say so. I was beginning to get tired, and the amount of revelations I'd heard made my head ache. An hour ago I'd been trying to force myself to accept the fact that Radleigh and I were not meant to be together, and now he was telling me I hadn't been in it alone.

"Come back to L.A. with me."

My stomach flipped over with excitement at the possibility of actually being with him. Of hearing him say he wanted me to be with him. But along with it, there was always doubt and I shook my head. "Too much has happened."

"What do you mean? Is there someone else?"

The idea made me laugh. "Of course not."

"You know, when I saw you with Miguel earlier, I thought maybe you-"

"What? I'd magically fallen in love with him and forgotten all about you?"

"Well…yeah."

Shaking my head again, I said, "I knew it was all a front."

"What?"

"Your gigantic arrogant streak. You're just as pathetic as me underneath it, aren't you?"

He laughed. "I don't think you're pathetic."

"Well that makes one of us."

Placing his hands on my hips, he gently sat me down on his lap. "Please don't make me go back without you."

"I need to think," I told him. "It's nearly four a.m, I have to meet my brother and nephew for breakfast in a few hours and I haven't been to sleep yet. Can we please pick this up again tomorrow?"

"Aren't you supposed to be going home tomorrow?"

Amazed at how he seemed to know so much without actually having asked me, I said. "Yeah, I'm supposed to."

"But you're gonna stay?"

I nodded. "There's still a lot to talk about."

He gently brushed my hair from my face and I shivered as his hand touched my cheek. After a slight hesitation, I put my arms around his neck, finally allowing myself to breathe in the familiar, freshly showered scent I'd missed while we were apart. "Will you stay here with me tonight?"

Just in case this all goes wrong again, I need you to stay with me tonight. I want that night you threw away.

"I didn't bring my pyjamas," Radleigh said facetiously.

"Me neither."

Radleigh let out a small groan of frustration. "Don't be such a tease."

I laughed. "I'm actually not kidding, but I can throw something on if you can't control yourself!"

"I can barely control myself when you're fully dressed. But I'll risk it."

Rolling my eyes, I stood up but the beginning of something resembling happiness started to consume me. Things were far from being sorted out, but this was more than I'd ever expected.

I slipped my bathrobe down over my shoulders, and hung it over the back of the chair, fully aware Radleigh's eyes were following me.

"Anyone would think you were expecting company," he said, of my perfectly matched black lacy bra and knickers.

"Well, I was considering bringing Bryce back here after we'd finished at the club," I teased. "So I thought I should be prepared. I didn't want him to see me in my grey granny pants."

"Very funny," he said as I climbed into the bed.

"Oh, come on. I wouldn't sleep with him, nor would he want to sleep with me. He's your friend, and he's married."

"Would you like a shovel?" he asked, looking over his shoulder at me. "Or are you okay digging that hole by yourself?"

"No, no," I giggled. "I'm doing fine on my own."

He stood up and took off his t-shirt but left his jeans on, then got into bed beside me.

"Radleigh, seriously. You know there's nobody other than you who I-"

"Want to show your underwear to?" He grinned.

"Right."

His face became serious again and after a second or two, he said, "Come here."

I flicked the switch to turn the lamp off and shuffled across the bed, closing the gap between us. His arms encircled me and my heart began to beat more quickly as I felt his muscular form pressed up against me.

I was tired, but not so tired that I didn't realise how perfect the moment was.

His lips brushed against mine, making me shiver. He'd never kissed me that way before. It had always been frantic, or teasing or urgent. The urgency was different now though. It wasn't a desperate need to be ripping each other's clothes off, although I was positive we were. It was simply the need to be close. It was better than any kiss I'd experienced before.

"I love you, Leah."

I closed my eyes, letting the words hang in the air, letting them play in my mind before allowing myself to believe them.

"I love you too."

With one final kiss, I snuggled closer to him and, almost immediately, fell asleep with a smile on my face.

Chapter 25
Return Of The Ego

The next morning, I awoke to the tantalising smell of bacon and coffee. It seemed to fill my senses while I slept, and gently coaxed me into opening my eyes.

The first sight that greeted me was Radleigh sitting in the chair at the table by the window. As my eyes regained focus, I noticed that a little to the side of him was a tray with two enormous full English breakfasts on it, and two cups of coffee.

"Am I still asleep?" I asked, rubbing my eyes.

"No," Radleigh answered, turning to look at me. "If this was a dream your breakfast wouldn't be cold."

"It's cold?"

"I'm kidding. It hasn't been here for long. I was deciding on the best way to wake you up."

Pushing a rogue dirty comment out of my head, I said, "Nothing short of an earthquake can wake me when I'm sleeping. I-"

I stopped abruptly, having seen the clock out of the corner of my eye.

"What's wrong?"

"I was meant to meet Josh and Jamie for breakfast fifteen minutes ago!"

I scrambled to free my arms from the warmth of the duvet and reached out for my mobile phone to send Josh an apologetic text message telling them to go on without me.

"Did you tell him you're with me?" Radleigh asked.

"Not yet. Some things are best done face to face. Besides, I don't want him storming up here before I've properly woken up."

"I guess I shouldn't expect to be welcomed into your family then?"

With a small laugh I said, "First you have to win me over, then you can worry about Josh."

"I've already won you over. Now I need to make you admit it."

He'd *almost* won me over. But I needed to think about what the next step was before making any promises or commitments.

That's what today is about. All you have you have to do today is talk to him and be honest.

After we'd eaten breakfast, Radleigh went back to his room to get dressed. He took the majority of my things with him so I could check out of my room after I'd sorted things out with Josh, and when he was ready, we went down to face him.

Josh and Jamie were already waiting, and the difference in reactions on seeing us together was huge. While Jamie's face lit up, Josh's clouded over.

"I'd better handle this on my own," I said nervously, looking up at Radleigh.

"You sure?"

"Yeah."

"Okay. I'll go and see if I can add you to my room for the night."

I smiled up at him. "Okay. I'll see you in a minute."

He winked at me then headed over to the reception desk. I stared after him for a second, somewhere between excited and astounded he was mine. All I had to do was give him the word and we would be together. I was still having trouble believing any of it was happening. I thought for sure this was all some elaborate prank and at any second a camera crew were going to jump out from nowhere, proving I'd been well and truly "got".

I took a deep breath before approaching Josh and Jamie. The expression on my brother's face told me this wasn't about to be an easy conversation.

"Good morning." I hoped my cheerfulness would make him a little easier on me.

"Please tell me you met him in the lift," Josh said, without a hint of a smile.

"I didn't meet him in the lift."

Jamie beamed up at me. "Are you and Radleigh friends again now?"

"Yes. We're friends."

"Friends? It certainly looks like more than that."

I was very aware my nephew was eagerly listening to every word so I halted my response before I began. Although nothing had happened between us that would corrupt him, I didn't think he needed to hear the details.

I reached into my pocket and pulled out a five pound note. I handed it to Jamie. "Why don't you go to the shop and buy yourself a magazine for the journey home?"

There was a small newsagent type shop right by the hotel entrance, and when I pointed him in the right direction, he said, "Can I buy some sweets too?"

I laughed. "Yes, if you must."

"Yay! Thank you!"

Jamie darted to the shop and Josh said, "I take it you're not coming home today?"

"No. I'll catch a train home tomorrow."

"So what's going on? You two sorted things out?"

"Almost. Last night he came to see me after we got back from the club."

"And?"

"We talked. A lot. Christina wasn't so wrong about him after all." Josh didn't look nearly as happy at this news as I'd hoped. "This is a good thing, Josh. A really good thing."

He nodded. "I'm pleased for you."

"Right." I narrowed my eyes. "You look it."

"I'm not going to pretend I like him, Leah. Not after what he put you through over the last few months. But if you think it's worth giving him a chance, I wish you luck."

He sounded more sceptical than supportive and it annoyed me. Josh's opinion was important and without him backing me, there would be a dark cloud shadowing my good mood for the rest of the day.

Sensing my thoughts, he said, "Don't look at me like that. I don't have to like him."

"But you *did* like him."

"Before he messed you around."

"So you're not even going to give him a chance?"

"I won't make things hard for you. If this is what you want, fine. I can't forget that he hurt you though."

I knew he wanted to say more but I could tell by the uneasy look on his face that Radleigh was on his way over to us. I turned and greeted him with a smile. As he reached us I said, "Everything sorted out?"

He nodded. "Yeah, you have a place to stay tonight."

"Thank you."

In response, he smiled then looked nervously at Josh. "Hey."

Josh surveyed him for a second. "Hello."

The tension was unbearable and eventually Radleigh broke the silence.

"Listen, man, I know I'm probably the last person you want your little sister to be with but I wanna… I'm gonna take care of her. If she'll let me."

Once, my reaction would have been to tell him I could take care of myself and even if I *did* need someone to take care of me, he would be my last choice. And while I was perfectly capable of being on my own, I knew I didn't want to be.

And Radleigh was never your last choice.

"You'd better look after her," Josh said. "Because she's been through enough."

"I have to persuade her to let me first. She's pretty stubborn."

"Careful. She's careful."

"Okay." I stepped in between the two of them. "It's very flattering to be argued over by two men, even if one is my brother, but this isn't helping."

Josh nodded, grudgingly and I gave him a hug. He'd always been protective of me, and it meant a great deal to me that he accepted my decision without too many protests. As we let go of each other he said, "Leah, I think Freya's trying to catch your attention."

Turning my head, I saw her standing awkwardly by the lift. She'd promised to come and say goodbye to me and I knew Will, Bree and Miguel would be along soon too.

"I'd better go and tell her what's happening," I said. "Can you two please try not to kill each other while I'm gone?"

"We can do that," Josh answered.

I gave Radleigh's hand a quick squeeze as I passed, then made my way over to Freya, trying not to think about what the two of them might say to each other when I wasn't there to separate them.

"What's going on?" Freya asked with a curious grin. "Are you and McCoy-?"

"It's a long story. I'll fill you in later," I answered. "For now though, we're talking."

"But things are good? It's good talking, right?"

"Yes."

She let out a squeak of delight. "That's great!"

"It is. But there's a long way to go yet. I'm staying here an extra day and... we'll see."

"Stop playing it so cool! You're ecstatic, I can see it in your eyes!"

Closing my eyes, I leaned forward, my forehead resting on her shoulder. "I *am* ecstatic. I don't want to jinx it though, so shush!"

"You won't! I think there might be something in the air here."

My head snapped up. Freya's eyes twinkled, and I let out a gasp. "Did something happen with you and Will?"

She nodded. "He was kind of drunk but he... he said he's been in love with me for a long time, and thinks we should go on a date!"

It was my turn to let out a squeal. "That's fantastic! I want to hear all about it but I need to go and separate Radleigh and Josh before they start pulling each other's hair."

"It's okay. We'll talk later. Let's meet for drinks tonight."

I grinned. "It's a date."

After saying a brief goodbye to Josh and trying to explain to Jamie why I wasn't going home with them, Radleigh and I left the hotel and went for a walk around the city.

It's funny how, when you live in London, you don't take in how phenomenal it is. There's so much you take for granted because there's never any time to appreciate what's around you. With Radleigh though, it was like a holiday. We did the tourist thing of visiting Buckingham Palace then Trafalgar Square, Covent Garden and Oxford Street but Radleigh had one final request before we went back to the hotel.

"I want to go on that enormous wheel thing that overlooks the Thames," he said as we made our way through the masses of people in the street. "It looks amazing."

My heart stopped for a second and I looked at him, panic stricken. "The London Eye?"

"Yeah. Have you ever been on it?"

"No. I'm scared of heights."

"You are?" he asked, with a small laugh. "Wow."

"What? Is that so strange?"

He shrugged. "I guess not, I just never knew that about you before." He gave me a knee-weakening smile and added, "I still want to go on."

"Then you're on your own."

We made our way to the famous tourist attraction. The queue for the London Eye was insanely long. Hordes of people were waiting in line to get a full view of the city from the top of the wheel. Just looking at the height made me queasy.

"Oh, it looks like we won't be going on today." I smiled to myself.

"What do you mean? I thought British people loved to queue."

"Ha ha. That is a myth."

"Leah, come on. I really wanna go on. Please come with me. I'll look after you, I promise."

The part of me that couldn't resist him resurfaced.

"Okay," I agreed. "Okay."

We waited in line for a full hour, throughout which I continued to get more and more scared. If I'd been with anyone else I would probably have run away way before we got to the front of the line.

When we finally got there I gave one last panicked plea in the hope he'd take pity on me and take me back to the hotel. No such luck. Radleigh handed over the money and I knew there was no backing out.

"Jesus Christ," I muttered, as we stepped into one of the giant pods. "I think you're pure evil for making me do this."

With a small chuckle, Radleigh said, "It's good to face your fears."

"Face my fears? I'll have you know, I'm more than happy to live with my fear of heights. I don't need to conquer it by getting on an overgrown Ferris wheel!"

"It's supposed to be romantic."

"You don't need to be romantic now, you've already got me!"

As a few more people filed into the pod with us, Radleigh gently manoeuvred me away from them and grinned. "Maybe I haven't got everything I want from you yet."

"If I promise to do obscene things to you when we get back to the hotel, will you let me out of here?"

"No," he replied, laughing. "But you can do obscene things to me anyway if you like?"

"After this? Not a hope!"

A smile spread across my face and he pulled me close to him.

Wow, this feels good. We'd spent the night wrapped in each other's arms, but he'd done nothing more than hold my hand while we'd walked around the city. He hadn't even kissed me since the night before. Finally being pressed against him… it felt right.

I ran my hands down his back to the waistband of his jeans. "So, why did you bring me on here?"

"Partly so I can say I did something in London other than sleep, and partly so we can talk about the things we didn't have time to talk about last night."

"Ah, cunning. You dragged me up here where I can't escape so you can get some answers from me. And here was I thinking it was about you having your wicked way with me in public."

"Quit turning me on when I'm trying to be serious," he groaned.

"Sorry." I grinned.

"I want you to come back to America with me."

"Well," I said, my smile fading a little, "that was abrupt."

I knew the question of what would happen next was coming. He'd already asked me to go back with him, but I was hoping we'd talk more before it got brought up again. We hadn't solved anything. We'd admitted our feelings, but it was going to take more than that for me to uproot my life again.

"I'm sorry," Radleigh said. "That's what I want."

I nodded. "I know."

"You don't want to?" he asked, sounding surprised.

Return of the ego.

"I want to be with you," I told him, carefully. "I'm just… I'm not sure about moving back to America. I don't want to ruin this by pushing things faster than they need to go. We've already made enough of a mess of things."

"It's different now. We've argued, and we've apologised. Everything's good."

"You really think we can sort everything out with one conversation? Radleigh, we're talking about me making a huge move. Again."

His arms dropped from around my waist and he turned away from me. It was only then I realised we were quite a few feet higher than we had been. We'd been so engrossed in each other that the view over London was the last thing on our minds. With a sharp intake of breath, I instinctively reached out to him, just for something to hold on to. He shrugged me off, and I was torn between trying to keep control of my fears and trying to have the serious discussion with him. I couldn't easily do both.

I leaned back against the edge of the capsule in order to keep my balance while I got used to the fact that we'd moved, and took a couple of deep breaths.

We weren't anywhere near full height yet and I was already having a panic attack. My palms were sweating and my legs began to shake.

This was not supposed to happen. I was not meant to be arguing with Radleigh, but telling him how deathly afraid I am of heights and letting him calm me down.

"Well," I said, trying to keep a quiver out of my voice, "I guess this proves my point. We've not even been together for twenty four hours and we're already fighting."

He turned his head to look at me. "You're the one being unreasonable."

I closed my eyes for a second, in an attempt to steady myself a little then wiped my perspiring palms on my jeans, silently telling myself everything was okay. I squeezed my eyes closed again, willing myself to realise my fear was irrational. I was perfectly safe.

I had two options. I could suffer silently, or ask Radleigh for help.

"Radleigh, could you… I need you to hold my hand."

Once, a long time ago, I would never have asked and even if I had, I wouldn't have believed he'd be there for me. Even in the middle of our disagreement things had changed enough for me to know when I reached out for him, he *would* be there.

His hand closed over mine and he carefully drew me to him. I could tell he was still pissed off from the way he held me, but he *was* holding me.

That had to mean something, right?

"Have you ever been in a relationship with someone you loved so much you felt like you couldn't breathe without them?" I asked, my voice trembling almost as much as my legs.

"Not yet," he answered dryly.

"The last time I loved someone that way, I got screwed over. I've never been that girl. The girl who means everything to someone."

There was a long, excruciating silence, then Radleigh said, "You *are* that girl. You'd think I'd get sick of you always arguing with me, telling me you're not interested, challenging me. I can't get away with anything with you. I'm not tired of you yet and I don't see that happening."

That was so much what I needed to hear. I let myself sag against him, holding him tightly.

I knew what I wanted. I'd always known. Cornwall was my home only by chance. L.A was where I belonged. Even when I left everyone and everything behind, I knew. But I'd needed time to heal. Time to be with my family, to gather up the bits of me that were broken. Radleigh was offering me the final piece. The piece that would cover up the last gaping hole inside me and I wanted to take it.

God, I wanted to take it.

Take it. It's all yours. Those doubts in your head... they're nothing but excuses. He's made all the moves to show you he loves you. Now you need to do the same. Be honest. But don't let him go.

I took a deep breath. "I want to be with you. In L.A. But I need a little time. If I come back right away, I'm scared it'll be too much. Too fast. I know the distance is big, and it's not that I don't think we'll work out, but... I just think we should take it slow."

Radleigh kissed the top of my head. "I didn't expect you to fly back with me right away."

"I'll need to get my stuff packed up again, and search for a job."

"You don't need a job. You can-"

"What? Stay at home and clean your enormous house?"

"What makes you think my house is enormous?"

I looked up at him. "Radleigh McCoy, don't you dare try and tell me size isn't important to you."

"Okay, so it's huge," he admitted with a grin. "You don't have to clean it, though. I have a housekeeper."

Shaking my head at the very different lifestyles we led I said, "I need to find work. I'm not the stay at home type. Maybe one day in the future if I had children to look after but-"

Radleigh burst out laughing. "You accused me of rushing things, and here you are talking about having children!"

I narrowed my eyes. "If you continue to make this conversation difficult for me I will make sure you aren't capable of fathering children. Ever."

"I'm not the one making this difficult." He slid his hands down to my hips. "And I would love to have children with you, by the way. You'd look really sexy pregnant."

If I hadn't been aware of how sick I would feel if I moved, I would have turned away from the devilish smile on his face. As it was though, I was pretty much rooted to the spot, and the corners of my mouth twitched.

"Are you really that guy I met in the training ground restaurant on my first day at work, who offered me a night of casual sex?"

"Oh, very clever. Are you that girl who spent weeks saying she wasn't interested in me, only to keep me awake all night after a drunken night out at a wedding?"

"We were both guilty of misleading each other. But now we're being honest. I think we need to take this slowly."

He leaned in close to me, and just before his lips brushed against mine, he stopped.

"Slowly," he repeated, with his trademark mischievous grin.

Feeling his warm breath against my cheek made me shiver, and I nodded. It was all I was capable of doing at that moment.

"I can do that," he said.

I tilted my head back slightly, waiting for the moment our mouths would meet but it didn't come.

"Is there something you want, Leah," Radleigh asked, his hand stroking the back of my neck.

"Well," I began, nonchalantly, "since you've been in London, we haven't… I mean… you haven't-"

My words were cut off as he finally gave me the kiss I'd been anticipating for so long.

It was just like the first time he kissed me. The intensity, the passion. Except it was better. It meant so much more than the first time. It wasn't about some passing physical attraction anymore, not that that attraction had diminished in any way. But along with it were real feelings. Feelings we had taken far too long to admit. As his hands ran through my hair, I couldn't quite remember why that was.

About The Author

Kyra Lennon is a self-confessed book-a-holic, and has been since she first learned to read. When she's not reading, you'll usually find her hanging out in coffee shops with her trusty laptop and/or her friends, or girling it up at the nearest shopping mall.

Kyra grew up on the South Coast of England and refuses to move away from the seaside which provides massive inspiration for her novels. She published her first novel in July 2012, and her novella, *If I Let You Go* and *Blindsided (Game On Book 2)* soon followed.

Made in the USA
Columbia, SC
24 November 2017